Two Little Dickie Birds

Birds

A Bernie Fazakerley

mystery

Judy Ford

Two Little Dickie birds

Published by Bernie Fazakerley Publications

Copyright © 2015 Judy Ford.

Cover design by Acepub

ISBN-10: 1-911083-13-9
ISBN-13: 978-1-911083-13-9

DEDICATION

To the staff and supporters of Action for Children
(formerly the National Children's Home); to all those
children, in days gone by, who sold Sunny Smiles, raising
money to give other children a better start in life; and to
children in care everywhere.

CONTENTS

ACKNOWLEDGMENTS

Lucy and her friends all enjoy reading *Hairy Maclary from Donaldson's Dairy*, Lynley Dodd, 1983, Mallinson Rendel Publishers Limited, New Zealand,
ISBN   978-0-14-330615-3.

Two Little Dickie Birds is a traditional nursery rhyme, dating back to the eighteenth century. See, for example, http://allnurseryrhymes.com/two-little-dickie-birds/.

The Wheels on the Bus is an anonymous nursery rhyme. See, for example, http://www.bbc.co.uk/learning/schoolradio/subjects/earlylearning/nurserysongs/U-Z/wheels_on_the_bus.

Every effort has been made to trace copyright holders. The publishers will be glad to rectify in future editions any errors or omissions brought to their attention.

CHAPTER 1

The call came through early one Thursday in September. It interrupted the chaos of the Johns family breakfast, deflecting Detective Inspector Peter Johns from the task of unjamming the toaster and causing his wife, Angela, to look up anxiously from her bowl of muesli. Two early-morning rowers had found a body in the Thames and called '999'. A senior officer was required on the scene right away.

Peter ran his hands through his faded, once-red hair, feeling a mixture of annoyance at having his routine disrupted and excitement at the prospect of something more interesting to investigate than the sequence of petty thefts and drink-induced assaults that had been coming his way recently. He made a hasty telephone call to his sergeant before resuming his meal, gulping it down, eager to be off.

The doorbell rang and Angela got up to answer it, almost colliding in the hall with her son, Edward, who was hurrying downstairs, pulling on his sweater as he did so. He was also heading for the front door. Angela got there first and opened it to reveal her friend Bernadette, always known as Bernie, and Bernie's small daughter, Lucy. Lucy looked up with a big smile, blue eyes sparkling, and raised her arms, inviting Angela to pick her up. The sun shining

1

in through the open door caught her golden curls and made them glow like a halo around her head.

'Aunty Angie!' she called happily.

Angela picked Lucy up and carried her into the kitchen, while Edward helped Bernie to bring in a buggy and a large bag of toys and childcare equipment, which they stowed in the front room.

'I think I've brought everything you could possibly need,' Bernie said, speaking in the unmistakable Liverpool accent, which she had still not lost after twenty-six years in Oxford.

'It certainly looks like it,' Eddie agreed with a grin. 'How long did you say you were leaving her for? A week, was it?'

When they joined the others in the kitchen a few minutes later, Angela had returned to her muesli, while Peter was sitting at the table eating toast and drinking tea. Lucy was standing by his chair with her arms reaching up to hold him round the waist. She was very fond of 'Uncle Beter'.

'Hi Bernie!' Peter greeted her, through a mouthful of toast, which he was eating as rapidly as he could. 'I've got to rush off I'm afraid. There's a body washed up in the river and I've got to get over there.'

Bernie nodded understandingly. Her own husband had been a police officer too. He had been killed while on duty a few months before Lucy was born. Peter and Angela were Lucy's godparents and played a large part in her upbringing.

'And I've got to get off now too,' Angela added, putting her bowl and teacup in the sink and checking in her pocket for her keys. 'Bye, bye Lucy. You be a good girl for Eddie now, won't you?'

Lucy nodded, letting go of Peter to turn and look towards Edward. He immediately caught her up in his arms and lifted her high above his head. She giggled with delight as he swung her round. He placed her on his shoulders and her fingers gripped his tight, wiry, black curls.

'Careful!' Peter warned. 'There isn't room in here for that sort of thing.'

Eddie obediently lifted Lucy down and placed her on the floor. She immediately set off down the hall in pursuit of Angela, who was standing by the front door, fastening her coat over her nurse's uniform. Seeing Lucy approaching, she bent down and kissed the little girl, her dark skin contrasting markedly with Lucy's pale complexion as their faces touched. Eddie hurried after Lucy and took her hand as his mother let herself out.

'Bye, bye Aunty Angie!' Lucy called, waving her other hand vigorously as Angela walked the few feet down the path and turned right, along the road, heading for the bus stop. Lucy and Eddie were still standing in the doorway, watching her retreating figure when Peter squeezed past them, his car keys in his hand. Lucy waved him off as he climbed into his car and drove away.

Once his parents had both gone, Eddie looked at Bernie.

'Hadn't you better get off too?' he asked. 'You don't want to miss your train.'

'There's no rush,' Bernie assured him. 'Now, are you sure you'll be OK with Lucy all day? I've brought some of her favourite toys and half a dozen disposable nappies and a change of clothes, just in case. They're all in the bag in the front room. Is there anything else you think you'll need?'

'No. We'll be fine,' Eddie said firmly. 'Won't we, Lucy? I've got some new picture books from the library to show you and then, later on, we'll go to the park. We're going to have a great day!'

'Swings!' Lucy said, clapping her hands at the mention of the park, 'roundabout!'

'That's right,' Eddie agreed. 'We'll go on the swings and the roundabout and the slide.'

'Sounds as if you've got it all planned out,' Bernie admitted, resisting the temptation to offer any further advice. She realised that Eddie wanted to take responsibility for Lucy's welfare while she was away at a daylong conference in London. He had often acted as baby-sitter over the two and a half years since Lucy was born, but this was the first time he would be in loco parentis for a whole day and he was determined to demonstrate that he was capable of doing so without help. 'I'm sure you'll get on just fine. Just let me help out by washing up the breakfast things before I go.'

'There's really no need,' Eddie protested. 'I can sort everything out this afternoon while Lucy has her nap.'

'Better not to rely on her settling,' Bernie advised. 'And there's no point in me going for my train just yet. Come on,' she continued, putting on rubber gloves and turning on the tap in the sink, 'you must let me do something to help. I feel that I'm always putting on you and never doing anything in return. I don't know how I'll manage when you go back to university.'

'OK. You wash and I'll dry,' Eddie conceded. 'And Lucy – you can help to put things away, can't you?'

'Yes,' Lucy nodded eagerly.

Eddie handed her a carton of butter from off the table and showed her where to put it in the fridge, while Bernie emptied the teapot and started washing the crockery.

'Do you think this body in the river will turn into a murder enquiry?' Eddie asked.

'I doubt it. It will probably be a tragic accident – someone having too much to drink and then fooling around near the river and falling in. At least it's outside term time, so it's not likely to be an undergraduate.'

Bernie was mathematics tutor at one of the Oxford colleges and was therefore pleased that the victim was probably not one of the students at the university. Accidents and suicides among the undergraduates generated bad publicity and extra work for the academic staff.

'So you don't think it'll stop Dad taking me to Manchester on Saturday?'

Eddie was studying computer science at the University of Manchester. His father was due to drive him there to start the second year of his course in two days' time.

'I shouldn't think so. Even if the investigation's still ongoing, I would have thought they could spare him for a day. He's had that Saturday booked off for months. Anyway, don't worry: if he does get called into work, I'll be happy to drive you – provided you don't mind Lucy coming too.'

Soon the job was done, although, if pressed, both Bernie and Eddie would have had to admit that it would have been quicker if they had not had to spend so much time finding items with which Lucy could safely be entrusted and directing her as to where to put them.

'And now, it must be time for you to head to the station,' Eddie said, as he held Lucy in a standing position on a chair so that she could reach to wipe the table with a dishcloth.

'OK, OK, I know when I'm not wanted,' Bernie pretended to grumble. She kissed Lucy briefly. 'Good bye, love. Mind you behave yourself for our Eddie. I'll be back before your bed time.'

CHAPTER 2

In a small flat at the top of a converted Victorian villa in another part of Oxford, Detective Sergeant Paul Godwin was also washing up after breakfast. He had still been asleep when Peter's summons came through on his mobile phone, which he had left lying on the small table next to his bed. He was to meet his commanding officer at the Riverside Centre, a local authority outward-bound facility to the south of the city, where a body had been washed up by the recent stormy weather.

Bleary-eyed, he hastened to get up, knowing that Peter would be heading for the crime scene at once. He took a brief shower, as much to wake himself up as for the sake of cleanliness, and then shovelled down a bowl of cereal and a glass of orange juice. He hesitated for a moment, wondering whether to leave the glass and bowl unwashed until the evening, but his habitual tidiness got the better of him and he washed the bowl, spoon and glass meticulously and put them away before carefully locking the flat and hurrying downstairs.

As he expected, Peter's car was already there when he arrived at the centre. He parked his own vehicle and walked down the sloping lane towards the river. There was an ambulance pulled up on the grass and two uniformed officers guarding the path that led along the bank to the right. Paul recognised them as constables Tracy Burton and Gavin Hughes.

Tracy was a few years younger than Paul and had been in the police service for just three years, having entered the graduate training scheme with a history degree from Exeter University. Paul, who had recently been transferred from South Oxfordshire, had only known her for a few months but he had already come to respect her for her calm competence, down-to-earth common sense and knowledge of the local area and its inhabitants. She was small and vivacious, with deep brown eyes and short black hair.

Gavin was a complete contrast in both appearance and character. Six foot three and heavily built, he moved slowly and gave the impression that his mind was similarly sluggish. He was dependable, in the same way that a St Bernard dog was dependable, but could not be expected to act on his own initiative. He had been a constable for seven years now, with no apparent desire for promotion – which Paul considered was just as well, since it was unlikely to be forthcoming.

They allowed Paul through their cordon and pointed along the path to where a team of Scenes of Crime Officers was intent on taking photographs and surveying the area for clues. Paul hurried along the bank, past clumps of bushes growing into the water, to where Peter was standing motionless, looking down at the body, which lay in a slight dip in the ground where it had been laid after being pulled out of the water. Pathologist Mike Carson was kneeling on the muddy grass next to it. He looked up as Paul approached.

'How're you doing?' he saluted him cheerfully in a soft Irish brogue. 'Come to join the party, I see! Nothing like a nice corpse to brighten up a damp and dreary morning.'

Paul nodded acknowledgement of the greeting, more

interested in surveying the body that lay at their feet. It was a man in his thirties, wearing navy trousers, a pale blue shirt with a tie and a sports jacket, all very muddy from having been hauled up the riverbank. His hair, which was shoulder length, was tangled with weed and small pieces of twig, presumably picked up during its time in the water. Paul judged that it was probably a light brown colour, but it was difficult to tell while it was wet. His eyes looked grey, but perhaps they would appear blue in some lights.

'Any idea who he is?' Paul enquired.

'He had a credit card in the name of Robert White,' Peter told him. 'I've asked Missing Persons to check if anyone of that name has been reported to them.'

'An accident, do you think?'

'Can't say yet,' the pathologist said, looking up from his kneeling position beside the body. 'The appearance is consistent with drowning, but there are also injuries which could have been inflicted during some sort of fight before he went into the river.'

He turned the body slightly and pointed to a wound on the back of the victim's head.

'This could have been sufficient to render him unconscious or even to kill him,' he explained. 'Depending on where he went in, it could have been caused by him hitting something as he fell, or he could have been attacked and then dumped in the river. We'll know more after the post mortem.'

'How long has he been in the water?' Peter asked.

'Difficult to say: maybe a day, maybe more. We'll know more after the PM.' Mike stood up. 'OK. You can take him away now. I'll leave the rest of my examination for when we get him back to the mortuary.'

While the corpse was being packed ready for transport, Peter led Paul down the riverbank to show him the place where the body had been found nestling under an overhanging bush. The ground was soft underfoot and there were footprints sinking deep into the mud, showing how difficult it had been to drag the heavy weight out of the water. A large branch was still lying in the water, caught up against the bank. Behind it, a mass of smaller branches, waterweed and grass had accumulated. This is what had caught the body and prevented it from being washed any further downstream.

'The river level's pretty high,' Peter observed, 'It'll be that rain we had over the weekend. The way it's running at the moment I'd say he could have gone in quite a way upstream.'

'You've seen this sort of thing before, then?' Paul asked.

'Don't get the idea that bodies in the river are commonplace,' Peter replied, 'but I've been around for a long time now and this isn't my first. However, I was also drawing on my experience of others things being washed away down the river. I remember a punt getting loose from Magdalen Bridge and ending up in the Thames: further down than this, in fact. So he could either have gone into the Thames somewhere upstream or else he may have started off pitching into the Cherwell somewhere between here and Mesopotamia.'

'Mesopotamia? I thought that was in the Middle East somewhere.'

'It's Greek for between rivers. The Cherwell splits into two and, of course, the erudite people of Oxford called the island in between Mesopotamia as a way showing off their classical education.'

Peter's mobile phone rang. Robert White's girlfriend had reported him missing the previous evening. Peter noted down the address of White's flat and the hair salon where the girlfriend worked. Then he put away the phone and headed back along the bank, calling after him for Paul to accompany him.

'According to Missing Persons,' Peter related to Paul as they walked back to the car park, 'a Gemma Markham reported White missing yesterday evening when he didn't come home after work. She hadn't seen him since the night before, but she thought he had just sneaked out early without waking her. She started to get worried when he didn't turn up for his evening meal. She rang his work and they said he hadn't been in all day. So then, she rang the station to report him missing. They made a note of it, but didn't take any further action because he'd probably only been gone about twelve hours at that time and there was no particular reason to suspect foul play.'

'So what now? Presumably we need to interview the girlfriend?'

'That's right. She left a mobile number, but under the circumstances, I'm reluctant to speak to her over the phone, so I think we'll go over to her place of work and try to see her in person. It's a hair salon right in the centre of Oxford, so we'd be mad to take two cars. I'll drop mine off at home – it's more or less on the way – and you follow me in yours and pick me up from there.

A few minutes later, Peter was climbing into Paul's car outside the Johns family home, in the Cowley Road area of East Oxford.

'Did you say her name was Gemma Markham?' Paul asked.

'Yes: that's right, why?' Peter detected a hint of anxiety in Paul's voice and wondered what it meant.

'Oh nothing!' Paul tried to speak casually, but did not quite succeed in hiding the emotion that was evoked by hearing this once-familiar name so unexpectedly. He was not quite sure what exactly he did feel: a mixture of excitement and foreboding at the thought that he might be about to meet someone who had made a deep impression on him as a young teenager but whom he had not set eyes on for more than fifteen years – half his lifetime. 'I don't suppose it's the same person. I used to know someone with that name, years ago. It was just odd hearing you say it like that.'

Never one to pry into his colleagues' personal lives – or

to volunteer information about his own – Peter said nothing. They drove on in silence, coming to a stop outside a rather flamboyant hairdressing establishment in the centre of the city.

CHAPTER 3

Peter approached the receptionist and showed his warrant card.

'I'm looking for Gemma Markham,' he explained. 'I believe she works here?'

'Ye-es,' the young woman answered uncertainly, glancing nervously around the shop. 'What do you want with her? Is there something wrong?'

'We'd just like to have a word with her, that's all. Is she in today?'

'Can I help?' a middle-aged man dressed in a lemon coloured suit with wide lapels came over to them, smiling broadly and pushing back his luxuriant auburn hair with one well-manicured hand. 'I'm Marcus, the manager. What can we do for you?'

'I'm Detective Inspector Johns and this is Detective Sergeant Godwin,' Peter answered, turning to face Marcus. 'We need to have a few words with one of your employees: Gemma Markham.'

'She's not in trouble I hope?'

'No, not at all. I'm afraid we have some bad news for her. Is there anywhere private we can take her?'

'Yes, of course. You can use my office. Walk this way.'

The manager led them with mincing steps through a door at the back of the shop and into a rather cramped office. As he followed behind, Peter felt an irrational annoyance at Marcus for having the appearance, voice and movements of the archetypal camp hair stylist. He hated the idea of putting people into boxes according to their race, class or profession and was frequently frustrated to find that, despite his determination to keep an open mind and reject all preconceived ideas about them, people often seemed determined to fulfil the expectations of every stereotype.

'Make yourselves at home,' Marcus said, waving his hand towards two chairs on either side of a narrow desk. 'I'll send Gemma in.'

A few minutes later, he returned, carrying a third chair and accompanied by a woman, whom Peter judged to be around thirty. She had dark hair, cut in a long fringe, which partially obscured her eyes and trembled at the touch of her eyelashes whenever she blinked. Peter noted with distaste that her face was painted like a china doll, with a thick layer of pale foundation cream and red smudges on her cheeks. Her chosen complexion looked out of keeping with the dark brown of her eyes and their long black lashes, which Peter correctly suspected of being not entirely her own. Why did women do this to themselves? He wondered. Surely, they must realise that no one would believe that this was what they really looked like. In any case, he considered that Angie's smooth, chocolate-coloured skin was infinitely more attractive.

Paul was also looking closely at Gemma's face, trying to work out whether she could be the fifteen-year-old girl whom he had known all those years ago. Her hair had been much longer then – hanging down her back almost to her waist – and her amateurish attempts at makeup had mainly consisted of experiments with different shades of lipstick and nail varnish. She seemed smaller than he remembered, but then, he had only been thirteen at the time and small for his age, so it should be no surprise that he had now overtaken her in height. Then she looked at him, her brown eyes wide open, and he knew!

'I'll leave you then,' Marcus said, turning to go. 'Take all the time you need.'

Peter waited until the door closed and then turned to Gemma.

'Sit down, please, Miss Markham,' he said, gesturing towards the vacant chair. She took her seat and looked at him expectantly.

'Is it about Rob?' she asked anxiously.' Has something happened to him?'

Yes, I'm afraid it has.' Peter paused for a moment before continuing. 'A body was found in the river this morning, which we believe belongs to Robert White.'

Gemma looked from Peter to Paul and then dropped her eyes and appeared to be contemplating something in her lap. She seemed very calm. Peter was not sure what to make of her. Was she expecting this? Or was it just taking time for the news to sink in? Or was she simply someone who did not show her emotions?

'Do you know how it happened?' she asked at last.

'That's what we're trying to find out. And that's why we're going to need to ask you some questions. And we'll need to see the flat where you both lived – in case he left anything behind that might throw light on what he was doing when he fell in.'

'You think it was an accident?'

'We don't know yet. We're keeping an open mind while we investigate to find out.'

'And you think I might be able to help you do that?'

'Yes. We need you to tell us as much as you can about him and about how he seemed when you last saw him. Then we can build up a picture of what may have happened. Did he seem unhappy at all recently, for example?'

'You mean you think he might have done it

14

deliberately?' Gemma looked up at Peter and he saw tears welling up in her eyes. 'You think he killed himself?'

'We don't think anything yet,' Peter assured her calmly. 'We're just exploring all the possibilities.'

Paul silently handed Gemma his handkerchief. She dabbed her eyes and nodded her thanks to him. He smiled back, wondering whether to tell her that he knew her. Had she recognised him too?

'Before we go any further,' Peter said, 'Can you tell me who Mr White's next of kin is? Does he have any family whom we ought to contact?'

'His parents, I suppose – but they're in Australia. That's where Rob comes from. He's over here on a research grant.'

'I see.' Peter looked at his watch and considered the time difference. It would be late evening in Eastern Australia by now. It would be better to inform the parents within the next few hours if he were to avoid waking them in the middle of the night to break the news.

'Miss Markham,' he said gently, looking directly at her. 'I wonder if you would mind coming with us to the mortuary to identify the body? We're pretty sure that it must be Robert White, but there's always the faint possibility that someone else robbed him of his credit cards before falling into the river himself. So I'd feel a whole lot better if you could confirm that we *have* found him before we start contacting his parents to tell them their son is dead.'

'Yes, of course.' Gemma dabbed her eyes with the handkerchief again, then folded it neatly and handed it back to Paul. 'I'm ready.'

'Thank you. We appreciate it,' Peter said, getting up. 'I'll go and explain things to your boss.'

Once the inspector was out of the room, Paul took the opportunity to speak to Gemma about their previous acquaintance.

'Do you remember me?' he asked eagerly. 'Paul

Godwin. We were together at Willowbank House – back in eighty-six. You took me under your wing.'

'Paul Godwin?' Gemma said slowly, pausing in her weeping as she struggled to bring back memories from what seemed like a very distant past. 'Paul – oh of course – Paul! Yes, I remember you. You were a couple of years younger than me, weren't you? I remember thinking you seemed very little and lost when you came. And those awful Bottinger boys picked on you.'

'That's right. And you saved my life.'

'Well, I don't know I'd go so far as that,' Gemma protested. 'I doubt they'd have actually killed you, but they did play some hateful tricks on you.'

'That wasn't-' Paul began, but he stopped as Peter came back in. The inspector took in the tableau of the two of them together and immediately realised that they were more intimate than was possible in the course of a mere five minutes' acquaintance. He said nothing, however.

'I've cleared it with your manager,' he said to Gemma. 'He's fine for you to take the rest of the day off to help us with our enquiries and come to terms with your loss. We've got a car outside, so we'll drive you to the mortuary. I've already rung ahead so they'll be expecting us. Then, after that, we'll go back to your flat and have a look round and a bit of a chat with you about Mr White.'

They went back out through the shop, which by now was busy with customers. The receptionist and the three hairdressing assistants looked up from their work as Gemma and the police officers emerged from the back room, and their eyes followed them as they trooped through the shop and out to the waiting car. Peter held the door for Gemma to climb in the back and then got into the front passenger seat.

A few minutes later, they arrived at the mortuary and were greeted by Mike Carson, who led the way to where the body lay, covered with a sheet.

'Miss Markham?' Mike said, looking at Gemma as he

took hold of the corner of the sheet. 'Are you ready?'

Gemma nodded, and Mike drew the sheet back to reveal the victim's face. His team had cleaned it, removing the river mud and weed that had been clinging to it when Peter and Paul saw it last. The eyes were closed and Gemma could almost have believed that he was asleep, except that there was something wrong about the colour of the cheeks and the complete lack of movement of the body beneath the sheet. She stared down without speaking for perhaps half a minute. Then she looked towards Peter and nodded again.

'Yes,' she said in a low voice, 'that's Rob.'

Mike replaced the sheet and led the way out of the room and back to the mortuary entrance.

'I'll be doing the post mortem this afternoon,' he told Peter, holding the door open for them to leave. 'Do you want to be there?'

'Yes. We'll both come. It'll be good experience for young Paul here – he was telling me the other day that he's never actually seen a PM.'

'Come around one-thirty then.'

Paul drove them back into the centre of Oxford to the flat in Gloucester Green that Gemma had shared with her boyfriend. She took them upstairs and unlocked the front door.

'First of all,' Peter said, as soon as they were inside, 'I'd like the address and telephone number of Robert's parents. I ought to let them know right away, now that there's no doubt that he's dead.' He looked at his watch again. 'Quarter to twelve: it must be getting on for midnight in Australia. I hope I don't have to get them out of bed.'

Gemma disappeared into the bedroom, leaving Peter and Paul standing in the small hall. They heard the sound of drawers being opened and closed. After a few minutes Gemma appeared, carrying a scrap of paper on which she had scribbled down an address in Melbourne and a telephone number.

'I think this is right,' she said, handing it to Peter. 'Rob always used to communicate with his family by email, and of course he knew the address anyway, without writing it down. I found this on the application that he made for the job here in the university. It could be out of date.'

'Thank you.'

Peter tried one of the doors and found his way into the kitchen. He sat down at the table and started dialling on his mobile phone. It seemed a long time before there was any answer, but eventually a rather irritated voice asked him what he wanted. Peter broke the news as carefully and sympathetically as he could. After years of experience, he still found it hard to choose the right words to tell relatives that their loved-one had suffered a violent and unexpected death.

He waited, as there was first a stunned silence at the other end of the line, then a whispered conversation as Robert's father relayed the information to his mother, who was evidently in the same room. Peter pictured the scene in his mind's eye: the two of them being awakened by the ringing of a phone at the bedside, the unexpected voice of a stranger making them think at first that they must still be asleep and in a nightmare, the shock of realising that the news was not a dream.

In this, he was mistaken. His mental calculations of the time difference had made him think that it was an hour or two later in Melbourne than it actually was and Bernard White's irritation was not caused by having been wakened, but by the telephone call having interrupted the shared shower that he and his wife, Samantha, were enjoying before going to bed. This was a practice dating back to their newly-wed days, which they had recently revived now that their two children had left home. They were both now wrapped in towels, standing awkwardly in the living room of their bungalow, wondering what to make of this unexpected and unwelcome news.

Then there came a torrent of questions: how had

Robert died? Was it an accident? When would the inquest be? What were the police doing to investigate? Peter responded calmly, conscious that he was unable to tell them any of the things they really needed to know, and wondering whether his anxiety to inform the next of kin at the earliest opportunity had been misplaced. Might he have done better to put off breaking the news until it was morning in Australia, rather than giving them a disturbed night during which they could do nothing productive? He assured them that the police were doing everything they could to find out the cause of their son's death and left them with his mobile number and instructions to ring him at any time if they felt the need. He would be in touch with them again, in any case, after the post mortem.

'Now, Miss Markham,' Peter said, turning to Gemma, who had followed him into the kitchen, and motioning her to sit down. 'We need you to tell us all about what happened. When did you last see Robert White alive?'

'The night before last.'

'That would be Tuesday?'

'Yes.'

'What time?'

'I don't know exactly. We'd been out for a meal and got back about ten, maybe ten thirty. We had a drink and sat around for a while and then went to bed. When I woke up, he was gone. But that wasn't all that unusual; he often went off to work early if he got an idea for his research in the night.'

'So when did you realise something was wrong?'

'When he didn't come back in the evening: he's usually in before me, but there was no sign of him when I got back. I waited a bit; then I phoned his work and they said he hadn't been in all day. I rang round his mates, but none of them had seen him either – which is when I got worried and phoned the police. But they didn't seem specially interested.'

'Most people who go missing like that turn up safe and

sound after a few hours,' Peter explained gently. 'We can't go looking for all of them. The difficulty is knowing which are the exceptions. Now, to go back to Tuesday evening: how did he seem then?'

'How do you mean?'

'Was he acting just as usual? Or did he seem depressed or excited? Did he appear to have anything on his mind?'

'I don't think so ...' Gemma paused, thinking. 'Well, I don't know. I suppose, looking back, maybe he was a bit down.'

'Do you have any idea why that might have been? Did he speak to you about anything that was worrying him, for example?'

'No.' Gemma shook her head.

'And your relationship? You hadn't had a row or anything?'

'No.'

'The meal out? That wasn't to make up after you'd fallen out?'

'No.'

'So, as far as you were concerned, everything was OK with Robert and if he was feeling depressed at all you don't know the reason for it?'

'Yes.'

'Right. Now, can you take us through the exact sequence of events on Tuesday night, starting from when you got home from work?'

'I got in about six,' Gemma said, 'or maybe it'd be a bit later. Rob was there typing up some notes on his computer. He was always working. I reminded him that we were going out and he said he hadn't forgotten and he'd be ready in a few minutes. Then I went into the bedroom to get changed. By the time I came out again he was ready, so we went out.'

'Where did you go?'

'A little place just across Folly Bridge: it's called *The Rabbit Hole*. Robert says they must be trying to make out that you get into Wonderland when go inside. You know – Alice and that.'

'How did you get there?'

'We walked. It's not far.'

'But it rained hard on Tuesday night,' Paul commented, making his first contribution to the interview.

'It didn't start until later,' Gemma explained. 'It was OK when we set out.'

'During the meal,' Peter resumed, 'did he speak about anything that was worrying him? Did he say anything that, in retrospect, might have indicated that he was unhappy or depressed at all?'

'No. I don't think so.'

'You left the restaurant what time?'

'I'm not sure. Nine thirty – ten o'clock maybe.'

'It must have been raining hard by then, so did you get a taxi back?'

'No. We walked. It's not far at all and we knew we were going straight to bed, so it didn't matter getting wet. Rob's,' she hesitated, 'Robert was used to being out in all weathers on field trips, so he doesn't believe in using a car just to keep out of the rain.'

'OK. You walked home together, and presumably, with the rain pelting down as it was, you won't have hung about, so you got back – what? – at about ten or ten fifteen?'

'About then.'

'And you had drink and then went to bed? Together?'

'That's right.'

'And you woke up in the morning and Robert was gone?'

'That's right – but I didn't think anything of it at the time, because he often goes off before I get up and he tries not to wake me when he does. It was only when he wasn't back in the evening that I started to wonder where he was.'

'And then you rang his work. Where *is* that?'

'The University – the Geography department. He's

working on a research project – something to do with climate change or ecology or something.'

'And they told you he hadn't been in all day?'

'That's right. That's when I *really* started to get worried, because he wasn't like that. He never missed a day's work. So when it got to half past eight and he still hadn't come home, I rang the police.'

'Thank you. That's all very clear.' Peter paused, unsure how best to put his next request. 'And now, please could you show us where he kept his things? We need to have a look through them to see if he left any clues as to where he was going or why. I'm sorry we have to do this,' he added, 'we'll try not to intrude on your privacy.'

Gemma led them into a small sitting room containing a two-seater settee, a desk and computer chair in the corner, and a television set on a low table under the window. On the wall hung two framed maps and two aerial photographs showing the same areas. The landscape looked unfamiliar to Peter and the strange names in the captions suggested that the regions featured were in some remote parts of Australia.

'Those are his books on the shelf over there,' she said, pointing to a small bookcase next to the television. She looked round vaguely, as if trying to remember something.

'And he left his laptop in its bag under the desk,' she said at last. 'I wish I'd noticed it yesterday morning. Then I'd have known there was something up. He never goes anywhere without it.'

Peter went across to the bookcase and ran his finger along the line of books. They were mainly concerned with his geographical research, but there were also a few novels and a book of poetry. Paul meanwhile retrieved the laptop from under the desk.

'We'll need to take this away,' he told Gemma. 'I'll give you a receipt.'

'OK,' Gemma nodded absently.

'And now, we'd like to see the bedroom,' Peter said

apologetically.

Gemma showed them into a medium-sized room furnished with fitted wardrobes down one side and a large, crowded dressing table against the opposite wall. On either side of the double bed, which was covered with a rumpled floral-patterned duvet, was a matching pair of bedside cabinets. On the left-hand one of these were a romantic novel, lying open and face down, a pair of silver earrings, a nail file and a pot of face cream. By contrast, the right-hand cabinet was empty apart from an electric shaver. Peter correctly deduced that Gemma occupied the left-hand and Robert the right-hand side of the bed.

A pair of jeans and a rather grubby jumper lay on a chair on Robert's side of the room and there was a pair of muddy walking boots underneath it.

'When he was found, Robert was wearing smart trousers and a jacket with a raincoat on top. Is that what he usually wore to go to work?' Peter asked, remembering that university staff usually dressed casually. The jumper, jeans and walking boots were much more likely attire for a day in the Geography department than the stylish jacket in which the body had been clad.

'Sometimes,' Gemma answered vaguely. 'It all depended.'

'On what?'

'On what he was doing, I suppose. I mean, he wouldn't wear that for going out to collect soil samples and that, but he might dress up a bit to impress the head of department if he had a meeting to go to.'

Peter filed this information away in his mind, still sceptical of the suggestion that a research assistant, particularly in a scientific discipline, would be likely to dress formally except under duress. He fancied that, wherever Robert White was bound that morning, it was not the Geography department.

'Can you show me where he kept his things?' he asked, gesturing towards the wardrobes.

'OK. Robert used this section,' Gemma said, opening the door at the far left-hand end of the bank of wardrobes to reveal a hanging space containing a dinner jacket and matching trousers, a formal business suit and three shirts. Then she opened the next door, behind which were shelves housing several pairs of neatly folded jeans, about half a dozen tee shirts, some shorts and an assortment of underwear.

Peter bent down and pulled out a cardboard box, which filled the bottom shelf. Inside, he found Robert's driving licence, birth certificate, a plastic wallet containing Australian currency and various insurance and financial documents.

'We'll take these with us as well, if you don't mind,' Peter said. 'Sergeant Godwin will give you a receipt for them and for the laptop. Now I think we've finished here,' he added straightening up. 'Here's my card. Give me a ring if you think of anything else that might help us to work out what happened.'

CHAPTER 4

'OK Paul,' Peter said, as they sat in a nearby pub eating their lunch, 'tell me how you come to know Gemma Markham.'

'I told you, it was years ago. I was only about thirteen.'

'So you're confident that there's no conflict of interest here?'

'Yes. We were both just kids, and it was only for a few months. I haven't set eyes on her for … it must be fifteen or sixteen years.'

Peter said nothing, but Paul got the impression that he was not satisfied. Eventually he felt compelled to go on, to fill the silence that had ensued.

'My mum was ill,' he said, at last. 'She couldn't cope with me at home, so she got me put into care for a few months. Gemma had lost both her parents and she was in care too. She's a couple of years older than me and she felt sorry for me and looked after me a bit. Then I went back to Mum and I haven't heard anything from her or about her since.'

Peter nodded without speaking, chewing slowly on his sandwich. After perhaps half a minute, he put it down and looked Paul direct in the face.

'I was brought up in the National Children's Home,' he said quietly. 'I know it's not always easy for new kids to settle in. I guess you were lucky to have someone to stick up for you.'

'Yes,' Paul answered, not sure how to respond to this unexpected revelation. He had never known Peter to speak about his background or personal life before.

'I'll take your word for it that your previous acquaintance with Ms Markham won't compromise your involvement in the investigation of her boyfriend's death,' Peter went on. Years of bullying at school and during his early years in the police service had made him reticent about his own time in care and he had no desire to publicise Paul's past by making an official report of his previous acquaintance with their main witness. 'But we may have to review that if it turns out that she's somehow directly involved in it. Meanwhile, you can help me by filling me in on her background – if you can remember it at all.'

'Like I said,' Paul began, searching his memory for information about this ghost from his past, 'both her parents had died, which was why she was in care. She'd been in the home for about six months, I think, before I arrived, but it may have been more. She'd been around for long enough to know her way to market anyhow. She must have been fifteen then. She was doing her GCSEs. I think her dad died first – yes, I'm sure of it. He died in some sort of accident when she was quite small and then her mum had a fatal accident as well, and that was when she was taken into care.'

'And now her boyfriend seems to have also suffered an accidental death,' Peter observed mildly. Paul was unable to work out whether or not he was implying that this might be more than just a coincidence.

'Yes,' he agreed at length, 'she's been very unlucky.'

'Did she ever talk about her parents at all?'

'Not that I remember – except,' Paul paused to think,

'there was this man who came round and asked to see her. He called himself a friend of the family. Gemma refused point blank to have anything to do with him, so the care workers sent him away. Then, afterwards, she told me that he had been trying to get her mother to marry him. I sort of got the impression that she – Gemma that is – must have been very close to her father and didn't approve of the idea of her mother having a boyfriend.'

'That figures. I can't imagine my kids being best pleased if anything happened to my wife and I went off and found a new stepmother for them,' Peter said, confident in his own mind that, were Angie to die, he could never contemplate re-marrying. Nevertheless, plenty of widows and widowers did have successful second marriages and perhaps Gemma's mother needed someone to share the task of bringing up a troublesome teenager. She may even have needed a new husband to give her financial security. Moreover, Gemma was growing up; maybe her mother feared being entirely alone when the time came for her to leave home.

'And then when her mum died,' Paul went on, 'I think maybe in a funny sort of way she blamed this friend.'

'Do you mean she actually told you that she thought he'd killed her mother?' Peter asked sharply.

'No, nothing like that. I think it was more that, if he hadn't been around, the circumstances that led up to her accident – whatever it was – wouldn't have happened.'

'She must feel that everyone she cares about is doomed to die a violent death,' Peter said quietly, thinking through everything that Paul had told him. 'I'd better see what we can do about organising some counselling or something for her.'

They sat in silence for several minutes, each lost in his own thoughts.

Peter was wondering whether Paul had been completely open about his past relationship with Gemma. During his own time in care, he had seen dozens of children come and go through the group that shared his house. There were a few of the longer-term inmates with whom he still exchanged Christmas cards and brief news updates each year, but most of them had long since faded to vague blurs in his memory. When it came to those who had stayed for only a matter of months before moving on, he would certainly have had difficulty recollecting any of their names. Yet Paul had displayed an emotional response to the mere mention of Gemma Markham, even before he met her and confirmed that she was his old companion. Perhaps he should be taken off this case; but then again, if Gemma had nothing to do with Robert's death, it hardly mattered that she was an old friend of one of the police team investigating it, and if she was in any way responsible, Paul's knowledge of her background might prove useful.

Paul was wondering why Peter had compared Gemma's resentment of the prospect of a new stepfather with a hypothetical scenario in which his children had lost their mother. Was he less sure that they would be unwilling to accept a replacement for him if he had died and his wife re-married? It seemed odd that he should have turned the situation round like that – almost as if he thought that his children might not have minded having a different father. Was it because he lacked confidence that he was a good father? Now he came to think of it, Paul realised that Peter often behaved as if he was not confident in his own abilities. Paul liked him because he never put other people down and was always willing to listen to ideas from the officers working under him. Was this because he was never really sure of himself?

'I suppose it was a local authority home you were in?' Peter said conversationally, hoping to draw out more information about the relationship that Paul had had with Gemma.

'That's right – Willowbank House, up the Woodstock Road. I think it's still there, though I haven't ever been back to see.'

'No. It doesn't do to go back,' Peter murmured thoughtfully.

'What about you?' Paul plucked up courage to ask. 'I mean – what happened to your parents to put you in care?'

'I don't know,' Peter shrugged. 'I was in the home from as early as I can remember. Nobody told me who my parents were or why they couldn't look after me and I never asked. When I was tiny I imagined that I was an orphan, but then, after I started to understand things a bit more, I assumed that I must have been illegitimate and my mother thought it was for the best.'

'I thought babies were usually adopted, aren't they?'

'Maybe nobody fancied me,' Peter shrugged again. 'There's a surprising amount of prejudice against red-headed kids.'

'I wouldn't say you were exactly-' Paul began. Then he stopped, realising that Peter's sandy grey hair could well have once been a fiery carrot shade and that it was not particularly polite to draw attention to the ravages of age by pointing out the change. 'I mean, it's not supposed to be a matter of foster parents choosing the bonniest baby, is it?' he finished rather lamely.

'No, but it would hardly work if you let people adopt a child that they couldn't stand the sight of, would it?'

'And didn't you ever try to find your parents?' asked Paul, curious to know, and also keen to move the conversation away from consideration of Peter's supposed deficiencies as a baby.

'No. I reckoned it was better to let sleeping dogs lie. Who knows what trouble it might cause if, say, my mum was married and hadn't told her husband that she'd had a baby before they met.'

'But aren't you even curious to know who she is?'

'No. It's what you do with your life that's important, not who your parents were. And the sort of person you turn out to be is much more to do with your upbringing than your genetics.'

'So you go for nurture rather than nature?'

'All the time; but you have to take responsibility for your own actions too. If I mess up as a dad, it isn't good enough for me to hide behind being a poor kid who never had a dad of his own to show him how to do it.'

Paul thought about this. He was not used to his boss talking about his home life, even in this oblique way, or engaging in philosophical debate. He thought about his own chaotic upbringing and was grateful to Peter for not having quizzed him on the exact circumstances that had led to him being taken into temporary local authority care.

His contemplation was interrupted by the sound of Peter's mobile phone. It was PC Jordan Fox, a young police constable whose beat covered the area of East Oxford where Peter lived.

'I'm sorry to bother you sir,' he said apologetically. 'I'm in Manzil Way Gardens. We've got a black youth here, with a young girl that we think he's abducted. I was taking him in, but he insisted on me ringing you. He says you can vouch for him.'

'Oh? What's his name?' Peter asked, puzzled. The neighbourhood was very mixed racially and there were a good number of black families amongst Peter's neighbours, but he could not think of anyone who would have been likely to call upon him as a character witness.

'That's just it,' the constable replied with a nervous laugh, 'he says his name's Edward Johns. He claims you're his father!'

'And what makes you doubt his word?' Peter asked coldly, suddenly realising what had happened and not liking it.

'Well, I mean ... like I said: he's black,' PC Fox answered, completely taken aback by Peter's response, 'and you're ... I mean ... Oh! I see ... I'm sorry, I hadn't thought of that ... Are you telling me that you have a black son?'

'My son, Edward, has dark skin,' Peter said calmly, but

with a menace in his voice which made Fox, listening on the other end of the line, wish fervently that he had been more careful about how he had approached the situation.

When a passer-by had drawn his attention to a young black man struggling to put a screaming white child into a buggy, he had jumped to the conclusion that the man had no business to be taking her away from the park. Then, when the man had claimed to be the son of a senior white police officer, it had not occurred to him that he could have been speaking the truth. His heart started beating faster as he realised his mistake and it dawned on him that his actions could well be interpreted as betraying racial prejudice.

'I'm sorry sir,' Fox apologised. 'I didn't think … and the little girl? He's got a fair-haired kid with him, about two years old. She seems very distressed.'

'Not surprising when she's just seen a clod-hopping great policeman arresting her best friend!' Peter retorted. 'Her name's Lucy Paige. Her mother's a friend of ours. Eddie's baby-sitting for the day while she goes to a conference in London. Are you satisfied now?"

'Yes sir. That's just exactly what he told me, sir. I'm sorry. I'll let him go now. I never thought …'

'No,' Peter commanded. 'You stay right there. I'm coming over. I'll be with you in ten minutes.'

He turned to Paul.

'I want you to drive me over to Manzil Way Gardens – it's a park on the Cowley Road – and drop me there before you go on to the post mortem. We don't want to keep Mike waiting, so tell him to start without me. I've got a bit of a family crisis to sort out, then I'll walk back home and pick up my car and join you.

CHAPTER 5

They left the pub and walked towards Paul's car in silence. Paul was trying to piece together what had happened, from having heard Peter's end of the conversation, not daring to ask for an explanation in case Peter thought he was prying into his family life. Peter did not trust himself to speak. for fear of betraying to Paul the intense anger that he felt towards PC Fox. After a few minutes, however, he realised that he would have to give Paul some sort of explanation for this abrupt change of plan and he started to wonder whether he might have been a little too hard on Jordan Fox. Perhaps it was only natural to jump to conclusions in the way that he had done.

'Tell me something, Paul,' Peter said tentatively, as they got into the car. 'What would you think if you saw a young man of Afro-Caribbean appearance putting a two-year-old fair-haired girl into a buggy in the park?'

'I'm not sure, sir,' Paul answered cautiously, trying to be honest, but not wanting to incriminate himself in Peter's eyes. 'I suppose I'd be surprised, because you don't expect young black men to be interested in looking after kids – especially not other people's.'

'And how could you be so sure the child wasn't his?'

Peter asked sharply.

'Well, sir, children usually look a bit like their parents, don't they?'

Peter sighed, but decided not to pursue the issue of inherited racial characteristics and the possibility that children may sometimes differ significantly in appearance from one of their parents.

'OK. Let's assume you're right and it is someone else's child. Would you arrest him for child abduction?'

'Not without more to go on than that.'

'Well then: suppose the child was screaming and looked as if she didn't want to go?'

'Then I'd probably start to think there was something wrong.'

'Even though kids that age are always throwing tantrums?'

'I don't know, sir. I don't have much experience of young children.'

'OK. Now, tell me this,' Peter said, getting to the nub of his concerns. 'Would you treat the situation any differently if it was the other way round? What if it was a young white man making off with a black kid?'

'I hope I'd do just the same, sir,' Paul replied promptly, anxious to dispel any possible accusation of racist bias. 'I mean: it'd still be a bit odd, wouldn't it? You expect kids that age to be with their mothers, don't you?'

'Or their fathers,' Peter pointed out, it suddenly occurring to him that Fox's actions could have been motivated by sexism rather than racism. He wondered briefly whether it was wrong of him to feel a sense of relief at this possibility.

'When our kids were small, my wife was working full time and I often took them out. Why would you assume there was something wrong just because it was a young man with the child?' he asked, determined to work out what could have made Fox believe that Eddie could not be the innocent child-minder that he claimed to be.

'But, we're not talking about the child being out with its father, are we?'

'And I'm saying there's no way you could tell that he wasn't the father.'

Peter paused, wondering whether he had already revealed too much personal information, but determined to make his point.

'Both my kids would be described as black,' he explained, 'but nobody ever accused me of stealing them from their real parents. In fact, there were some people who would drive me mad by telling me how much they admired me for taking in a couple of coloured kids – as if my kids were somehow less desirable just because of the colour of their skin!'

Paul could not think of anything to say. Peter waited for a few seconds and then took pity on him.

'Never mind,' he said reassuringly. 'You've told me what I wanted to know. I guess the constable was in a difficult position and was trying to put the child's safety first. I just wish he hadn't jumped to conclusions so quickly. Or maybe I just wish it wasn't my son on the receiving end!'

They pulled up outside the patch of grass that was Manzil Way Gardens. Peter looked across at the children's play area and spotted Eddie sitting on a bench just outside the low fence that separated it from the rest of the small park.

'There he is!' Peter said to Paul, who followed Peter's gaze and saw a tall police officer with his back to them, standing over a young man who appeared to be sitting hunched up on a bench clutching a bundle of what looked like old clothes.

Then Paul saw that there were a child's legs protruding from the bundle and he worked out that the toddler, whose welfare was at the centre of the incident, was curled up on the lad's lap, her face buried in his chest. A few feet away there was a cluster of people: a mixture of middle-aged women and younger ones with children in tow. They seemed to be watching the proceedings, presumably wondering whether an arrest might be imminent.

'Would you like me to wait for you?' Paul suggested. 'We've got time, and it would save you the walk.'

'No.' Peter shook his head. 'You'd better get over to the mortuary. We don't want to keep Mike waiting. All being well, I won't be long, but you never know. Tell Mike I'll be there as soon as.'

He got out of the car and Paul pulled away. Peter stood for a moment at the side of the road and then strode purposefully across to the bench where his son was sitting.

'Hi Eddie!' he greeted him. 'How're you doing?'

'I'm sorry Dad,' Eddie said looking up. 'I didn't mean for you to come out. I thought you'd be able to clear everything up over the phone.'

'No, no,' Peter said, shaking his head. 'I had to make sure you and Lucy were both OK. Now tell me what happened.'

Hearing the sound of his voice, Lucy squirmed round in Eddie's arms and favoured Peter with a radiant smile. He noticed that her face was blotchy and red and her nose was running. She held out her arms in an extravagant gesture of welcome and cried out, 'Beter!'

Peter picked her up and held her tightly to him. Then he shifted her in his arms so that she was facing towards Fox, who was standing awkwardly, not liking to interrupt this reunion and unsure what to do to placate the inspector after what had turned out to be a serious faux pas.

'Lucy,' Peter said solemnly, 'let me introduce you to PC Jordan Fox. Fox: this is Lucy Paige, my goddaughter. You probably knew her father, Detective Superintendent Richard Paige.'

'Yes,' Fox said eagerly, pleased to be on comparatively safe territory. 'I remember his retirement party – or rather, what was going to be his retirement party. He was killed while on duty, wasn't he?'

'That's right. Lucy was born about six months later. Her mum works full time at the university, so we help out with childcare – like today, for instance, when she had to go to a conference. Eddie's home from university at the moment, so he was the obvious person to look after Lucy. Now, Ed, you were going to tell me what happened.'

'I was pushing Lucy on the swings when it got to lunchtime,' Eddie related. 'I told her it was time to go, but she said she wanted more time on the swings. I gave her five more minutes and then said we had to go. I got her out of the swing, but she wouldn't go in her buggy. She started screaming and arching her back, the way she does, and I had to fight with her to get her in. A woman saw her crying and came over to watch, as if she was suspicious of what was going on, but she didn't say anything and in the end, she walked off. But then, when we finally set off for home, with Lucy still screaming, there was this policeman in uniform barring our way and wanting to know what I thought I was doing and where Lucy's mother was. I tried to explain, but he sounded so fierce that it frightened Lucy and made her scream even more. In the end, I thought the only thing was to ask him to ring you, because he'd have to believe what you said.'

'I see,' Peter said quietly when this long speech was over. He turned to PC Fox. 'See if you can get the lynch mob to disperse, will you? Tell them the show's over.'

Fox nodded and went over to the group of women, who started drifting away after he said a few words to them. Peter handed Lucy back to Eddie.

'Now Lucy,' he said firmly. 'Eddie's in charge today and what he says goes. So let's get you back home for your dinner, and no more fuss, OK?'

Lucy nodded hard and smiled up at Eddie, allowing him to fasten her into the buggy without fuss.

'I'm sorry sir,' Fox said to Peter, coming back after dispersing the crowd, speaking quickly, eager to retrieve his standing with the more senior officer. 'I ought to have believed him when he gave your name. I never thought. I should have realised that, with your background, it'd be natural for you to have an adopted son.'

'And what exactly do you mean by my background?' Peter asked with icy calm.

'I'm sorry. I've probably got that wrong too,' Fox gabbled, realising that he had made another blunder, but not quite understanding why. 'Adams told me that you were an orphan and grew up in some sort of children's home.'

'If you're hoping to progress in the police service then I would advise you to find a better role model than Adams,' Peter observed drily. 'There's a reason that he's never made it past sergeant. I don't care who knows that I'm a product of the National Children's Home, but neither you nor Adams have any business thinking that gives you a right to believe you know how it makes me feel about family life or anything else. And it certainly doesn't give you the right to suggest that my kids aren't my own flesh and blood, just because they happen to take after their mother more than me in terms of looks.'

He paused, watching Fox's face, which was registering puzzlement and then dismay, as he realised how badly he had misjudged the situation and how unfortunate his well-meant remarks had been. Peter suddenly felt sorry for him. After all, he was only young and he had probably never come across a mixed-race family before.

'Let me assure you,' Peter went on, speaking less seriously now, 'that in other ways he is very much his father's son. We are both, for example, very much inclined to become irritable when kept from our food. So I suggest that we take Lucy back home and get some lunch, while you carry on with whatever it was you were doing before all this kicked off.'

'Yes sir,' Fox said, standing aside to allow Eddie to push the buggy past him. 'And sir?' he added nervously, 'Will you be reporting this?'

Peter thought for a moment. He had no real intention of taking the incident any further, but he briefly toyed with the idea of leaving the young officer guessing by giving an inconclusive answer. Then he decided that Fox had already suffered enough and determined to put him out of his misery.

'I think our lords and masters have better things to do than to read reports from me about your indiscretions, don't you? Just try not to make assumptions about people based on appearances in future.'

'Yes sir. Thank you, sir.' He hesitated and then plucked up courage to ask, 'I'm still not sure, sir. What would you have done in my place? I mean, it could have been a real case of child abduction, couldn't it?'

'You know, that's a very good point,' Peter conceded, realising the justice of this statement. He thought for a few seconds. 'I think that I would have asked to accompany them home so that I could check things out. Come along with us now and I'll show you.'

They walked the short distance to the Johns family home at a brisk pace. When they arrived, Eddie let them in using his front door key.

'That's the first thing to notice,' Peter pointed out to Fox. 'Now we know that he's given you his real address or at least somewhere that he has legitimate access to. Now we need to inspect for signs that it's a suitable place for a two year old. We can also watch to see if Lucy seems to find it familiar or if she's frightened by anything here.'

They went into the hall and closed the door behind them. Eddie started undoing the straps that held Lucy in the buggy.

'Now, tell me what you see,' Peter urged Fox.

'The stair gate,' Fox said, looking round. 'That's to stop her climbing up and falling down, right?'

'That's right,' Peter agreed. 'That's a good sign, because you wouldn't bother with that unless you often had young children in the house. Now let's have a look in the front room.'

He led the way into the living room and showed Fox the toys and equipment, which Bernie had deposited there that morning. Fox looked around the room, taking in the worn three-piece suite, faded curtains and small television set. He had imagined that a detective inspector would have had more impressive furnishings. There was a bookcase against one wall with some photographs standing on top of it. Fox went over and looked at a large picture in a stainless steel frame standing in the middle. It was of a much younger Peter Johns, dressed in a grey suit and looking a little self-conscious as he stood next to a black woman wearing a long white dress and holding a posy of yellow and blue flowers. More flowers were entwined in her hair, which was braided in an intricate design across her head.

'Your wedding photograph?' he asked.

'That's right. And these on either side are Hannah's and Eddie's christenings. And then this is our most recent family portrait.'

Fox looked at a group photograph in which he recognised an older Peter sitting surrounded by his wife, son and daughter. His pale skin, with the red and white, blotchy complexion typical of the redhead, looked rather out of place beside their brown faces. Fox reflected that it must be strange for Peter being the odd one out in his own family.

'Now let's check out the kitchen,' Peter said briskly, leading the way back into the hall and along the passage to a room at the back of the house. He opened the door and stood aside to allow Fox to look in.

He saw Lucy standing on an upturned bucket in front of the sink while Eddie helped her to wash her hands. A beeping sound from the microwave announced that the stew, which Angie had left for their lunch, was ready. Fox watched as Eddie carefully lifted Lucy down and dried her hands before switching his attention to dishing up the food. Lucy went over to the small kitchen table and climbed on to a chair. Fox noticed, lying in front of her, a plastic cup with a picture of a rabbit and the word 'Lucy' on the side. Peter laid his hand on Fox's shoulder and looked past him into the room.

'There you are!' he said softly, speaking low so as not to disturb the peaceful scene. 'Clear evidence that the little girl feels at home here, and hence evidence that your suspicious young man was telling the truth when he said that he had been left in charge of her for the day.'

'Yes sir,' Fox mumbled, feeling increasingly foolish for not having dealt with the situation in a less confrontational way. 'I'm sorry sir. I'll know what to do next time.'

'Good. And now,' Peter went on, 'I'll show you out and you can get back to keeping the streets of East Oxford free of crime.'

He led Fox back to the front door and ushered him through. Then he returned to the kitchen.

'It's OK Dad,' Eddie assured him. 'There's no need for you to hang around. We're both fine now.'

'Are you sure?' Peter felt strangely reluctant to leave, although at the same time he was keen to return to the mortuary and the results of the post mortem on Robert White. 'You wouldn't like me to-'

'No Dad. Like I said, we're fine. It's no big deal, really.'

'Fox should never have reacted like that.' Now that the young constable was no longer there, Peter felt a resurgence of the anger that he had felt when he first heard about the incident. 'He shouldn't have jumped to conclusions, just because of the colour of your skin. And it's no good saying that wasn't a factor, because I know it was.'

'Look Dad, I said it's no big deal. Just forget about it.'
'But-'
'No. Think about how it looked: me and Lucy. It's only natural he should wonder what I was doing with her.'

'Whatever he thought, he ought to have known how to

handle it better,' Peter argued.

'Well, now you've shown him, haven't you? Please Dad! Forget about it. It doesn't bother me – really. I'm used to that sort of thing.'

'But you shouldn't be used to it! That is just the point. You shouldn't have to get used to being treated like that.'

Eddie abandoned the argument and busied himself with feeding Lucy. He could see that his father was not going to be convinced and that the best thing was to ignore his indignation and allow his anger to blow itself out. Peter stood indecisively in the doorway for a moment or two and then turned to go.

'OK then. I'd better get back,' he said over his shoulder. 'See you later.'

CHAPTER 6

The post mortem was in full swing when Peter arrived at the mortuary. He joined Paul, who was watching intently as the pathologist and his assistant took tissue samples and assessed the condition of the internal organs.

'It looks like he drowned,' Paul reported to Peter.

'What I said,' Mike corrected him, 'was that the appearance of the body is *consistent* with drowning. We won't know until we get the toxicology reports back whether that was the only, or main, cause of death. There is always the possibility that drugs or alcohol were involved. And there is also a significant wound on the back of the head, which was almost certainly inflicted before death and which could well have rendered him unconscious.'

'So, are you suggesting someone hit him before he fell – or was pushed – into the river?' Peter asked sharply.

'Could be – or then again, he could have hit his head as he fell. There are pieces of stone or grit in the wound, which could have come from a fall from a height on to a stone wall or a rocky outcrop along the bank. If the wound was inflicted in a fight, then I'd say that the chances are someone pushed him back hard against a wall, hitting his head against it, rather than someone coming at him from behind and hitting him over the head. There are some bruises on his back which would fit with that; but there's an outside chance that his assailant picked up a loose rock and hit him with it, I suppose.'

'Will the grit particles enable us to work out where he went in?' Peter asked eagerly.

'I don't know about that – not really my area – but I guess once you have an idea where that was, they may help to confirm it. I'll bag up all the pieces I can find and hand them over to forensics to check out. If you're lucky, they'll turn out to be from some unusual type of rock that will pinpoint exactly what he hit his head on. If you're unlucky it'll just be bog standard silica with no distinguishing features.'

'I thought most of Oxfordshire was limestone, not silica,' Paul observed quietly. 'That and Oxford clay.'

'Well, there you are then!' Mike declared cheerily. 'It looked like sand to me, but what do I know? Maybe it will turn out to be something unusual that tells you exactly where the incident happened. Now, I'd also like to draw your attention to these scratches here.'

He pointed towards the left-hand side of the victim's face. Peter and Paul leaned closer to see four scratches in the skin, each about an inch long.

'They could have been made by finger nails,' Mike explained, 'which might indicate some sort of a fight.'

'A woman?' Paul asked. 'Perhaps defending herself against him?'

'Could be,' Mike agreed with a shrug. 'In which case, she might still have traces of his skin under her nails – if you can find her and persuade her to let you look. But then again these scratches could have been caused by something else – or they could have happened earlier and have nothing at all to do with him falling in the water.'

'And do you have any better idea when he died?' Peter asked.

'Well, the contents of his stomach indicate that it wasn't long after his last meal.'

'Which was?'

'Have a look for yourself!' Mike said cheerfully, picking up a large bowl and holding it out towards Peter, who took a step backwards, shaking his head.

'Just tell me what you found,' he urged.

'Well, I haven't done a proper analysis yet, but just with a visual inspection, I'd say bacon featured quite a lot – and potato – and green beans – and then what looks like pineapple and some sort of pastry I think – and there's a faint smell of coffee.'

'Sounds more like dinner than breakfast then, would you say?'

'Well, there you have me. I cannot venture to give an opinion on what an Australian might habitually eat for breakfast, but I'm guessing that green beans would be unusual. Bacon though – that could be breakfast could it not? But then the pineapple is making me think maybe it's more like gammon maybe. The pieces look quite thick for rashers – here, see!'

Peter once more declined to view the proffered stomach contents, muttering that he would take Mike's word for it that the corpse's last meal had been gammon and pineapple with green beans.

'We can check with the girlfriend what they had for dinner that evening,' he said to Paul, 'but it does look as if he must have gone out and got himself killed almost immediately after they got home.'

He turned back to address Mike, who had returned to his dissection of the body and was intent on inspecting the liver.

'When you say he died soon after his last meal, how long exactly do you mean?'

'Now "exactly" isn't a word I like to use,' Mike said without looking up. 'I would say that he probably died *approximately* one hour after he finished eating, but it could have been less, could have been more, it all depends.'

'And what would you say was the longest time that could have elapsed between his meal and his death?' Peter pressed him.

'I'd say two hours – maybe three at the outside.'

'Thanks. That's certainly not what I was expecting. We definitely need to follow up on that with the girlfriend.'

'Are you thinking she maybe did it?' Mike asked, for the first time showing some interest in the case beyond his examination of the body.

'Not at all,' Peter said hastily, 'but it does call into question her story that they went to bed together and she only discovered he'd gone out when she woke in the morning.'

The rest of the post mortem proceeded without giving any further insight into when or how Robert White had died. At the end, Peter and Paul left the mortuary, having gained the impression that the likeliest scenario was that Robert White had somehow fallen into the river and drowned during the night, possibly after some sort of fight, perhaps with a woman. Mike promised to send them a full report as soon as the various laboratory tests had been completed.

'Did you get things sorted out with your son?' Paul asked, once they were outside where they would not be overheard.

'Yes. I don't think that young constable will be quite so hasty in future.' Peter sighed, 'I'm afraid it may have a lasting effect on Lucy's willingness to trust policemen in uniform, though. She seemed quite traumatised by the whole business.'

'I've been thinking about what you said about "would I intervene if I saw a child being taken away apparently against its will?" Do you remember the James Bulger case? The little boy who was abducted and murdered in Liverpool.'

'Actually, it was Bootle,' Peter said, remembering that

Bernie had been very definite about this distinction. 'But, yes – I remember it very well. Eddie was the same age as Thompson and Venables, and I found it hard to get my head round the idea of boys that seemed no different from him doing a thing like that.'

'Well, if you remember, there were a whole load of people who saw them with him, but they just assumed that he was their little brother, so they didn't do anything to stop them dragging him off to where they killed him. I was still a green PC myself when it happened, and I remember discussing how dreadful it was that nobody had lifted a finger to help. So I guess I'd want to step in if there was any chance something like that was going on – even if it did mean appearing heavy-handed sometimes.'

'So you're saying that attitudes have changed since the days when I got away with Hannah flinging herself in the floor of the supermarket and screaming herself blue in the face just because I wouldn't let her fill the trolley with pink toilet rolls?' Peter asked, remembering a famous incident from Johns family shared memory. 'I suppose now the store detective would have demanded to see her birth certificate and my passport to establish that she really was my daughter!'

'Oh! At least!' Paul joked, pleased to have detected a lighter tone in Peter's voice, which made it clear that he was no longer viewing the subject with the seriousness that had been evident earlier in the afternoon. 'After all, most murders are committed by members of the victim's family, so I think you'd probably get a visit from social services the next day to check it really was pink toilet rolls, and not something more sinister, which had made her cry!'

'They're not called the terrible twos for nothing!' Peter commented, 'as any parent will tell you. We should have known better than to let Eddie out in public in charge of a toddler – they are guaranteed to cause embarrassment one way or another.'

He looked at his watch.

'It's too early to go back to White's flat. I would rather wait until the neighbours are home from work so we can ask them if they heard anything during the night. So let's go to the Geography department and see if any of his colleagues can tell us why he might have gone wandering the streets at dead of night.'

CHAPTER 7

The School of Geography and the Environment was housed in the Oxford University Centre for the Environment, which was an unimposing brick-built structure in the middle of the university science area. The receptionist, who greeted them as they entered, showed them to the office that Robert White had shared with another post-doctoral research assistant, Claire Chiao. Claire looked up from her computer as they entered, with an expression of surprise on her face at the unexpected intrusion. As her surname suggested, she was of oriental appearance. Peter made the introductions.

'Good afternoon. I'm Detective Inspector Peter Johns and this is Detective Sergeant Paul Godwin. We're investigating the death of Robert White. I believe he worked with you?'

'Well, we were working on different projects,' Claire said, looking round at them in wide-eyed bewilderment. She spoke without any trace of an accent and Peter correctly deduced that she had been born and raised in southern England. 'But what do you mean, investigating his death? What's happened?'

'I'm sorry. I thought you would probably have heard.

Robert White's body was recovered from the Thames early this morning.'

'Are you saying he drowned?'

'It's looking that way, but we're still not sure exactly what happened. That's why we want to speak to the people here who knew him. Can we ask you a few questions?'

'Sure. Fire away.'

'When was the last time you saw him?'

'The day before yesterday,' Claire answered promptly. 'I left at about five and he was here, putting away some research papers he'd been reading.' She pointed in the direction of a tall metal filing cabinet. 'He was very organised: he always put things away neatly so he could find them again later.'

Peter looked round the room, taking in the two desks. The one at which Claire sat was covered with untidy piles of books and papers. A yoghurt pot held an assortment of pens and pencils; two mugs, both with brown tea stains visible on the inside, stood amidst a jumble of items including a stapler, scissors, headphones and a calculator. The other desk was bare, apart from a large computer screen, a keyboard and a mouse. These had all been pushed tidily to the back, leaving a clear space in front of the chair, which was stowed neatly under the desk. Peter tried the draws of the storage unit beneath the desk. It was locked. He turned to Paul.

'Do you remember if there were any keys found on the body?'

'Yes, there was a ring with the keys of his flat and about half a dozen others. I remember thinking that one of them looked as if it was for a suitcase or a filing cabinet and there were a couple that might fit these drawers.'

'I think Carol Benjamin, Professor Baxter's secretary, has a spare set of keys for all the cupboards and drawers in this part of the building,' Claire put in helpfully. 'Would you like me to ring her?'

'Yes please. I'd like to have a look in here, in case he left anything that might throw some light on his state of mind when he went home on Tuesday evening. And if there are any personal items, they ought to be given to his parents.'

'Have you informed his parents,' Claire asked anxiously. 'You do know they're in Australia?'

'Yes,' Peter assured her. 'I rang them as soon as we were sure it was him. Now, if you could just put me on to the secretary that you mentioned ...'

Claire obediently dialled the extension for him and soon Peter had explained to Carol why he was there and what he needed. She promised to bring the keys immediately. Peter turned back to Claire and continued his questioning.

'How did he seem when you saw him? I mean what sort of mood was he in on Tuesday? Happy? Anxious? Depressed?'

'Much the same as usual, I think,' Claire said, shrugging. 'I'm afraid I didn't really think about it.'

'There was nothing that, looking back now, could have suggested that he might have been thinking of taking his own life?'

'Is that what you think happened?'

'We don't know – that's why I'm asking. Was there anything?'

'No. I don't think so.'

'Tell me about his day. Do you know what time he got in, and what he was doing on Tuesday?'

'He was already here when I got in at half past eight. He had a cup of coffee half drunk, so I guess he probably got in not long before that and made it for himself first thing. He had a meeting with his supervisor, Dr Abbott, in the morning and then he spent some time working on a research paper they were writing together. I don't know what he was doing in the afternoon, because I was out of the office. I'm working on a project that involves collaboration with a group of scientists in Brazil and we were holding a video conference. I only got back just before five. That's when I saw Rob filing his research papers. I just popped in to pick up my coat and bag and went off home.'

There was a knock at the door. Paul opened it and saw three figures standing in the corridor outside. They introduced themselves as Carol Benjamin, Professor Arnold Baxter, the head of the research group of which both Claire and Robert were part, and Dr Chris Abbott, Robert's supervisor. They crowded into the office, which suddenly felt very small. Paul had to ask them all to stand back so that there was room for him to open the drawers beneath Robert's desk, using the key that Carol handed to him.

The top drawer contained nothing of interest: just pens and pencils, a ruler, stapler, hole-punch and other small items of office equipment. Paul closed it and opened the second drawer.

'What have we here?' Paul said in a tone of surprise. He put his hand in and took out a passport and a paper wallet bearing the name of a travel agent on the outside. He handed the passport to Peter and opened the wallet himself to look inside.

'Why would he keep his passport here in the office instead of in his flat?' Peter wondered.

'He'll have had to bring it in as ID when he first joined the department,' Claire suggested. 'Maybe he just never got round to taking it back home.'

'This is a one-way ticket to Australia,' Paul said, holding up a document that he had found in the wallet, 'dated two weeks next Wednesday.'

'Well yes, of course,' Dr Abbott said, in a tone which suggested that the police appeared to him to be very slow on the uptake, 'his contract ends at the end of the month. He was going back home.'

'That's strange! His girlfriend didn't mention that.' Paul

exclaimed. 'You'd have thought it would be something that would have been uppermost in her mind.'

'Do you know how he felt about the move?' Peter asked. 'Was he pleased to be going home, or sorry not to be staying on here?'

'Well, it was his choice,' Dr Abbott replied, still sounding as if he were being asked to state the obvious. 'We offered to renew his contract, but he turned it down. You can draw your own conclusions.'

'He was a good worker then? You were pleased with what he did?'

'Yes,' Dr Abbott's tone started to thaw a little. 'He worked very hard and was good at what he did. He was very dedicated to the project. In fact, at first I thought he was rather too dedicated: I started to worry that he didn't have any outside life. He would be here at all times of the day and night, beavering away. So I was pleased when he acquired a girlfriend who forced him to keep more regular hours.'

'He's been going back to his old ways a bit recently though,' Claire put in. 'not as bad as before, but he's always in before me in the morning and hardly ever leaves before six now.'

'How long has that been going on?' Peter asked.

'I'm not sure,' Claire answered, frowning with concentration. 'It happened gradually – maybe two or three months – maybe a bit more than that.'

'It's probably just that he's been trying to finish everything off before he leaves,' Dr Abbott suggested. 'When he came to me and told me he'd decided not to take the new contract, I could see he was torn between wanting to see things through and wanting to go back home.'

'So the offer was for him to continue working on the same project?'

'Essentially, yes. Technically, it was a new project, but it was developing the stuff that we had been doing already. I was a bit annoyed with Rob, actually, because we'd named him on the grant, thinking he would stay on, so it made things a bit difficult for us when he decided not to stay after all.'

'OK. I think I'm getting the picture now.' Peter looked round at the assembled group before addressing Dr Abbott again. 'Tell you what: is there somewhere that you and I can go to talk while Sergeant Godwin finishes off in here? As his supervisor, you must be the person who knows most about Robert White's likely state of mind at the time of his death.'

'You can come back to my room if you like,' Dr Abbott suggested. 'It's only two doors down the corridor.'

'I'll leave you to it,' Professor Baxter added, opening the door to go. 'I'll be in my room if you need me.'

Carol Benjamin also left, after presenting Paul with a further two keys – one to the filing cabinet and one for a tall cupboard in the corner of the room – and instructing him on how to find her office in order to return them when he was finished.

Peter followed Abbott to an office a little way down the corridor. It was larger than the one that Robert and Claire had shared, and contained three huge desks – two of them piled high with papers and the other set up as a computer workstation – three filing cabinets and a tall bookcase. Abbott and his guest sat down at a small round table on which lay copies of several geographical journals.

'Dr Abbott,' Peter began, taking out a notebook and pen as a way of indicating his intention to record salient points from their conversation, 'I'd like you to tell me whatever you can about Robert White. We need to get a picture of who he was and what he was like, in order to piece together the events that led up to him ending up in the Thames sometime between Tuesday night and the early hours of this morning. So let's start with the basics: when did he come here to work on your research project?'

'Just coming up to three years ago. It was a three-year

project, which ends this month. By about eighteen months into it, we realised that there was plenty of potential for extending the work, so we started working on applications for funding to continue beyond the end of the three years. We got confirmation that we had the money a few months back and it was then that Rob started hinting that maybe he wouldn't be staying on to do it.'

'Do you have any idea what prompted his change of heart?'

'No,' Abbott shook his head. 'I couldn't understand it at all. He insisted that he was still enjoying the work and he had this girlfriend that he was living with in Oxford, so it didn't make a lot of sense to me, but maybe he had reasons for wanting to go back to his family in Australia.'

'But, if he did, he didn't tell you what they were?'

'No.'

'And what will you do now – to find someone to work with you on the new grant?'

'We've already advertised. We've got interviews coming up next week.'

'Going back to Robert White: you said you were pleased when he acquired a girlfriend – when was that exactly?'

'I can't really remember – probably about a year into the grant, so about two years ago now. She's a hairdresser, which seemed a funny choice to me, but they appeared to hit it off OK.'

'And more recently? Did they still seem to be happy together?'

'As far as I know. He didn't talk about his private life to me.'

'Not even to say what he was planning to do about Gemma when he went back to Australia?'

'No. I did wonder, but I didn't like to ask and he didn't volunteer any information.'

'And his demeanour, generally, over the last few weeks? Did he seem depressed at all?'

'No. If anything I'd say he seemed more settled in his mind than he had been. I think he was anxious while we were waiting for the grant to come through, not knowing what to do if we got it – whether to stay on or to go back, I mean – and then it was a weight off his mind when he was able to tell me that he'd made the decision to go.'

'So you're saying that, a few months ago he did seem, if not exactly depressed, at least somewhat anxious, but that more recently he appeared to be happier?'

'Yes. I think that about sums it up.'

'So you wouldn't have expected him to attempt to take his own life?'

'Good God, no! Is that what you think happened?'

'We really don't know. That's why we need to ask the questions. Now, tell me: when was the last time you saw him?'

'The day before yesterday – in the morning. We met together to discuss some changes to a paper were writing, then he went away to work on it. He emailed it to me during the afternoon and we were supposed to be meeting again to put it to bed yesterday, but he didn't turn up.'

'Did that surprise you?'

'It did. I had never known him to miss an appointment before. It was completely out of character – and not to have contacted me to let me know either!'

'Did you take any steps to find out what was wrong?'

'I emailed him first, and then rang his room and Claire told me she hadn't seen him all day. We both agreed that it was very odd, but there didn't seem to be anything to be done about it. We just assumed he'd turn up.'

'You didn't try ringing him at home, or on his mobile?'

'Come to think of it, Claire did try the mobile, but it was switched off.'

'And the last time you met? Did he seem just as usual? Not excited about anything – or worried?'

'I suppose so,' Abbott shrugged, looking rather uncertain. 'I don't think I was taking much notice. We were both concentrating on the paper. We wanted it finished so that we could get it sent off before he went back to Australia.'

'OK.' Peter got up to go. 'I think we'll leave it there. Here's my card. Let me know if you think of anything else that might be useful to us.'

Paul meanwhile set to work emptying the drawers of the under-desk storage unit and thumbing through the contents of the filing cabinet. Claire obligingly gave him a large plastic carrier bag into which he put the few personal effects that Robert White had left behind: a pair of sunglasses, a calculator, a half-eaten tube of polo mints, a mobile phone charger and a framed photograph of Gemma, which Paul was surprised to find in the bottom drawer hidden beneath a waterproof jacket. Why was the picture not displayed on his desk? Paul wondered. Surely, that was a more natural place to keep it; but perhaps he took it out each day and then locked it away for safe keeping overnight.

'Now, you were telling us,' he said, turning to Claire, 'that Robert had recently started coming in early and going home late. Do you agree with Dr Abbott that this was just because he had a lot of work to do?'

'I expect so,' Claire answered cautiously. 'I didn't ask him.'

'But you had no reason to suspect it was, for example, because he was having trouble at home and wanted to get out of the flat?'

'Not at all: I'm quite sure that he and Gemma were very happy together. That's what made it so odd that he turned down the offer to stay; but maybe she was going over there with him?'

'So you thought that he was content with life and looking forward to the future? Is that how you would sum up his state of mind when you saw him last?'

'I suppose so.'

'Did he say anything about what he was doing on

Tuesday night? Any plan to go out?'

'He said he was taking Gemma out for a meal. I think it was their anniversary or something.'

'He didn't say that he needed to go anywhere else at all?'

'No. What sort of thing do you mean?'

'Well, we think he may have gone out during the night – or very early in the morning. Did he ever come into work during the night? If he suddenly thought of a new idea, for instance?'

'No, I don't think so,' Claire looked puzzled. 'But I suppose he might get up in the night if he wanted to ring home when it was daytime in Australia.'

'Yes,' Paul agreed, 'that's an idea! And he might have gone out of the flat so as not to disturb Gemma. Thank you – that's a very clever thought.'

At this point Peter returned, and the two police officers left the building, having first locked the drawers and returned the keys to the secretary's office. Paul waited until they reached the seclusion of the car before telling Peter about Claire's idea as to why Robert might have gone out late on Tuesday night.

'Of course,' Peter pointed out, 'there could be an additional reason for wanting to be out of the flat when he telephoned home, quite apart from not disturbing Gemma's sleep. What if he still hadn't told her that he was going back? She didn't tell us, and you would have thought it would have been something at the forefront of her mind, wouldn't you? That is – if she knew!'

CHAPTER 8

They climbed the steps, between a shoe shop and a newsagent, that led to the flats where Robert White had lived with Gemma. It was half past five in the evening by now and the residents were starting to return home after work. Peter and Paul managed to speak to several of the neighbours, who all confirmed that Robert and Gemma had been living there together for some months – nobody seemed very clear exactly how many – and appeared to be happy together, as far as you could tell from outward appearances. Only one of them remembered being aware of their return on Tuesday evening. The witness was a small, dark woman in her twenties called Amber O'Brien, who lived in the adjoining flat. She confirmed that it must have been about ten fifteen when she heard voices outside in the corridor, off which the front doors of the flats opened. She recognised Gemma's voice and heard her addressing Robert by name, quite distinctly.

'I think maybe they'd had one or two,' she reported. 'I heard laughter, and then Gemma shouted out "Rob!" and then something like, "Here: give them to me!" I think he must have been fumbling with the lock – or maybe he dropped his keys – anyway, she said something about how clumsy he was and then I heard the key in the lock and then after that the door banged shut.'

Peter thanked Amber and they moved on to make their call on Gemma. Judging by the redness of her eyes, she had been crying, and throughout the interview, she seemed more subdued than when they met her that morning. Presumably, the reality of Robert's death was starting to sink in.

'Is there someone who could come to stay with you for a few days?' Paul asked anxiously. 'One of the girls from the salon, for example?'

Gemma shook her head. 'No. I'll be fine,' she insisted. 'I don't want people fussing around.'

'We've just come from the Geography Department at the university,' Peter told her. 'We found this in his desk.'

He held out the air ticket. Gemma took it and looked at it expressionlessly.

'Yes?' she said at last. 'What about it?'

'You knew he was going back to Australia?'

'Yes, of course. You don't think he wouldn't have told me, do you?'

'We were just surprised that you didn't mention it when we spoke to you before,' Paul explained gently, keen not to allow her to think that they suspected her of deliberately concealing information out of some ulterior motive. 'It must have been quite a big thing in your life.'

'Well yes,' Gemma looked round at them both with eyes wide, 'but hearing about Robert's death sent everything else out of my mind.'

'What were you planning to do when he'd gone?' Peter asked bluntly, ignoring the hard look that Paul gave him.

'I was going to go out and join him, of course. We'd talked it all over and decided that if we were going to make a life for ourselves together it would have to be in Australia. Robert had started to get worried about being so far from his family – particularly his parents. He didn't want his sister to be left to look after them on her own when they got old, and he wanted our children to be able to see their grandparents. I don't have any family – my parents died when I was a kid – so it was a no-brainer. Only, Robert had things out sort out before I could go over there. He didn't even have a job! So he was going to go home, break the news to his parents, get a job and a house sorted for us, and then arrange for me to join him.'

'And how long did you expect it to take? How long before you emigrated?'

'Six months – maybe up to a year. Robert was very keen not to do things in too much of a hurry.'

Peter still looked dissatisfied with her answers, but said nothing. Paul sought to put her mind at rest.

'That all makes perfect sense,' he said reassuringly.

'Yes. Thank you sergeant,' Peter said firmly. 'Now, can we talk about Tuesday night?'

'You said before, that you and Robert went to bed together at about ten thirty,' Paul said, remembering that they had agreed that this statement was unlikely, given that, in all probability, Robert had died only an hour or so after they finished their meal together. 'Are you sure about that?'

'Did I say that?' Gemma asked. 'I meant that I went to bed and I assumed that Robert came soon after. I was dead tired, so I went to bed and fell asleep. Robert said he was going to have a shower and then come to bed too. So I thought he had.'

'So you couldn't swear that he didn't, in fact, decide to go out for a breath fresh air before coming to bed?' Paul asked eagerly.

'No. I suppose not,' Gemma looked round at them both apologetically. 'I'm not a very good witness, am I?'

'You're doing fine,' Paul assured her. 'Everyone finds it difficult to remember things when we start asking questions.'

'That's right,' Peter agreed. 'So the main thing is to be completely honest when you can't remember things. It's much better if we know that we don't know something than if we think we have some facts which turn out not to be true after all.'

Gemma nodded, unsure whether she had quite followed this.

'Now Gemma,' Peter went on, 'I'd like you to think back to that meal that you had with Robert on Tuesday night. Can you remember what he had to eat?'

'Oh yes!' Gemma said confidently. 'He had what he always had when we went out to eat: gammon steak.'

'With pineapple?' Paul asked.

'Yes – that's right. And there was mashed potato and beans to go with it, and then we both had Bakewell tart for dessert and Robert finished up with an espresso, but I was afraid that coffee would keep me awake, so I had a liqueur instead.'

'Was that all you drank?'

'Well, we shared a bottle of wine with the meal and Robert had a lager while we were waiting. But we weren't drunk – we just had enough to relax us a bit, that's all.'

CHAPTER 9

Peter returned home that evening to a rapturous reception from Lucy, who never attempted to hide the fact that her godfather was her favourite person in the entire world. As soon as she heard his key in the lock of the front door, she dropped the crayon with which she was colouring in a drawing she had made, got up and ran out into the hall to greet him. Peter bent down and picked her up as she ran towards him with arms outstretched.

'Lucy! Hasn't your Mum come for you yet? I was afraid you would have gone home before I got back. Come and let's sit down and you can tell me what you've been doing.'

They went into the kitchen, where Eddie was sitting at the small table while Angie was busy in front of the cooker, preparing an evening meal for her family. She turned and smiled at Peter as he came in and sat down at the table with Lucy on his lap.

'How did you get on with your body in the river?' she asked.

'I'm not sure. One or two things don't quite seem to add up, but on balance, I'd say it's shaping up for a suicide, or maybe an accident: still more work to do on it though. Now, Lucy, tell me about your day – after you got back from the park, that is.'

'You won't tell Bernie about that business in the park, will you?' Eddie asked anxiously. 'She might not like to leave Lucy with me again, if she knew about it.'

'Don't be ridiculous! You don't think for a minute that our Bernie would stop trusting you to take good care of Lucy, just because some none-too-bright young copper gets his knickers in a twist about seeing her throwing a screaming fit in public, do you?'

'No, Dad, that wasn't what I meant,' Eddie replied, with irritation in his voice. 'I meant that she might not like to ask me to look after Lucy because she didn't want to risk putting me in an awkward situation again. You know what she's like: she'd probably decide that it was her fault that PC Plod tried to arrest me!'

'Alright,' Peter conceded. 'I suppose there's no point giving her an excuse for thinking that she might have been imposing on you. And in the end there was no harm done.'

'I'd say it may have been a rather useful experience for that young constable,' Angie put in, always one to put the best possible construction on every event. 'He must have learnt a lot about thinking before he acts and not taking everything at face value.'

'He ought to know those things already,' Peter grumbled. 'It's part of his basic training.'

'But learning something in a training course isn't the same as coming up against it in real life. There are lots of things that I thought I knew from my nurse training that were quite different when there was a real patient in front of me!'

'And there was that crowd of women,' Eddie added, pleased that his mother was backing his side of the argument, 'all wanting him to do something to protect the little golden-haired girl from the wicked black man. He had to do something.'

'But that's the whole bloody point!' Peter exploded suddenly, unable to prevent himself raising his voice as he looked across the table at his son. 'Of course he had to do something, but what he ought to have done was to show them that it was wrong to assume that the golden-haired girl is always innocent and the black man is always wicked. He should have called their prejudices into question instead of sharing them.'

In the silence that followed this uncharacteristic outburst, Lucy's voice came high and quavering, as if she were about to break into tears.

'Beter,' she said timidly, twisting her neck to look up at his face, 'why are you cross?'

'I'm sorry, sunshine,' Peter apologised, his anger dispersing as quickly as it had come and being replaced with remorse that he had frightened his beloved goddaughter, 'I didn't mean to shout. I'm not cross with anyone. I just sometimes wish … I wish the world was different from how it is sometimes, that's all. Now, why don't we have a look at these drawings of yours?'

He stretched out his arm and pulled a pile of papers across the table so that he and Lucy could study them together.

'That's my mam,' Lucy explained, pointing at the first picture, which showed a group of five stick people with disproportionately large heads standing in a line, smiling and holding hands. The face on the left, to which Lucy was pointing, was distinguished by large spectacles. 'And that's me,' Lucy added pointing at a much smaller figure with curly yellow hair standing out round its head, 'and you, and Angie and Eddie.'

Peter looked as she pointed out a tall man with orange hair and red cheeks, towering over the rest of the group and then two brown-faced people, one wearing what he recognised as a nurse's uniform, the other taller and slimmer dressed in a red football strip, with a rather oversize ball at his feet.

'Why's Eddie wearing Liverpool colours?' Peter asked.

'Mam says that Spurs are rubbish,' Lucy declared

bluntly.

Peter and Eddie exchanged amused looks at two-year-old Lucy's partisanship.

'Hey, Lucy,' Eddie said, leaning across the table towards her, 'did I ever tell you about when your mam took me to Wembley to watch Liverpool thrashing Sunderland in the FA cup?'

'Yes,' Lucy said promptly. 'Liverpool won two-nil and you had a pie and a can of coke.'

'Oh dear, Eddie,' Peter grinned, 'just turned twenty and you're already sounding like an old man repeating all his best stories to anyone who'll listen!'

There was a ring at the door and Eddie hurried down the hall to let in Bernie, who was full of apologies for returning so late.

'I couldn't get away,' she explained. 'An old DPhil student of mine was there and he just wouldn't stop talking – telling me all about his new job and the research he's doing and why I ought to go over to Ireland to pay him a visit.'

Lucy looked round at the sound of her mother's voice and a frown appeared on her face.

'I can't go home yet,' she said firmly. 'I'm busy.'

'Now that's no way to greet your mother!' Angie said, putting on a tone of mock horror. 'Don't you worry: you can both stay to dinner and go home afterwards – there's plenty.'

'Are you sure?' Bernie sounded dubious. 'We've already imposed on your hospitality quite enough for one day. Lucy and I can perfectly well get our own supper when we get home.'

'Ma-am!' Lucy shouted out reproachfully. 'I said I'm busy!'

'Alright, alright! Pardon me for breathing! Now what is it that's so important?'

'I'm showing Beter my pictures.'

'You're showing them to who? I mean, to whom?'

Bernie asked. She had recently been trying to get her daughter to pronounce Peter's name correctly, thinking that what had been cute when baby Lucy had first attempted to name her godfather would become an embarrassment when she was older.'

'*Peter*,' Lucy said after a short pause, making a big effort to get the name right. 'I'm showing *Peter* my pictures.'

'That's better.' Bernie said, coming over and kissing her daughter briefly on the cheek. 'And have you been a good girl for Eddie?'

'Yes,' Lucy declared confidently, smiling up at Bernie. Then she seemed to remember something and her face became anxious. She looked round uncertainly at Eddie and Peter. 'At least,' she added, 'I tried my best.'

'No one can do better than that,' Bernie reassured her, wondering what had happened to make Lucy suspect that she had done wrong, but making no attempt to find out.

'She was very good,' Eddie assured her, quickly. 'We had a great time together, didn't we, Lucy?'

'Now Lucy,' Angie broke in, 'the dinner's going to be ready in a minute, so do you think you could take Peter in the dining room and help him lay the table? There isn't room for all of us in here. You'd be being a big help if you did that.'

'Are you sure it wouldn't be better if we went, and left you to have your dinner in peace?' Bernie put in, aware of the disruption that their presence was having to the normal routine of the house.

'No. It's no bother,' her friend assured her. 'And if your conscience is still bothering you afterwards, you can always help with the washing up!'

'OK,' Bernie grinned. 'Now is there anything I can do to help with getting things ready?'

CHAPTER 10

Meanwhile, back in his one-bedroom flat down the Abingdon Road, Paul was preparing his own evening meal. He rather prided himself on being able to cook, and made a point of buying fresh produce and creating his meals from scratch, rather than relying on frozen ready-meals or tinned food. However, interesting recipes were rarely designed for a single person living alone and he frequently had to freeze a large part of what he had prepared, to keep it for another occasion. He was standing in front of the freezer now, looking at the labels on the numerous plastic pots to decide which to heat up for his dinner.

Eventually, he selected a shepherd's pie, which he warmed up in the microwave and ate accompanied by fresh cauliflower. This was the sort of meal he remembered eating while he was living in the care home where he had met Gemma Markham. One of the care workers would dish it out to them and they would sit around the big table: ten or twelve children of varying ages all cast adrift from their families for one reason or another. Some of them, like him, knew – or thought they knew – that they would only be there for a short while. Others, like Gemma, had no family to go back to after whatever crisis had brought them there.

As he ate, he reflected on the strange coincidence of his having come across Gemma again after all these years. He wondered what she had been doing during that interval. Sixteen years was a long time – long enough for him to finish school, complete his police training, make the move into CID and gain promotion to sergeant. Had she gone into hairdressing straight from school? Or had she tried other jobs first? Had she had other boyfriends before Robert White? Presumably, she must have done – she was, after all, over thirty by now. On the other hand, he was only two years younger and had never managed to maintain a relationship with a woman for long enough to get to the stage of sharing a flat, so maybe White could have been the first.

How would she cope with losing him? She had always appeared surprisingly calm about her parents' deaths, but Peter had suggested that having been through bereavement twice before might make things even worse for her now. Fancy Peter having been brought up in care! Everyone spoke of Peter as the ultimate family man, always eager to get home to his loving wife and two kids. Had it been hard for him to make the transition from being one among a dozen kids in a care home, where relationships were always transient and shallow, to being a husband and father? Or perhaps it was precisely *because* he had not enjoyed a real family life as a child that Peter always preferred a quiet evening at home with his wife to a night out with the lads. Was it because, when he was growing up, there had never been anyone for whom he had been that one special person, that Peter would decline any invitation to drinks after work in favour of heading back to the family home?

Paul suddenly felt very alone and, for the first time since he had departed from his parents' home a decade earlier, wished that he were part of a family himself. He found himself envying Peter, who, he imagined, would now be relaxing with his wife and son – and maybe his daughter too, for Paul was unsure whether she was still living at home. They would be talking over the events of the day, perhaps laughing at the way PC Fox had tried to arrest Eddie and had then had to back down when he discovered that the boy was telling the truth about his relationship with the little girl.

Who was that girl? Paul wondered. Not a relative, since Peter had none and she surely could not be related on his wife's side. Paul was not an expert in genetics, but he was convinced that the laws of heredity dictated that the mother of the young man in the park, with his fuzzy black hair and smooth brown skin, could not also be close kin to the little girl with the mop of yellow curls who had been huddled in the young man's lap. A neighbour's daughter, perhaps, with a single mother who went out to work and could not afford professional childcare? He had watched the scene for long enough before driving off to have seen the child's joyful recognition of Peter. If this were a soap opera, it would turn out that Peter was the child's father, but Peter was famous for his loyal devotion to his wife and Paul could not believe that he had ever been unfaithful to her.

It must be nice to have someone so pleased to see you. Whoever the child was, Peter evidently played an important part in her young life. Would Paul ever have anyone who would greet his arrival with such clear pleasure?

He washed the dishes and dried them meticulously before putting them away. Then he looked round at the empty flat and decided to go out for an hour or so and find some company. There was a pub, about fifteen minutes' walk away, which was popular with off-duty police officers; he would go and see if any of his colleagues were there.

It did not take long to find a small cluster of men whom he recognised, standing near the bar, talking and laughing. They were mostly uniformed officers and mostly young single men like himself. Married men like Peter, Paul reflected, did not need to come here: they would all be at home in the bosom of their family, watching television, putting children to bed or helping teenagers with their homework.

The notable exception was a thickset man in his fifties whom Paul identified as Sergeant Mark Adams. Twice married and twice divorced, Adams was now rumoured to be living with a woman half his age, but that evidently did not prevent him from enjoying a few pints with his mates in the evening. He was leaning against the bar with a half-empty glass in his hand recounting an amusing incident that had taken place that morning. Paul was too late to hear what it was about, but the nervous laughter from the group when Adams reached the punch line made him suspect that the joke was, at best, in dubious taste. Adams was known for his opposition to 'political correctness gone mad' and had several times been in trouble for his attitude towards female officers and ethnic minorities.

'Hello there!' Adams called out when he saw Paul approaching. 'It's Godwin isn't it? We don't often see you here.'

Paul smiled in acknowledgement of the greeting, but could not think of a reply. He ordered himself a half pint and stood rather awkwardly with it in his hand looking round at the group.

'Do you all know DS Godwin?' Adams asked them. 'He was transferred from South Oxfordshire, back in – when was it?'

'June,' Paul filled in for him.

'That's right. So he's only been with us three months. Working with DI Johns – is that right?'

'Yes.'

'How're you finding him?'

'We get on OK,' Paul answered guardedly. He was aware that Peter had a low opinion of Adams and suspected that the feeling was mutual. There was no point in antagonising the man by suggesting that he and Peter were particularly good friends.

'Jordan was just telling us about a run-in he had today with Peter Johns,' one of the young constables piped up from the back of the group. 'A bit of bother over arresting one of his kids.'

'Let's hear it,' Adams urged, looking round for Fox, who reluctantly stepped forward and recounted the story of the incident in the park. He wished now that he had not mentioned it to his friend, fellow-constable Aaron King. He had never intended it to be shared any further. Paul watched Fox's evident discomfort at being forced to repeat the story in front of an older and more senior officer, trying to work out whether this was because Fox was embarrassed at having made a blunder or nervous of being perceived as critical of the inspector's treatment of him or just unused to being the centre of attention.

'Anyway,' Fox brought his narrative to a conclusion, 'he was quite nice about it all in the end, so I guess I was lucky really. Some people would have put in an official complaint.'

'I'd say you're the one with the right to complain,' Adams said in a decided tone. 'You weren't to know it was Johns's kid.'

'That isn't the point though, is it?' Paul said without thinking. 'The point is how to safeguard the little girl without wrongfully arresting the man who was with her.'

He immediately regretted having intervened when Adams turned on him angrily.

'I suppose you were there, backing Johns up?'

'No, I had to watch a post mortem. I dropped him at the park and then went on to the mortuary.'

'Of course you did! I don't suppose he wanted you there to see him harassing Fox.'

Out of the corner of his eye, Paul noticed Fox opening his mouth as if to protest, but then he appeared to change his mind and clamped it shut again.

'It wouldn't do for you to know about the way he is about coloured people,' Adams continued, getting into his stride now. 'He's always been the same. I remember way back when he first started going out with that coloured nurse. I mean to say – I can understand him going out with her. It stands to reason don't it, a coloured girl *and* a nurse, it's got to be good for having a good time, but he had to go and *marry* her! And so now he's got himself lumbered with a string of coloured kids and he goes round blaming the likes of Fox here for questioning why one of them's making off with a white girl! I ask you!'

He turned back to the bar and put down his empty beer glass. 'Same again, love!'

'I think we're supposed to say "black" now, not "coloured",' ventured a young earnest constable, breaking the awkward silence that followed this outburst.

'Don't give me that political correctness crap!' Adams growled, taking a long pull on his pint before continuing. 'What difference does it make what we call them? We all know that more crime is committed by coloured youngsters than any other group and it's bloody obvious that a black teenager dragging a white girl away from the swings in the park has got to be suspicious. Who was the kid anyway? Did Johns answer you that?'

'He said her father was Detective Superintendent Paige, sir,' Fox answered nervously. 'You know – the guy who got killed while on duty a few years back.'

'That figures,' Adams said complacently. 'Paige and Johns always were thick as thieves. Between you and me, Johns would never have made it in CID if he hadn't been Paige's blue-eyed boy. I always wondered about those two, but with Johns supposedly being the happily married man …'

He paused to take another long draught from his glass and to allow his audience to draw their own conclusions from what he had said.

'Mind you,' he went on, 'I never believed that was

conclusive. What's to stop him liking his bread buttered on both sides?'

He laughed a drunken laugh and one or two of the other joined in, but Paul noticed that Fox was looking red with embarrassment and had started working his way towards the edge of the group, as if he were planning to leave, but trying to do so without being noticed.

'Of course, the kid wasn't born until about six months after Paige died,' Adams went on. 'I always wondered who the father really was. I mean to say – Paige was well past it. We'd got his retirement party all organised – had to turn it into a wake when he took that tumble off the roof. I never bought the idea of him suddenly marrying some woman from the university after all those years as a "bachelor gay" as they say! You know what I reckon?'

He looked round hopefully, but nobody expressed interest in his theory.

'I reckon,' he said emphatically, draining his glass and setting it down with a bang on the counter. 'I reckon he married her for Johns to have. Johns was the younger man y'see, so Paige'll have been worried he might get tired of him, and, like I said, I reckon Johns is AC-DC, so Paige had a lot of potential competition. Johns already had that coloured wife of his, but it stands to reason he's not going to be satisfied with her; so Paige, he fixes him up with a nice white girl – a bit younger, but old enough to be afraid of being left on the shelf – and there you are! All nice and cosy!'

Paul felt himself going hot and cold with anger. His heart was racing and beads of sweat appeared on his forehead. He wanted to tell Adams what he thought of his insinuations, to tell him that it disgusted him to hear him speak in that way about a man whom he respected and liked, to tell all the others that it was nothing but a pack of lies. Nevertheless, he held back, unsure how to express his feelings and anxious that any intervention from him could make things worse rather than better. Then he saw Fox walking towards the door and that decided him. He gave up the futile idea of arguing with Adams and hurried to catch up with Fox as he slipped out into the street.

'Don't take any notice of Adams,' Paul said in a low voice, coming up beside Fox and walking alongside him. 'It's the drink talking.'

Fox did not answer, so Paul had another go at engaging him in conversation.

'Who was that superintendent they were talking about – the one who was killed? Can you tell me about him?'

'DS Richard Paige,' Fox answered, increasing his pace very slightly and speaking without looking at Paul. 'I never knew him. He was killed before I joined the service - about three years ago now – but I heard about it on the news and I took an interest because my mum was a scout at the college where it happened.'

'And what exactly did happen?'

'The way I heard it, he was making an arrest and the man ran for it across the roof of the college – it was one of those old lead-covered ones – and when Paige cornered him, he pushed him off the roof, or maybe it was just an accident, I don't know. Anyway, he fell to his death. The papers just said, married with no children. I never knew about the kid until today.'

'Not surprising that Peter Johns took an interest in her under the circumstances,' Paul said thoughtfully.

'You mean because he was an orphan himself?' Fox asked.

'I meant, because of feeling sorry for the widow bringing up a kid on her own – but what do you know about Peter having been in care?'

'Adams told me, ages ago,' Fox admitted sheepishly.

'You don't want to take everything Adams says at face value,' Paul advised, feeling irritated with Fox for his naïve acceptance of the sergeant's often vindictive gossip but at the same time sympathising with the discomfiture which he was evidently feeling now. 'Like I said, the drink makes him say things he doesn't mean and a whole lot more than he ought to say.'

'But Johns admitted it to me today,' Fox protested and then immediately wished he had said nothing. 'I mean – it came up and he told me it was true.'

'I'd say *admitted* is a funny word to use,' Paul said coldly. 'What exactly is there to *admit* about growing up in a care home?'

'I didn't mean -' Fox broke off, unable to think of anything to say.

'Never mind,' Paul sighed. 'Forget it.'

They walked on for a minute or two in silence. Then Fox plucked up courage to ask, 'what did Johns say about me? I mean – after he got back this afternoon?'

'Not a lot: just enough to explain why he had to go rushing off, leaving me with a suspicious death on my hands. I don't suppose he wanted to show you up in front of me. He didn't even tell me your name. I wouldn't have known it was you if you hadn't blurted out the whole story to your friends.' Paul thought for a few moments, before going on. 'Look Fox: I haven't been here for long, but I think I know Peter Johns well enough to know that ... Well, all I can say is you'd do a whole lot better modelling yourself on him than following the likes of Sergeant Adams.'

'Yes, I know,' Fox said humbly. 'He was very fair with me, even though I could see he was upset for his son. But,' he went on, remembering his first anxious weeks in the police service, 'Adams was very good to me too when I was new here. Like you said, it's the drink that's the problem with him – and someone told me his girlfriend just left him, so it's not surprising if he-'

'Nothing excuses the sort of things he said this evening,' Paul cut across the young officer's train of thought. 'Those stupid things about Peter fathering a child with his friend's wife – those are the sorts of things that stick in people's minds after they've forgotten where they heard them, and then they get passed round and eventually everyone's saying "there's no smoke without fire" and lots of people get hurt! And that's apart from his blatant racism and his deplorable attitude to women. Stop making excuses for him and recognise that Adams is a dinosaur and the sooner his sort goes extinct the better!'

CHAPTER 11

Peter and his family finished their meal and Bernie, having helped Angela with the washing up as agreed, took Lucy back to their home in Headington, complete with the pile of drawings that Lucy had made and which she was now determined to share with her mother. Once the guests were gone, Eddie retreated to his room in the attic of their small terraced house, and Peter and Angie settled down for an evening in front of the television.

They were just on their way to bed when the telephone rang. It was Robert White's father. It was Friday morning in Melbourne and he was ringing to say that they were booked on a flight that evening and would be arriving at Heathrow the following day. Peter immediately promised to meet them there and bring them to Oxford. Ignoring his wife's head-shaking and gesticulations towards the ceiling, he went on: had they arranged accommodation, or would they like him to book a hotel for them? No, it was no bother; leave everything to him.

The call ended and Peter put the phone down. He turned to his wife, who gave him a look of mingled reproach and admiration.

'I know, I know,' he said hurriedly. 'I'm supposed to be driving Eddie to Manchester on Saturday; but these people have just lost their son. They have a right to expect to speak to the officer in charge of the investigation.'

'You could have sent Paul Godwin to meet them at the

airport and arranged to see them when you got back from Manchester,' Angela pointed out. 'A few hours wouldn't have made all that much difference.'

'It might to them. And they deserve to see the senior officer, not to be fobbed off with a detective sergeant.'

'You're always saying what a good man Paul is – and he could probably do with the overtime; sergeants are always short of money.'

'And I'm already in hot water over my overtime budget after that missing person case last month. So Paul would have to do it in his own time and it'd be unfair for me to ask him.'

Angela gave up the argument. She had known at the outset that she could not win – and deep down she wouldn't have wanted Peter to give in and put his personal life ahead of what he saw as his duty – but she had felt obliged to make the case on behalf of their son, principally so that Peter would be prepared for the inevitable confrontation when he broke the news to Eddie.

'I'll ring Our Bernie in the morning,' she said a little later, as she lay in bed waiting for Peter to finish putting on his pyjamas. 'I'm sure she wouldn't mind taking Eddie up to Manchester.'

'You can't spring something like that on her at such short notice,' Peter protested. 'No: he can go on the train and we'll take up anything he can't manage next weekend. Students never used to be taken everywhere in a car.'

'A lot of students these days have their own cars,' Angie reminded him, 'as Eddie has pointed out to us more than once.'

'And they all have rich Mummies and Daddies who can afford to pay for the insurance and the road tax. Besides, where would he keep it? It's hard enough finding a parking space in this road for one car, never mind a fleet! And if he thinks we're letting him drive around central Manchester at all times of day and night-'

'OK, OK.' Angie interrupted with a grin. 'I've got the

message, loud and clear. I'm just trying to prepare you for the battle to come!'

Eddie's reaction the following morning, when his mother persuaded him out of his bed and down to the kitchen in his pyjamas to hear the news before his parents went off to work, was exactly as they had predicted.

'Oh Dad!' he complained, 'I knew this would happen! As soon as I heard about that body in the river, I knew you'd be saying you had police work to do instead of driving me up to Manchester. What's the point of saying you've booked the time off and are definitely going to do it, when you know that something's bound to come up?'

'I'm sorry, Ed. But think about it: these people have just lost their son-'

'But why does it have to be *you*? There are enough police officers about: someone else could have done it. I mean, you're only talking about going to Heathrow and collecting them; it doesn't exactly need a high-powered detective inspector does it? Why can you drive them from Heathrow, but you can't drive me up to Manchester?'

'It's nothing to do with driving anyone anywhere – it's a matter of them being able to talk to the person in charge of investigating their son's death. It's-'

'Oh forget it, Dad! I'll ask Our Bernie. She said she'd take me if you got tied up.'

'You'll do no such thing! Our Bernie's got quite enough on her plate with a full-time job and a toddler to look after – you can't go around asking her to give up a day to take you off back to university! What's wrong with the train, for goodness sake?'

'Well, for a start-'

The telephone rang.

'I'll get it,' Angie said, glad of an excuse to get away from the row. She went out into the hall to answer the call. It was Bernie.

'Hi Angie! I'm glad I've caught you before you go out. I wanted to put a proposal to you.'

'Yes?'

'I was wondering if I could drive Eddie up to Manchester tomorrow instead of Peter. You see, I met an ex-colleague at the conference yesterday and she was complaining that she had never had the chance to see Lucy and why couldn't I bring her on a visit some time? Then it occurred to me overnight that she's at UMIST now, so if I took Eddie back tomorrow, I could call in on her. But, before I suggest it to Eddie, I wanted to check with you first that Peter and Eddie won't mind. I wouldn't like to be getting in the way of any father-and-son bonding opportunity!'

'Well now, Bernie, it just so happens that Peter has to be elsewhere tomorrow after all. Something's cropped up with this suspicious death that he's investigating.'

'Now, why am I not surprised?'

'So, if you really don't mind spending the whole day ferrying our son all that way, we'd be very grateful.'

'That's settled then. Tell Eddie I'll be round this evening to pack the car, so we can make an early start in the morning.'

Angie returned to the kitchen to see her husband and son sitting in silence glaring at one another across the table.

'That was Our Bernie,' she told them. 'Apparently she needs to go to Manchester to see an old friend up there and she's wondering if she could be permitted to combine it with taking Eddie back to uni tomorrow.'

'See, Dad! I told you Our Bernie wouldn't mind.'

'Are you sure it was Bernie's idea?' Peter asked sceptically.

'Absolutely,' Angie assured him. 'I never said a word about it. She must be psychic.'

'Rubbish!' Eddie snorted rudely. 'She's been married to a policeman, that's all!'

CHAPTER 12

Peter and Paul spent most of Friday morning co-ordinating a search of the riverbanks for signs of where Robert White had fallen in, and organising a programme of visits to premises near the river, in the hope of finding someone who had seen him on Tuesday night or Wednesday morning. Over pie and chips in the police canteen, they talked through what they knew so far.

'The thing I don't get,' Paul said, 'is why he went out again. It was a foul night and he had no reason to – or not that we know about. Why didn't he just tuck himself up nice and warm in bed and wait until morning to go and do whatever it was he wanted to do?'

I suppose if he went out with the intention of killing himself, he wouldn't be bothered about getting a bit cold and wet while he was doing it,' Peter suggested. 'But why would he want to? He was doing nicely for himself by all accounts and looking forward to going back to Australia, as far as we can tell.'

'Maybe he was regretting turning down the job here. It may have seemed a good idea at the time and then he changed his mind.'

'You'd think if that was the case he'd have asked his supervisor if there was any chance of him having the job after all,' Peter said, sounding unconvinced. 'They haven't got anyone else and they would clearly have liked him to stay on, so I bet he could have had the job if he'd asked. It doesn't make sense for him to top himself without even mentioning it to anyone.'

'Does topping yourself ever make sense though, sir? Don't we have to assume that, if he killed himself, it was because he wasn't thinking straight when he did it?'

'OK. So you're saying that, despite his work colleagues being convinced that he was actually feeling a lot happier recently than he had for a while, he was sufficiently depressed – just in a general way, without any reason – that it prompted him to wander out in the dead of night in the pouring rain and jump into the flooded river? I suppose the idea is that he did it while the balance of his mind was disturbed – disturbed by what, exactly? Surely, even if he was depressed, there'd have to be some sort of trigger to make him go off like that?'

'Does it really matter what it was?'

'I don't know – maybe not, but I'm trying to think what I'm going to say to his parents tomorrow.'

'Surely they'll understand that depression is an illness and it makes people behave irrationally. Will they really want to know why he did it?'

'I think they will. I think they'll want to know why he did it and why nobody realised in time to stop him doing it and what *they* could have done to stop it happening.'

'I don't see *they* could have done anything: they were thousands of miles away.'

'Nevertheless,' Peter shrugged. 'If we tell them their son killed himself, that's the first thing they'll think of – followed by, why didn't anyone here notice he was suicidal and do something about it, such as informing them, for instance.'

'He's a grown man,' Paul argued, 'they can't expect-'

'Do you think parents suddenly stop worrying about their kids when they reach the age of eighteen?' Peter demanded with an uncharacteristic hint of anger in his voice.

Paul sat in silence, remembering the way Peter had

interrupted his work in order to rush off to rescue his own son from the hands of Constable Fox. What was it like to care that much for someone else?

'That's not how it is,' Peter went on, returning to his normal calm. 'And so I need to try to understand what was going on in Robert White's head when he went out on Tuesday night and didn't come back.'

'Perhaps he got to thinking about what it would really be like being back in Australia without the woman he'd been sharing his life with for maybe two years?' Paul suggested tentatively.

'Ah yes, Gemma. What do you think about the way she changed her story after she heard that he must have died on Tuesday night and not on Wednesday morning?'

'She didn't exactly change her story,' Paul argued, finding himself strangely unwilling to admit that the young woman could have been less than completely frank with them. 'She just realised afterwards that she couldn't be sure that he'd ever come to bed after all.'

'I'm sure I'd always know whether I was sleeping alone or in company,' Peter said doubtfully.

'But she told us she was dead tired, and she'd been drinking. She probably doesn't remember much about that evening if the truth be known. She probably told us what she would have expected to happen – what usually did happen – when they got home, not expecting us to question it or to read anything more into it. She was probably embarrassed to admit that she couldn't remember.'

'If it wasn't for the neighbour being so confident that she'd heard them both coming in together, I'd be wondering if Gemma could have come back without Robert and he could have had some sort of accident on the way home from the restaurant. As it is, we're stuck with the idea that, for some reason we can't understand, he went out again that night.'

'Mm,' Paul agreed. 'And it must have been pretty well

straight away – as soon as Gemma was in bed – to have got himself killed before his stomach started digesting that gammon and pineapple.'

'I wonder …,' Peter paused from this own meal with his fork in the air. 'I wonder if there's any possibility he could have had another helping of gammon and green beans on Wednesday. Don't you remember? Gemma said that he always had the same thing when he ate out. Suppose he met someone on Wednesday morning and they went to lunch together somewhere. Then the stomach contents wouldn't prove that he died on Tuesday night at all!'

'And whatever that meeting was about could have been the thing that made him decide to take his own life,' Paul chipped in, glad to have found a way of diverting attention from Gemma's apparent inconsistent testimony. 'But this is all speculation. We have no evidence that he went anywhere or met anyone on Wednesday, and if he knew he was going to be somewhere else on Wednesday morning, why didn't he let anyone at the Geography Department know?'

'Maybe whoever it was accosted him on the way to work,' Peter suggested, reluctant to give up this line of reasoning. 'And as far as evidence is concerned, didn't I see something about a waiter at the Head of the River saying that a man answering White's description had been there round about lunch time on Wednesday?'

'You know, you may be right! Andrews and Philipson were covering that area; we'd better check their report.'

'And cross-reference with any sightings there may have been of him on the way to the pub that morning. And that may give us a possible area to concentrate on for trying to work out where he fell into the river. I'm not an expert, but I would have thought that, with the river flowing so fast after the rain, a body that went in at the Head of the River at lunchtime on Wednesday could easily have been washed down to the place where we found him by

Thursday morning.'

Peter hastily finished his meal and got up to go. Paul abandoned his remaining chips and followed. Soon they were both sorting through the file of reports from the team of officers who had been out interviewing potential witnesses.

'Here it is sir!' Paul said holding out a page of handwritten notes. 'It says here that a man answering White's description came into the Head of the River pub at about quarter past twelve on Wednesday in the company of an older man. They had lunch together and then went out – still together.'

'Does it say what they had to eat?'

No. I don't suppose they thought to ask. They interviewed the waiter yesterday afternoon. We didn't know until later that White's last meal was so significant.'

'And we hadn't issued people with a photograph of White at that stage either,' Peter mused in a dissatisfied way. 'So the waiter was just going from a description, which might well have sounded like any number of people. You had better go back and talk to this waiter again. Take a photograph of White and ask him about what they ate and get a proper description of the other man.'

'Right you are, sir,' Paul said, getting up to go.

'I'll stay here and go through the reports that have been coming in from the house-to-house team this morning, in case they've turned up anything. Come back and report to me as soon as you're done.'

As it turned out, Paul did not return to the police station after his interview with the waiter, because there were developments which warranted Peter coming down to the river to view the scene for himself. As Paul emerged from the pub, unfurling his umbrella to fend off the heavy rain, a uniformed officer accosted him. He recognised him as the earnest young constable who had corrected Adams' use of the word 'coloured' in the pub the night before.

'Sir! There's something down here I think you ought to

have a look at.'

Paul followed him the short distance down the road to Folly Bridge.

'We got a call from DI Johns,' he explained somewhat breathlessly, 'saying he wanted us to do a forensic examination of the bridge and the area of the bank near the Head of the River.'

The road crossing the river here had pavements on either side for pedestrians, who were prevented from falling in the water by a stone parapet. Paul saw that the path on the downstream side of the bridge was cordoned off with police tape. He lifted it up and bent to pass beneath it to where a section of the parapet had been marked with white chalk. A photographer was just backing away, having taken several close-up pictures of the stonework and now intent on a wider view to put them in context.

'See here, sir?' the constable said, pointing. 'The forensics people say these marks look like someone climbed up on to the parapet fairly recently. And if you look down …' he added, standing on tiptoe and leaning over the wall.

Paul leaned his elbows on the wall and peered down. He saw a boat with two scenes of crime officers in it. They waved to him and pointed at the base of one of the stone pillars that supported the bridge. Paul could see nothing of interest, but he gathered, from their shouts, and from a commentary provided by the constable, that they had found traces of what looked like blood on the stonework.

'Get it back to the lab,' he instructed them, 'and while you're about it, take a sample of the stone – it may match with the fragments in the victim's head wound.'

He turned back to the young police officer at his side.

'Good work constable …?'

'King, sir – Aaron King.'

'Well, Constable King, I'll give DI Johns a call. He'll want to see this for himself. You just carry on guarding the site and moving on members of the public who want to gawp at us will you?'

'Yes sir!' King said eagerly, excited by the thought of being part of an investigation into a suspicious death. Up until now, his police work had revolved around a rather tedious mixture of shoplifting, drunken revelry and teenage vandalism. This was much more exciting. You never knew – it might even turn out to be a murder enquiry.

He was even more gratified when Peter, who arrived a few minutes later, in response to Paul's summons, came over to speak to him. True, he was only letting him know that the examination of the bridge parapet was now over and the public could be allowed back on the other pavement, but somehow he managed to convey the impression that he considered Constable Aaron King to be an integral part of the investigation – unlike some members of CID who made it very clear that they looked down on their uniformed colleagues.

After checking that all the forensic evidence was safely on its way for analysis, Peter turned to Paul.

'Now, tell me about your interview with the waiter,' he said, having first drawn him into the centre of the deserted beer garden, where they would not be overheard.

'Not much to go on, I'm afraid. He looked at the picture and said it may have been the man he saw on Wednesday or it may not. I showed it round to some of the other staff, but none of them recognised him. I've got a more detailed description of the other man, but it's still pretty vague. I've asked him to let us know if either of the men come into the pub again – so we can eliminate them.'

Peter's mobile phone rang. It was Mike Carson.

'I thought you'd want to know the results of the toxicology tests on your body in the river,' he said cheerfully.

'You sound as if they told you something,' Peter responded. 'Fire away.'

'There was a high level of alcohol in his blood – as you were probably expecting – but there was also something else.'

'Which was?'

'Flunitrazepam.'

'Which is?' Peter forced himself to remain calm in the face of the rising irritation that he was feeling. Why did Mike insist on playing these games instead of coming out with the salient points immediately?

'You probably know it as Rohypnol.'

'The date rape drug?'

'That's the one!'

'So you're saying someone drugged him before he fell in the river?'

'Well, it's not for me to say how it came to be in his system, but he certainly must have taken it, or been given it, shortly before his death.'

'How shortly?'

'Difficult to say. Nothing is certain in pathology, as you know. Different subjects may metabolise the drug differently, but it has quite a long half-life, so it could have been taken as much as a day before death.'

'A whole day?' Peter queried in surprise. 'Are you serious? Or is this just an example of your pathological aversion to committing yourself to anything definite?'

'OK. The chances are that he took it sometime between fifteen minutes and twelve hours of his death, but you can't rule out the possibility that it was longer ago than that.'

'And what exactly would the effects have been?' Peter asked. 'I mean, if he took it and then went to work, say, would people around him be likely to notice there was something wrong?'

'I'd say the amount he appears to have taken would most likely have sent him to sleep within thirty or forty minutes. He certainly would have been likely to be noticeably drowsy. Though, of course everyone reacts differently: there are cases recorded where it has a paradoxical effect and makes people more aggressive, talkative and violent.'

'Or suicidal?' Peter asked.

'Well, I'm not sure if there's ever been any recorded link to suicide, but it has been known to increase anxiety and cause confusion, so I couldn't completely rule it out. However, the most likely effect is that of sedation – which is what the drug is for, after all. It used to be prescribed for insomnia.'

'Used to be? Is it not anymore?'

'Not under the NHS, but you might be able to get a private prescription. I would be surprised, though, if any doctor in the UK prescribed it for insomnia unless it was very bad indeed. The long half-life makes it unsuitable for most people, because of still being under the influence the morning after. There are other more satisfactory treatments, and most doctors would be anxious about the possibility of it getting on to the black market – which is a much more likely source for him to have got it, I'd say.'

'Going back to these paradoxical side effects that you talked about: could he have taken it on Tuesday night, as a sleeping pill, and then, instead of it sending him to sleep, it made him so confused and anxious that he decided to go out somewhere and then he might have had a fatal accident?'

'That's a possible scenario. Did you have anything specific in mind?'

'We think he may have jumped off Folly Bridge. We've got some blood samples for you from the stonework at the bottom of one of the arches. I was thinking: maybe he got it into his head that he'd left something behind at the restaurant – they'd been eating at The Rabbit Hole – and he started walking back to get it, and on the way, under the influence of the drug, he climbed up on the parapet and fell in.'

'It's not impossible,' Mike said cautiously.

'Flunitrazepam, especially in conjunction with alcohol, does impair your inhibitions. Once he got back to the bridge, it might have made him decide to show off by climbing on to the wall; and once he was on the parapet it might well affect his balance and make him more likely to topple in. But remember – there is nothing in the science to support that hypothesis: all I can say is that he took the drug at some point during the twenty-four hours before he died. Now if you've quite finished your cross-examination, I have other things to do: you're not the only one with a body, you know!'

CHAPTER 13

That evening, Paul was washing up after dinner when his mobile phone rang. His heart started beating faster as he recognised Gemma's voice.

'Can you come over?' she asked, 'I've got something I think you ought to see – it's to do with Robert.'

'Yes, of course: I'll come right away.'

Leaving the unwashed crockery in the sink, he left the flat and hurried downstairs and out into the road. As he went, he pressed familiar buttons on his phone to bring up Peter's number, intending to tell him about Gemma's call. Then he changed his mind. Gemma had been given both of their numbers and she had chosen to ring him. Perhaps she would feel more relaxed and able to talk if he went alone. Moreover, he had promised her that he would go at once – if Peter wanted to be there too, that would mean a delay. In addition, whatever it was that Gemma wanted to show him might not be important enough to justify dragging Peter away from this family in the evening: it would be much more sensible for Paul to go alone and report back to Peter later.

His car was parked a few yards away. He got in and drove to Gemma's flat. She was waiting for him and opened the door the moment he knocked. She seemed calm, but Paul thought he could detect some redness about her eyes, which suggested she had been crying. She led him into the living room and told him to sit down. Then she handed him a piece of paper. It was part of a narrow-lined

A4 sheet, torn jaggedly across at the top.

'I found this,' she said flatly.

Paul took the paper and looked at it. There was a message written on it in neat handwriting.

'I'm sorry Gemma. I can't go on like this any longer. I feel like I'm in prison. I have to get away. Please try to understand and don't be angry with me – or not for long. Love, Rob.'

Paul looked up at Gemma, who sat watching him with a look of anxiety on her face.

'I take it this is Robert's writing?' he asked.

'Yes: I'm sure it is. And the paper looks like it's come from one of the pads he used for taking notes for his research.'

'And where did you find this? I mean, how come you hadn't found it before?'

'It was tucked behind the toaster. I usually have toast for breakfast, so I suppose he thought I would be bound to find it there. But I overslept on Wednesday and was late for work, so I didn't have time for toast; and then yesterday I was so anxious about what had happened to Rob that I didn't really know what I was doing. I can't even remember whether I had any breakfast. But then I spotted it this evening, just poking up, wedged between the toaster and the wall.'

Paul re-read the note to himself. This seemed to put the state of Robert White's mind during the hours immediately preceding his death beyond doubt.

'It looks as if he must have gone out on Tuesday night with the express intention of ending it all,' he said at last. 'I'm really sorry. I realise how that must make you feel.'

'Thanks.' Gemma nodded and gave a brief smile. 'I keep thinking: why didn't I see it coming? He seemed quite all right. I didn't lie to you when I said he wasn't depressed or anything. He really didn't seem any different from usual.'

'No, of course you didn't tell lies,' Paul reassured her

hurriedly. Then, remembering what Peter had said about the parents of a suicide blaming themselves for not having prevented it, he added, 'and you mustn't imagine that it's your fault that he killed himself or that you could have done anything to stop him. You weren't to know what he was thinking.'

'I'll have to keep this,' he went on, folding the paper and putting it in his pocket. 'And I'll have to show it to my boss. One good thing is that this ought to put an end to the investigation, I think – which reminds me: we think we've found where he went into the river.'

'Have you?' Gemma asked eagerly. 'How? Tell me about it.'

Paul explained about the scuffmarks on the bridge parapet and the blood stains on the stonework below.

'So, put together with the note you've just given me,' he concluded, 'it looks as if he must have decided to end it all that evening after you'd gone to bed. So he writes the note and leaves it for you to find in the morning, slips out of the flat and down to the river, which is running fast because of all the rain, climbs on to the wall and jumps to his death.'

They sat together in silence for a few minutes, neither of them able to think of anything to say. Then Paul remembered the toxicology report.

'Gemma?' he asked, trying to choose his words carefully, aware that he ought not to reveal too much detail about the case to her and unsure how his question might be received. 'Did Robert ever have trouble sleeping?'

'No – I don't think so. Why do you want to know?'

'We think he may have taken some sleeping tablets before he died. I wondered whether that was something he did regularly.'

'If he did, he didn't tell me about it. Is that what killed him? How did he end up in the river?'

'No, no. I didn't mean that,' Paul said hastily. 'But the drug might have made him woozy and not really knowing what he was doing and that could have been how he fell.'

'So it might not have been deliberate you mean? Even after what he wrote?' Gemma asked.

'Yes, no, I don't know,' Paul felt flustered. He wanted to be able to tell Gemma that it was all just a tragic accident, but she was too intelligent to be taken in by his incoherent argument. 'We need to consider all the possibilities. Did Paul take pills or drugs of any kind? Did you ever suspect he might be taking drugs recreationally?'

'No. he wasn't like that. He was very keen on healthy living. He wouldn't …' Gemma's voice tailed off and she appeared to be thinking. 'There were his hay fever tablets,' she said, after a short pause, 'but he hasn't taken any of those since the summer.'

'Can I see?'

'If you like. They're in the bathroom cabinet: on the top shelf, in a glass bottle.'

Paul went into the small bathroom and looked inside the wall cabinet. On the top shelf, he saw some packets of aspirin and paracetamol, a tube of antiseptic cream, a box of sticking plasters and a small brown glass bottle. He picked up the bottle and looked at it. There was no label on it. He opened it and looked inside. It was about a quarter full of some green tablets. He returned to the living room and held the bottle out towards Gemma.

'Are these the ones?'

'Yes – that's right.'

'It's funny that there's no label on the bottle. If these were prescribed for him, you'd expect it to have his name and instructions for how and when to take them.'

'I don't know,' Gemma shrugged her shoulders. 'I never asked about them. He just got them out from his luggage when the pollen count went up in the summer. I suppose he must have brought them with him from Australia. Maybe they do things different over there; or maybe he put them into a different bottle to bring them over here.'

I'd better takes these away for analysis,' Paul said, putting the bottle in his pocket. 'Now, what did you mean when you said he got the tablets out of his luggage? What luggage?'

'He had a big suitcase which he brought all his stuff over in from Australia,' Gemma explained. 'It's under the bed. Do you want to see it?'

'Yes please.'

Gemma led the way into the bedroom. Paul noted that the duvet was now smoothed down tidily over the bed and Robert's clothes and boots were no longer visible. Gemma bent down and pulled out a large suitcase from under the bed. Paul knelt down next to her and opened it.

The case was less than half-full. Presumably, most of the contents had been taken out and stored elsewhere in the house. Paul carefully examined what was left: a spare pair of walking boots, a snorkel and swimming mask, a pocket-sized Bible, which looked new and unused, and a heavy winter coat. There was nothing there of any significance to the investigation.

'I think it might be a good idea to pack all his things in here,' he said, getting up. 'Then it'll be easy for his parents to take them away when they come.'

'Yes, I suppose so,' Gemma agreed, looking rather subdued at the thought of meeting Robert's parents. 'I suppose they'll want to come here to see where he lived. What do you think they'll be like? I mean, I've never met them; I don't even know how much Robert told them about me.'

'I don't know,' Paul confessed, trying to think of something reassuring to say. 'Peter – that is, DI Johns – was the one who spoke to them. I expect they will just be rather overwhelmed and shocked by everything. I'm sure there's no need for you to worry. After all, they must recognise that you and they are going through similar emotions at the moment.'

They sat on the floor together for a few moments.

Then Paul got up and walked across to the wardrobe.

'Tell you what,' he said brightly, 'let me help you to pack away his things.'

He started to empty Robert's section of the cupboard, placing the clothes, neatly folded, in the suitcase. Gemma stood up and watched him for a few seconds before disappearing through the door. She returned carrying a pile of books.

'These had better go in at the bottom,' she said, laying them in the suitcase and going back for more.

Soon the wardrobe was empty and the suitcase was full. Paul fastened it closed and pushed it back under the bed.

'Thanks,' Gemma said flatly, looking rather dismally at the empty shelves and hanging space. 'Now, can I offer you a drink?'

'A coffee would be nice,' Paul responded, closing the wardrobe door so that Gemma would not be disturbed by seeing its emptiness. 'I'd better not have anything stronger, because I'm driving.'

'Of course,' Gemma smiled, 'it wouldn't do for a policeman to get nicked would it?'

They both laughed nervously. Then Gemma ushered Paul into the living room and told him to sit down while she got the coffee. He sat looking about him, wondering whether he ought to make his apologies and leave. He wasn't supposed to socialise with witnesses, but it seemed callous to go off and leave her alone in the empty flat with its empty wardrobe and empty bookcase as constant reminders that her boyfriend had killed himself only days before.

Gemma came back and put down two mugs on the small coffee table in front of the sofa. She sat down beside Paul. He moved up to make room for her to sit without touching him.

'It's quite like old times,' she commented. 'Do you remember that old bench at the bottom of the garden at Willowbank? Where we used to go to get away from

Bongo and his gang?'

'Yes, of course I do,' Paul laughed, 'the old wooden bench with the weeds growing so high that no one could see we were there. It was the one place I felt really safe – especially when you were there with me! You were very good to me,' he went on, speaking more seriously now, 'I don't think I'd have survived if you hadn't been there. The others all seemed so awful.'

'Well, Bongo liked picking on anyone smaller than him, and the others were all afraid of him …'

'Except you,' Paul put in. 'You weren't afraid to stand up to him.'

'Well, I was older and the care workers all liked me and felt sorry for me because of the way my parents died, so I knew they'd be on my side if it came to a fight.'

'I still thought you were tremendously brave the way you talked to him. Nobody else dared to say the things you said.'

'I don't want to waste the evening talking about Bongo. Don't you remember any of the good times we had at Willowbank?'

'Good times?' Paul repeated, taken aback. His own memory of his time in care was of perpetual misery, intimidated by bigger, more confident boys and in constant fear of doing something wrong that might be reported back to his parents.

'Yes. Don't you remember? What about that trip to Whipsnade zoo? You enjoyed that, didn't you?'

'Yes, I suppose so – except for the way Bongo kept making fun of everyone by comparing them to different animals.' Paul sat for a moment, remembering his childhood. 'Why was he called Bongo? I never understood.'

'Apparently someone said he must have come from Bongo-Bongo land and the name stuck.'

'Didn't anyone stop it? I mean – it's not acceptable to call people names based on their race.'

'I don't know,' Gemma shrugged. 'It was all before I got there. I suppose if Bongo didn't mind … I mean he seemed pleased with the name, didn't he? Anyway – let's forget about Bongo. Tell me what you've been doing since you left Willowbank. How did you end up becoming a policeman?'

The time passed pleasantly and Paul was sorry when he looked at his watch and realised that it was time he was gone. He felt a pang of guilt at the thought that his assertion that he had no conflict of interest in this case was starting to look unconvincing. He had to admit that he had enjoyed Gemma's company and hoped that she might be willing to carry on the acquaintance after the investigation into her lover's death was over.

Eventually he made his excuses and left. It was far too late to take the suicide note to Peter this evening; he would do it the next day – or perhaps it could wait until Monday? No, he must tell Peter before he spoke to Robert's parents again, and before they went to the flat and spoke to Gemma.

CHAPTER 14

'Thanks for taking me,' Eddie said to Bernie as they headed north around the Oxford ring road. He was in the front passenger seat while Lucy was strapped in her safety seat in the back, occupied, for the time being, with hunting for treasures in a brightly coloured fabric bag that one of Bernie's friends had made for her. It had numerous separate compartments fastened by a variety of different mechanisms: zips, Velcro, buttons and drawstrings. Bernie had prepared it for the journey by putting a toy or treat inside each compartment; now they would see how long it would be before Lucy's interest waned and the inevitable question was asked: are we nearly there?

'No need for that,' Bernie assured him. 'I told you: this ex-colleague of mine has been on at me for ages, wanting to see Lucy.'

'Come off it! We both know that isn't why you suggested driving me up. I just hope your friend won't be too put out at having you both turning up on her doorstep at such short notice!'

'I don't know what you mean!' Bernie protested, pretending to be offended. 'I'll have you know she was very pleased to hear we were coming. Her kids are about the same age as Lucy, so she's interested in comparing notes.'

'She's younger than you then,' Eddie commented, remembering the discussion during the run up to Lucy's birth of the perils of embarking on motherhood after the age of forty.

'Less of your cheek, young Edward!' Bernie exclaimed in mock indignation. 'Our age is none of your business – although, as it happens, Harriet is a few years my junior. She's got three kids: a girl about Lucy's age and two older boys about two years apart. So I'm sure we'll all have a good time together, and you don't need to start thinking I'm only going up there for your benefit.'

'Dad thought I ought to go on the train.'

'Well, he has a point. When I was your age, I always came up to Oxford by train. My family didn't even have a car!'

Yeah – and you all wrote with quill pens, and calculators hadn't been invented, and you were all grateful for what you could get what with the war having only just ended and-'

'Hang on! Less of that! We're talking the nineteen seventies here. The war had been over for thirty years. But you're right in a way – we did have less stuff to bring: no computers and printers, just books and clothes and a kettle.'

'Anyway, I don't see why Dad couldn't have taken me like he promised,' Eddie returned to his real grievance. 'He's always doing it. I don't know why I keep believing that this time he might actually *do* what he says he's going to do.'

'Don't be too hard on him, Eddie. It is his job, after all. I know he feels bad about letting you down.'

'He's only collecting a couple of people from the airport,' Eddie insisted. 'It's not even real police work.'

'It's two people, whose son has just been found dead in the river,' Bernie pointed out. 'They'll be wanting to know how it happened.'

'But there must be plenty of other people who could do it,' Eddie refused to be convinced. 'People who were *supposed* to be on duty today. Why does it have to be Dad –

when he *promised*?'

'Eddie,' Bernie said patiently, 'has it not occurred to you that the reason your dad feels obliged to bend over backwards to help these people is because he's imagining all the time what it would be like for him and your mum if *you* were the body lying in the mortuary fridge after being dragged from the Thames?'

'Do you really think so?' Eddie asked in surprise.

'Yes, I do,' Bernie answered with a finality in her voice that made it clear that there was to be no more discussion. 'And now,' she went on, 'tell me about the incident with the policeman in the park on Thursday.'

'How did you know about that? They promised they wouldn't tell you.'

'Lucy showed me her picture – the one with the big bad policeman in his tall helmet who wanted to take you away to prison!'

'It wasn't like that.'

'No, I'm sure it wasn't, but that's how Lucy described it to me; so now I'd like to know what really happened – so I can try to explain to her that policemen are really nice kind people who help you!'

Eddie told the story again, as briefly as possible, playing down his own fear during the moment when he had actually believed that he might be arrested and taken off to the police station to answer a charge of child abduction.

'Of course, I should have known better than to get Dad involved,' he concluded. 'He always gets this sort of thing out of proportion. I told him afterwards it was no big deal, but he didn't want to let it go.'

'Of course not: he's your dad – it's his job to worry about it when people give you a hard time.'

'Well, I wish he wouldn't,' Eddie grumbled.

'Oh Eddie! Give him a break. It's only natural that he wants to protect you – and only natural that he resents anyone except members of your immediate family suggesting that you might be anything other than the most wonderful young man who ever walked the earth!'

'Stop taking the mick!' Eddie laughed in spite of himself. 'Dad doesn't think anything of the sort!'

'I didn't say he did. I just said that, as your father, he will be dissatisfied unless everyone else thinks it – or at least pretends to.'

'But anyway,' Eddie resumed, refusing to be diverted for long from his main complaint, 'I don't see why he has to make such a fuss about things. Mum doesn't. She just says, "Take no notice" and carries on as if nothing had happened.'

'Well, it's different for your Mum – she's black.'

'What's that got to do with it?'

'It's difficult to explain,' Bernie said slowly, wondering whether this had been a rather unwise remark to have made.

'You're always saying that everyone's the same underneath,' Eddie persisted. 'I remember your Sunday school lessons. "Don't judge people by outward appearances," you said. So how come you're telling me that it's because she's black that Mum can behave sensibly when that sort of thing happens, whereas Dad always has to start pontificating about the race relations act and unacceptable behaviour and all that?'

'Well, of course, being a policeman, he's bound to think in terms of the law,' Bernie began.

'Maybe, but that isn't what you were talking about. You said he and Mum treated things differently because she's black. Being in the police is nothing to do with that.'

'OK, OK, I'll try to explain what I mean. Just give me a minute to think, will you?'

Bernie remained silent for several minutes. Eddie waited impatiently. Lucy began singing to herself in the back of the car, 'the wheels on the bus go round and round ...'

'OK,' Bernie said at last, taking a deep breath before going on. 'Let's start with an example. Say you came home from school and told your mum that some of the kids had been calling you names because of your colour.'

'I never would,' Eddie interrupted.

'No, but just suppose you did. She could say, "I know how it feels, but the best thing to do is just to ignore it. When people do that to me, I just take no notice and carry on. It's not worth making a fuss about." But your dad – he can't say "I know how you feel" or "this is what I do when it happens to me" because he doesn't know what it feels like and he can't point to himself as an example of how to cope. All he can do is to try to imagine how bad you feel and to get angry with the people who are making you feel like that.'

'I suppose so,' Eddie said reluctantly.

'And there's another thing,' Bernie went on. 'You and your mum can tell yourselves that the people who say and do those things are just acting out of ignorance. It's only natural to be afraid of the unfamiliar, and when people are frightened they say things they don't really mean. They're only repeating things they've heard other people say, without really thinking about it. It's not personal, it's just the way they've been brought up to think. But your dad knows that none of those excuses really work, because he's just like them – born white and brought up in a predominantly white society – and yet he doesn't act like them and he knows that everyone has to take responsibility for their own actions. So he can't say to you, "don't hold it against them – they can't help it," whereas your mum can, because, to her, *they* are the unfamiliar other. Do you see what I'm getting at?'

'I think so.'

'And, of course, in this case there's an added dimension because of the police being involved. Your dad is a senior officer; he's obliged to take notice if a member of the force appears to have been discriminating against a member of the public because of his race. He can't choose to ignore it just because it happens to be his son on the receiving end.

The last thing Thames Valley needs is an accusation of institutional racism.'

'Does that mean he'll have to make an official report?' Eddie asked. 'He told Constable Fox he wasn't going to. I wouldn't want him to be in trouble about it.'

'Well then, in that case he won't. I expect he thinks he's made his point and there's no need for it to go any further. Just knowing that your dad is disappointed in him is probably punishment enough don't you think?'

'I'm not so sure about that,' Eddie laughed. 'It would be for me, but he's not Constable Fox's father is he?'

'I can only go by what Richard told me, but I definitely get the impression that Detective Inspector Johns is very well-regarded in the force. I don't think a young officer would want to feel he'd lost his respect.'

'I used to blame your Richard for calling Dad out to work at all hours of the day and night. When he finally made it to inspector I thought it would all change, but it didn't.'

'I'm sure Richard didn't make it any easier for Peter to get time with his family,' Bernie laughed, 'but you've got to remember that policing is a vocation – like being a doctor or a nurse or a priest – you can't pin it down to normal hours of work and go home on the dot regardless of what's going on.'

'I remember how you used to ring Mum to find out where Richard was when he didn't come home. I guess at least Dad usually calls to say he'll be late.'

'That was before we were married. Even Richard improved once he knew I was worrying about him in an official capacity! But, yes – I'd say your Dad does his best to balance police and family responsibilities. He's a good man as well as a good police officer – you'll come to appreciate that one day.'

'You really like him, don't you?' Eddie said suddenly, detecting a subtle change in Bernie's tone of voice.

'Both of your parents are my very best friends. I owe

them an awful lot.'

'I guess they owe you too. If it wasn't for you they'd probably have had a juvenile delinquent on their hands!'

'Don't talk daft!' Bernie reproved him, flushing red with embarrassment.

'I mean it. I was so mixed up and angry when I was in year eight! If you hadn't insisted on building that computer with me and pushed me to stick it out at school, I don't know what I'd have ended up doing. Mind you – you should have seen Dad's face when he saw that soldering iron you gave me for my birthday! I'm convinced he thought I'd burn the house down with it.'

'Poor old Peter!' Bernie laughed. 'He always did go a bit over the top with the health and safety stuff. I told him: a soldering iron's one of the most useful bits of kit there is; every fourteen-year-old should have one.'

'Did you have a soldering iron when you were fourteen?'

'Unfortunately not, and it wouldn't have been so much use in those days because computers were still monsters that took up a couple of rooms and needed constant expert attention. However, I did have a most magnificent Meccano set. Sister Teresa told my parents that I had the makings of an engineer, so they persuaded the whole family to give me bits. Dad was the youngest of thirteen, so there were plenty of aunts and uncles and cousins to contribute and it made quite a collection.'

'Have you still got it?'

'No. it went to the Sally Army with everything else when my dad died. I didn't think: I should have kept it for you and Hannah, but she was only a baby at the time and you were just a twinkle in your mother's eye!'

Eddie was spending his second year at university in a shared house with five other students. When they pulled up outside the Victorian terrace, they were greeted by a small, slim young woman wearing a green hijab. She introduced herself as Samira Iqbal, speaking in a strong

Yorkshire accent.

'This is Our Bernie,' Eddie said vaguely. 'She gave me a lift up. And this is Lucy,' he added, picking Lucy up and holding her so that her face was level with Samira's. Say "hello" to Samira, Lucy.'

'Hello Smeera,' Lucy said obediently, favouring Samira with a wide smile.

'Hello Lucy,' Samira said, returning the smile.

'I'm Eddie's godmother,' Bernie said by way of explanation.

'Godmother *Angie*!' Lucy exclaimed indignantly.

'Yes Lucy, that's right: Angie is *your* godmother and I'm *Eddie's* godmother.'

'Hey Lucy! Get this,' Eddie shouted in delight. 'My mum is your godmother and your mum is my godmother, so that must make me your *godbrother*! I'd never thought of it like that before.'

'Am I your godsister?' Lucy asked seriously, picking up the reasoning with surprising quickness.

'I don't think that are any such things as godsisters and godbrothers,' Bernie told her, 'but if there were, then that's what you'd be, sure enough.'

None of the other flatmates had arrived yet. Bernie's early start meant that they were the first to get there that morning. Samira had come over on the Trans Pennine Express from Bradford two days earlier. Bernie smiled when she heard that this student, at any rate, was not above travelling by train, but she tactfully said nothing. She and Eddie were soon busy unpacking the car and carrying his possessions upstairs to his room, while Samira took Lucy out to play in the small garden at the back of the house. As usual, Lucy managed to endear herself to her new acquaintance and they were both sorry when Bernie came looking for her to tell her that they were ready to go. Her friend, Harriet, was expecting them for lunch at her home in Wilmslow.

Lucy gave both students a hug and a rather wet kiss by

way of goodbye and then consented to be strapped into her car seat again. Then she waved to them as they drove off until they turned the corner and the house was out of sight.

CHAPTER 15

After waving Eddie goodbye, as Bernie drove him away shortly after breakfast, Peter wondered what to do until it was time to start out for the airport. Eddie had shown him how to monitor flight arrivals on their home computer, using the internet connection that Bernie has insisted on them having installed after Eddie had declared his intention of studying computer science. Robert White's parents had given him their flight number and he had checked it shortly after he got up and then again after breakfast. Everything pointed to them arriving on time, so now there was nothing more to be done until it got closer to the time when he would need to set out on the journey to Heathrow.

His wife was working that day, so he was left alone in the house with nothing to do except turn over in his mind what he had learned so far about Robert White and his movements during the last days of his life. What could he say to the lad's parents when he met them? They would want answers where he still had only uncertainty to offer.

He determined to make himself useful about the house during this period of inaction and set off upstairs to his son's attic bedroom with a view to stripping the bed and washing the sheets. As usual, the room was chaotic. Eddie's discarded clothes from the previous day lay in a heap on the floor. The duvet was piled up at one corner of the bed with a pair of pyjamas lying beside it. The dust on the desk was made more prominent by the clear patches where a computer and printer had been removed. A cactus, which had been standing on the windowsill, lay on the floor beneath, surrounded by compost, which had spilled from its pot. Next to it lay a lone training shoe, its partner, who knew where? Drawers and cupboards stood open from where they had been ransacked the evening before in preparation for Eddie's return to university.

Peter took the cover off the duvet and carried it down the attic stairs with the sheet and pillowcases and his son's dirty clothes. He added them to the already nearly full linen basket, which he then carried from the bathroom down to the kitchen. He loaded the washing machine and then went back up to the attic, carrying a brush and dustpan. He closed the cupboard doors, pushed shut the drawers and wiped the dust off the desk. Then he brushed the compost off the carpet and set the cactus back in its place on the windowsill.

Robert White's parents must have gone through a similar experience, he reflected. They too must have seen their son leave home: first temporarily, while at university and then for good. Had he come to England direct from living with his parents? Or had he moved out before that? Either way, in all probability they had a room like this, back in their Melbourne house: somewhere that was full of their son's possessions – or else starkly empty because he had taken them away to his new life elsewhere. Had they been looking forward to welcoming him back into their home at the end of his three years in England? What dreams had been shattered by the news that he would never be coming back, after all?

He was in the process of getting the clean washing out of the machine when his mobile phone rang. He snatched it off the table, where he had left it, and looked at the display. What could Paul want? It was not like him to ring on a Saturday when neither of them was on duty.

'I'm sorry to bother you at the weekend,' Paul

apologised, 'but there are a couple of things I think you ought to see before you meet the parents today.'

'OK,' Peter considered what to do. He did not usually encourage his work colleagues to visit him at home, but that seemed the easiest way of enabling Paul to share whatever it was. If they met at the police station they were sure to be drawn into other things and their day off would go by the board. 'Bring them over to my house. You know where it is, don't you?'

'Yes sir. I'll come over right away – if that's alright with you,' Paul added anxiously.

'Yes, of course; the sooner the better.'

Within twenty minutes Peter heard the sound of a car drawing up outside and, looking out, he saw Paul coming up the short path to the front door. He hastened into the hall to let him in. They sat down together in the front room and Peter looked at Paul enquiringly.

'Gemma Markham called me last night,' Paul explained. 'She wanted to show me this.'

He handed over the torn sheet containing Robert White's suicide note. Peter read it in silence, his face becoming more serious as he did so.

'Why didn't she show this to us before?' he asked, looking Paul directly in the eye. Paul felt uncomfortable. He sensed that Peter was considering whether or not he was becoming too close to their key witness and ought to be taken off the case.

'She *said* she didn't notice it before,' he answered, deliberately putting a degree of scepticism into his voice as if he doubted that Gemma was being completely frank in that assertion. 'Apparently it was hidden behind the toaster and she didn't have any toast until yesterday.'

'You said you had two things to show me,' Peter said, after considering Paul's response for just long enough to convey the impression that he did not necessarily believe in Gemma's explanation.

'Yes. This is the other one,' Paul said, getting out the

bottle of tablets from his pocket and handing it to Peter. 'She said that he told her they were for his hay fever, but there's no label on them and I thought the colour might be significant ...'

'Yes,' Peter opened the bottle and tipped a few of the tablets out on to his hand. He had never seen Rohypnol tablets before, but he remembered having been told that they contained a blue dye to make it easier to detect when they were dissolved in a drink. These were a dull olive green colour. He put them back in the bottle and screwed on the lid.

'We'd better get these analysed, he said. 'I think you may be right and they are Rohypnol, but they just *might* be some hay fever remedy – maybe a herbal concoction that comes in a plain bottle without any instructions.'

'I'll get them off to the lab,' Paul said, pocketing the bottle again. 'What about the note? Do you want to take it with you to show his parents?'

'Yes, I suppose so. They'll want to see it, and in any case, I'd like them to confirm that it's in his handwriting. It's always possible ...' He trailed off, unwilling to put into words the suggestion that Gemma could have forged the note. Perhaps she had been surprised at the thoroughness of the police investigation and was worried that, if it was not concluded quickly, it might turn up aspects of her own involvement that she did not want anyone to know about.

'I wonder why he tore the sheet off halfway down like that,' Peter mused, turning the note over in his hand. 'Why not pull it off the pad at the top and use the whole sheet?'

'Maybe he wrote it on the bottom half of a sheet that already had something on it,' Paul suggested, 'and then decided he only wanted Gemma to see the note and not whatever was already on the pad. She said it was one of the pads he used for his work, so maybe it was confidential or something – or maybe he had a false start at writing the note and didn't want to waste paper by starting again on a fresh sheet.'

'You're right,' Peter said with a smile. 'I'm probably reading too much into it. There are all sorts of perfectly reasonable explanations. OK. You get those tablets off to the lab – tell them we want the results on Monday – and I'll take care of the note.'

Paul went off, leaving Peter still turning over in his mind how he was going to introduce to Robert White's parents the possibility – now the likelihood – that their son had committed suicide. Would it make it better or worse for them to think that he might have been under the influence of a drug when he took the decision to end his own life?

He finished getting the washing out of the machine and took it out into the back yard to dry. As he pegged Eddie's jeans and tee shirt to the line, he was suddenly struck by the thought that he had no way of knowing the states of mind of his own children: Hannah in her nursing job in Leeds and Edward in Manchester.

Eddie certainly did not appear depressed – just angry with Peter for not making time to transport him back to university – but could he be sure? Peter had investigated a number of suicides among the student population of Oxford and knew that they often felt under a variety of different pressures – through being unused to failure or being crossed in love or getting into financial difficulties or just generally being young people unused to being away from home.

Hannah never seemed to want to communicate with them much anymore, but maybe she was just busy with her work and with whatever social life she had up there. Last time she visited, she seemed happy enough, but that might just be a façade. What was her life like in faraway Leeds? Did she have friends to whom she could turn if she were worried about anything? Did she have a boyfriend? Peter was surprised and dismayed at how much they had lost touch.

He decided to ring her flat. If she was not on shift this

weekend, she might be at home. The phone rang out several times before it was answered by a man's voice, speaking with the unmistakable accent that told Peter that, whoever it was, his formative years had been spent in the West Midlands. He asked to speak to Hannah.

'OK, I'll get her. Who shall I say is ringing?'

'Tell her it's her Dad.'

'OK. Right. There's nothing wrong is there?'

'No, no, just a social call.'

Almost immediately, Hannah's voice came on the line.

'What is it Dad? Is there something wrong?' she asked anxiously.

'No: I just had a few minutes spare and I thought it'd be nice to catch up with you. It seems like a long time since we spoke.'

'You mean I ought to have rung.'

'No, of course not. There's no reason why it should always be you ringing us. I was just wondering how you were and what you've been up to.'

'Well I'm fine.'

'Good. And the job? You're still enjoying it?'

'Yes. The job is fine too.'

'And you've got plenty of friends up there? You never get lonely?'

'Yes, Dad: I told you – everything is just fine. What's this all about?'

'I'm sorry, love,' Peter apologised, feeling rather foolish. 'Alright, I'll come clean. We've just pulled a young lad out of the river – not much older than you, with his whole life ahead of him – and it set me wondering what made him do it. His parents are arriving from Australia today and of course they had no idea it was coming.'

'OK Dad, I get the picture,' Hannah interrupted. 'Look – just take my word for it: I'm fine, my job is fine, my friends are fine and my flat is fine. Life is just fine, in every way. And I have no plans for jumping in any rivers. OK?'

'Yes. I'm sorry. I'll let you get on. I expect you're busy.

But,' Peter hesitated before adding, 'but you would tell us if there was anything wrong, wouldn't you?'

'Yes Dad,' Hannah sighed and looked up to the ceiling. 'I promise.'

'Thanks. Bye then.'

Hannah put the phone down and looked at her boyfriend, Laurence, with an expression of amused irritation, shaking her head at the strange behaviour of parents.

'What was all that about?' he asked.

'My dad is a police officer,' she explained, 'which means that he tends to see rather too much of the dark side of life.'

'Unlike nurses and paramedics,' Laurence suggested with a smile. He was a paramedic, whom Hannah had met while working in the Accident and Emergency department.

'He's investigating the death of some young man who's drowned himself in the river in Oxford and he seems to have got it into his head that I might be feeling suicidal and not telling them.'

'Aren't you pleased he cares?'

Hannah did not answer, so Laurence went on.

'I think it's only natural that he should worry about you.' He said, coming closer and putting his arms around Hannah. 'I'm sure I'd worry if I had a beautiful daughter like you. I bet he's scared some predatory male will come along and take advantage of you.'

'Like you, you mean?'

'That's right.' Laurence held her tight and kissed her on the neck. 'I bet he's sitting there imagining them all buzzing around you like bees round a honeypot.'

Hannah giggled and returned his kiss.

'Have you told your parents about me?' Laurence asked, suddenly more serious. 'He seemed taken aback when I answered – although he didn't say anything.'

'No,' Hannah admitted, feeling rather guilty, 'I haven't got round to it. I was afraid they might fuss – want to meet you, that sort of thing.'

'Don't you want them to meet me?'

'Well, yes – eventually, but there's no rush, is there?'

'Don't you think they'll approve of me?'

'No, it's not that. Don't be silly! And anyway, I don't need their approval for who I go out with.'

'Is it because I'm white?' Laurence asked suddenly.

'What!' Hannah gasped in amazement, flabbergasted by this suggestion. 'What on earth has that got to do with anything?'

'I thought you might be worried that your parents wouldn't like you taking up with a man from outside your own community. I don't mean I thought they might be racist,' he added hastily. 'I meant they might be concerned that it would be difficult for you to be in a mixed-race relationship.'

Hannah burst out laughing. She hugged Laurence to her and laughed until the tears came, unable to speak. He stared at her in bemusement. Eventually she managed to get out a few words between the peals of laughter.

'Oh Laurence! You have no idea how funny that is!'

'Why? I don't understand.'

Hannah let go of him and headed for the bedroom.

'Wait there!' she called back over her shoulder. 'I'm just getting something to show you.'

A few minutes later, she returned carrying a photograph in a cardboard frame. She handed it to Laurence.

'This is my graduation photo. That's my dad, standing next to me, and my mum on the other side. Believe me, they really don't have any hang-ups about mixed-race relationships!'

CHAPTER 16

As he drove back from the airport with Robert's parents, Peter was struck by the differences between them. Bernard and Samantha White were a couple of stark contrasts. He was large and slow; she was small and vivacious. He sat next to Peter staring silently ahead with his pale blue eyes; she chattered eagerly in the back, leaning forward over Peter's shoulder to ask him questions, her black curls brushing his cheek. Her deep brown eyes were red-rimmed, but whether from weeping or from lack of sleep Peter could not tell.

At present, she seemed not so much grief-stricken as excited and anxious about the immediate practical issues: when could they see Robert's body? Would there be an inquest? How soon could the funeral take place? Should they bury him in England or repatriate him to Australia? Then she turned to the police investigation and wanted to know what more Peter could tell them about what had happened. He fended her off with non-committal words while promising to give them a full account later in the day, after they had settled into their hotel and had a chance to rest.

However, Mrs White refused to be put off. She persisted in asking for more details. How could Robert have drowned? She wanted to know. He was such a strong swimmer. He was a surfing champion back home and an experienced scuba diver. And he was used to river swimming too. Even in flood conditions, it was hard for her to see how he could not have survived. Were the police considering foul play?

'We are keeping an open mind,' Peter assured her patiently, well aware that this platitudinous remark would not satisfy her maternal anxiety that all was not being done to obtain justice for her dead son.

'Be quiet Sam!' Bernard White barked out suddenly. 'The man's promised to tell us everything later. Give it a rest, can't you?'

'As regards how he came to drown,' Peter went on, trying to think of a way of filling the awkward silence that followed this outburst and deciding that he might as well take advantage of Samantha White's loquaciousness to ask a few pertinent questions, 'there is evidence that he had taken a sedative before he fell in the river. Do you know whether he was in the habit of taking sleeping pills?'

'No,' Samantha replied, sounding puzzled. 'I never knew him to have trouble sleeping. Even when he got depression – that was way back when he was a teenager – it never affected him like that.'

'Your son had a history of depression?'

'I suppose you could put it like that,' Samantha agreed, 'but he'd been absolutely fine for years – hadn't he, Bernard?'

'Yes,' Bernard agreed laconically, brushing his fair hair out of his eyes and continuing to stare out of the window.

'When you say he had depression as a teenager,' Peter persisted gently, 'do you just mean that he seemed depressed or was he actually diagnosed medically? Was he prescribed any medication?'

'Yes: it got so bad in the end we took him to our doctor and he gave him some antidepressants, but he wasn't on them for long. He had CBT and that worked wonders for him. And of course, he was an adolescent – he grew out of it. He hasn't taken anything for it for years now.'

'Do you remember exactly what it was that the doctor

prescribed or what the tablets looked like?'

'No. It was a long time ago. They were just some sort of mild anti-depressant – white tablets as far as I can remember. What does it matter now?'

'He had some tablets in his possession: green ones in a brown glass bottle with no label on it. We're getting them analysed, but I was wondering if they might have been familiar to you – if perhaps he'd brought them with him from home, or if he'd asked a doctor here to prescribe the same drug that he'd had before.'

'They don't sound the same at all to me,' Samantha said, shaking her head. 'And you've got to remember, this is fifteen or more years ago we're talking about.'

'His girlfriend says he told her they were for his hay fever. Does that ring any bells with you?'

'No,' Samantha looked puzzled. 'I can't understand that at all. Robert never suffered from hay fever.'

'Perhaps it came on after he came to England,' Peter suggested. 'The pollen over here would be different. But I take it he didn't mention it to you?'

'No,' Samantha shook her head again.

'If you ask me,' Bernard said belligerently, contributing to the conversation for the first time, 'you shouldn't believe everything that girl says.'

'Oh? What makes you say that?' Peter asked mildly, trying not to sound overly interested in this opinion.

Bernard said nothing, so after a minute or two his wife answered for him.

'We think they fell out,' she explained. 'About eighteen months back, after they'd been seeing each other for a few weeks, Robert was completely obsessed with her. She was the apple of his eye and he was determined they were going to settle down together permanently. Every time we spoke it was Gemma this and Gemma that.'

'You'd think the sun shone out of her-,' Bernard added morosely.

'Yes, well never mind that,' his wife put in hastily.

'Then, it was maybe four or five months ago, he suddenly seemed to cool towards her. He didn't say anything, but I definitely got the impression that there was something wrong and he was anxious to get away from her. He still wouldn't hear a word said against her, mind you – but things just weren't right, I could tell. And then he told us he was giving up the job in Oxford and coming home for good. He still didn't say anything, but I think he was running away from her.'

'But you've no idea at all what it was that she'd done to upset him?'

Samantha shook her head silently.

'We think he went out late at night last Tuesday,' Peter said, remembering, 'between, say eleven and midnight, which would have been Wednesday morning in Melbourne. He didn't by any chance telephone you?'

'No,' Samantha said firmly. 'We heard nothing from him after his weekend email on Sunday.'

'I see. We *had* thought that maybe he went out so as to be able to ring home without disturbing Gemma – or so as to speak in private – but it looks as if we were mistaken.'

'He may have rung Marian,' Samantha suggested, 'or one of his friends.'

'And Marian is?'

'Our daughter – Robert's sister. She's married now and living in Sydney.'

'Could you check with her? It'll come better from you. If she gets a call from the police it may worry her, and the chances are it's nothing.'

'Yes. We promised her we would ring to let her know we'd got here. I'll do it as soon as we get to the hotel.'

'Which is right here,' Peter said, pulling up in front of a small hotel in North Oxford. 'I hope this is alright for you. It's a family-run place and a bit more personal than the big ones in the centre. I'll leave you to get settled in and then, if it's alright with you, I've got a few more questions. Do you mind if I come back a bit later this afternoon?'

'Not at all,' Samantha assured him, giving him a brave smile. 'We'd like to help all we can, wouldn't we Bernard?'

'Yes, of course,' Bernard acquiesced gruffly, lifting their suitcases out of the boot and starting off towards the hotel entrance.

Peter gave them until about half past three before returning to the hotel. He knocked on the door of the couple's room and listened for a response, conscious that, after such a long journey, it was entirely possible that they would have fallen asleep. He came prepared to abandon the interview until the evening or even the following day if necessary.

The door opened and Mrs White stood there looking surprisingly refreshed, her hair damp from the shower. She had changed out of the jeans and sweater that she had worn for the journey and was now wearing a blue knitted dress, drawn in at the waist by a white belt; her legs were bare and she had slippers on her feet. She smiled when she saw Peter and made way for him to enter the room.

He husband was sitting in a narrow easy chair, which looked too small for his large frame. He had not changed out of his travel-stained grey flannel trousers and open-necked shirt. His blond hair was ruffled and the fringe fell across his face. He looked tired and depressed.

Peter indicated to Samantha that she should take the other easy chair, while he pulled out an upright chair from beneath the dressing table and sat down facing them both. He reached into his pocket and pulled out the scrap of paper containing Robert White's suicide note.

'Gemma found this in the kitchen of their flat,' he said, handing it to Samantha. 'Is it Robert's handwriting?'

Samantha looked down at the note. She read it without speaking and then hurriedly passed it to her husband who fished in his shirt pocket for a pair of glasses, before studying it. Peter watched them, waiting for a reply. Tears welled up in Samantha's eyes and she wiped them away with the back of her hand.

'Yes,' she said in a small voice. 'Yes: Robert wrote that.'

'But why?' Bernard demanded in a voice that sounded unnaturally loud in the silence of the room and then cracked suddenly as he repeated, 'why? He had everything arranged! He was coming home. Why did he have to …?'

'I suppose his depression must have come back,' Samantha said, trying to make sense of what she had just read. 'What a pity we weren't there to spot the signs!'

'It's that Gemma's fault, I'll bet,' Bernard growled. 'He was fine until he met her.'

'You don't know that,' Samantha argued, trying to be fair. 'It could have been the depression that made him think she wasn't acting right by him.'

'Your wife's right,' Peter agreed. 'Nobody can know what was going on inside his head and nobody need be to blame. Depression is an illness. It can strike anyone.'

'So what do you think happened between them?' Samantha asked.

'I can only tell you what other people have told me,' Peter said, not wanting to get drawn into giving an opinion, but also hoping to discourage the Whites from attributing blame to Gemma and perhaps making a scene when they visited the flat to collect their son's belongings. 'According to his work colleagues, he seemed happy with Gemma and they commented that her influence stopped him overworking, which they thought was good for him. She seems genuinely puzzled and upset about his death and she told us that they were planning for her to go over to Australia and join him once he'd got himself re-established with a job there. The neighbours hadn't heard any rows and they all said that Gemma and Robert seemed to be a very united couple.'

'He never said anything to us about bringing Gemma over,' Samantha said in a surprised tone. 'I definitely got the impression that they were splitting up and that was why he decided to come back.'

'Did he actually say that?'

'Well, no – it was more what I read between the lines. I may have been wrong …,' Samantha's voice trailed off into silence and she looked from Peter to Bernard with a haunted expression on her face. 'Oh Bernard! We should have been there for him.'

'Now honey, that's plain nonsense,' her husband said, speaking more gently than Peter had heard him do before and putting out his hand to take hold of hers. 'He was thirty-three for God's sake! You can't expect to keep him clinging to our apron strings now he's a grown man.'

'I know, I know,' Samantha responded, squeezing his hand and looking into his eyes with tears in her own. 'It's just that I can't help feeling we ought to have seen it coming and been able to do something. And why didn't he say anything to us?'

'Try not to blame yourselves,' Peter urged gently. 'I know it's hard, but in these situations it's best to try to accept that it's nobody's fault and there was probably nothing that anyone could have done. Now, I think the best thing for you is to try to get some rest,' he added, getting to his feet. 'I'll arrange with Gemma for you to go over tomorrow to pick up Robert's things from the flat, and on Monday I'll take you to see his body. If there's anything else in the meantime, you know how to reach me.'

'Yes – thank you,' Bernard answered distantly, as if he were thinking of something else.

'You've been very kind,' Samantha added. 'There's just one thing you might be able to help us with right now,' she went on. 'I was wondering – with it being Sunday tomorrow – can you tell us where there's a church service we could go to? We don't know Oxford at all.'

'Well now, that's an interesting one,' Peter smiled. 'In the city of dreaming spires the question isn't so much where to find a church as which particular brand you'd like to choose! We've got them all: Church of England – including Anglo-Catholic, Evangelical, charismatic and all the shades in between – Roman Catholic, Methodist, Greek Orthodox, Russian Orthodox, URC, Quakers, Salvation Army, you name it. What sort of thing were you looking for?'

'We're members of the Uniting Church back home, so we're pretty ecumenical-minded – just somewhere prayerful.'

'Well,' Peter said, playing for time while he thought through the options, 'there's a parish church just round the corner from here, and there's a Baptist church over on the Woodstock Road, or you could go into the centre of Oxford and there are all sorts there …'

'Do you happen to know which church Robert attended?' Samantha asked.

'No, I'm afraid not. None of the people we talked to mentioned him going to church. Gemma would know. If it's important to you, I could ring her.'

'No, don't trouble yourself,' Bernard interrupted. 'My wife always set great store by the kids going to church regularly, but Robert had other priorities – he put saving the world ahead of religion. I doubt he ever got round to going to church while he was in Oxford.'

Peter looked at him. This was the longest speech Bernard had made since they had met. Then he looked at Samantha, who was twisting her hands together in her lap anxiously and staring down at the floor.

'If you like,' Peter suggested, 'I could pick you up and take you to the Methodist church down Cowley Road where we go.'

The Whites both answered at once.

'No – we wouldn't want to intrude on your family,' Bernard said quickly.

'Yes – I'd like that,' Samantha replied, equally fast. 'You're very kind.'

'Not at all,' Peter assured her. 'I've got kids of my own. I'll pick you up at about ten – the service is at ten thirty.'

As Peter got into his car to return home a few minutes

later, he wondered what had made him suggest the idea of taking the Whites to church with him. It was not even as if he were a regular attender himself. He was still technically a member, but he rarely made it to the Sunday morning services any longer – not since the children had grown too old to be expected to go to Junior Church, which took place in the hall at the back. An increasing agnosticism made him feel hypocritical about joining in the hymns and prayers and he was aware that his continued involvement was more out of loyalty to Angie, for whom religion was still the foremost influence in her life, and nostalgia for the church of his childhood.

He sighed at the way he had been provoked by Samantha White's anguished expression and her husband's apparent lack of sympathy into breaking his usual rule of keeping home and work separate. He would have to ask Angie to brief the preacher and door stewards, he decided; otherwise, the Whites might be subjected to unwanted attention as visitors or potential new members. Was this the week in the month when they held a bring-and-share lunch after the service? He could not remember, but he had better check with Angie. Maybe Eddie was right and he ought to have delegated the task of fetching Robert's parents from the airport to a more junior officer, who would not have allowed himself to get so involved in their grief.

CHAPTER 17

Paul's Sunday started badly and got worse. He was awakened at half past six by a crash, which sounded ominously close to his bed. As he lay, listening intently, trying to identify the sound and its origin, he became aware of a dripping sound. It seemed to be coming from the living room, which lay next to his bedroom. He got out of bed and hurried round to look.

As soon as he stepped into the room, he became aware of a cold dampness under his bare feet. Looking down, he saw that the carpet was sodden. Then he looked round the room and saw a scene of devastation. The whole room appeared to be covered with a layer of yellowy-grey fibres. In places, this was accompanied by lumps of some creamy-coloured substance. The sound of dripping was louder here, but, at first, Paul could not see where it was coming from.

Worst hit was the N-gauge model railway layout that occupied the large alcove to the right of the chimney breast. It was now buried beneath a heap of debris, which on closer inspection Paul identified as plaster. He looked up and saw a gaping hole in the ceiling, through which water was trickling and dripping down on to his precious model.

Papier-mâché hills had collapsed under the deluge. The signal box lay partially submerged as if a landslide had occurred. The station building was smashed and small figures lay in front of it like the victims of a bomb attack.

Paul stepped forward and inspected the damage more closely. The transformer, thankfully disconnected from the mains overnight, was lying in a pool of water. Water was dripping over the edge of the table on to the floor beneath. Paul bent down and pulled out the box of rolling stock, which he kept stowed there. The locomotives and carriages were all sopping wet and there were two or three inches of water in the bottom of the box.

Paul stood up again and stared round the room, taking it all in. Then the continued dripping sound reminded him that something should be done to halt the disaster. The water must be coming from the loft above. Perhaps there was a leak in the roof, which had allowed water to build up in the space above his flat during the recent heavy rain until its weight was sufficient to cause the plaster to collapse with this devastating effect.

He went out into the small hall, off which led the four rooms that made up his attic flat, and stared up at the loft access hole in the ceiling above. Then he decided that he could do nothing useful while still barefoot and attired in pyjamas. He went back into his bedroom and started putting on his clothes. Looking upwards as he thrust his head through his pullover, he noticed a dark stain on the ceiling in that room. It looked as if the water had affected the plaster here too. He got up on a chair and looked more closely. The plaster was bulging ominously.

Paul put off investigating the loft in favour of averting a second disaster in the bedroom. He fetched a bucket and a screwdriver. Coming back into the bedroom, he positioned the bucket beneath the stained plaster and climbed back on to the chair. He thrust the screwdriver into the soft plaster making a small hole through which a stream of water began to pour. Satisfied that the water would now drain out harmlessly into the bucket, Paul turned his attention once more to getting up into the loft.

A few minutes later, he was standing on a chair trying to reach the square of plywood that covered the loft access. He had never had cause to go up here before and was unsure how it worked. A little experimental pushing resulted in the wooden sheet moving up into the loft and coming to rest to one side of the entrance. He was disappointed to discover that there was no loft ladder, leaving him with the problem of how to get up through the hole and into the roof space above. He needed something taller to stand on.

He vaguely remembered having seen an old wooden stepladder in the garden shed, which the tenants of the flats shared as a storage place for bicycles and other outdoor equipment. He went downstairs and retrieved it, trying not to make a noise as he carried it back up the narrow staircase, for fear of waking the other inhabitants, it being still early on a Sunday morning. He set the ladder up beneath the loft access and climbed up to look inside.

It was all blackness up there and Paul could see nothing at first. Then he noticed a patch of light at one side, close to the wall that separated the house from the next one in the terrace. As his eyes became used to the darkness he made out the shape of the chimney and saw that the light was coming from a hole in the floor. He looked up at the roof above, but could see no chinks of light there. He contemplated climbing up into the loft, but then decided that it would be a mistake to attempt to navigate his way around the unfamiliar space in the darkness, so he climbed back down and went into the kitchen in search of a torch.

Back on top of the ladder, he shone the beam around the interior of the loft. The rafters were dusty and covered in cobwebs. Between them was a layer of glass-fibre loft insulation. That explained the fibres which he had seen littering his living room. Next to the chimney, and partially above the hole in the floor, stood a large rectangular object, which Paul decided must be the header tank for the ancient hot water system that supplied hot water and central heating to the four flats that occupied the converted house. It looked as if this must be the source of the problem.

He climbed carefully up into the loft and made his way slowly across to the tank, treading cautiously to avoid stepping between the rafters and falling through the plaster to the room below. He shone his torch on the tank and eventually identified a leak between the tank and the outlet pipe. It had evidently been going on for some time before enough water had accumulated in the space above Paul's flat to break through the plaster and cause the flood in his living room. He lifted the lid of the tank and saw that water was coming in through the inlet pipe to replace that which was leaking out. He held up the ball cock and observed that this stopped the flow. He let go of the ball and the tank continued to fill up. Paul looked round the loft for some means of keeping the ball raised.

Eventually he found a piece of copper pipe lying between the rafters and used it to prop up the ball and prevent more water entering the tank. Then he groped his way back to the loft entrance and was just letting himself down through it on to the stepladder when he became aware of a hammering on the door of his flat.

'Hang on! I'm coming!' he called, hastening down the ladder and squeezing past it to reach the door.

It was Janice, the young woman who occupied the flat below. She stood at the top of the stairs which led up to his flat, dressed in a frilly pink nightdress covered, rather inadequately, by a flimsy-looking dressing gown, with fluffy blue slippers on her feet. She looked at him belligerently.

'There's water dripping off the light in my kitchen,' she complained. 'Have you left a tap running or something?'

'No, it's the water tank in the loft,' Paul explained. 'It's brought the plaster down in my flat and now it must be leaking through the floor into yours. I've wedged the ball cock so it won't fill up any more, but there's a whole tankful still leaking out. We'd better turn the hot water off to stop the boiler running dry and then the tank will have to be fixed.'

'But what about my kitchen?' Janice demanded. 'It's dripping all over the toaster!'

'We'd better turn off your lighting circuit for a start. You can't have water dripping through a live light fitting. Would you like me to come down and have a look?'

Paul slipped into his bathroom and turned on the hot tap, with the aim of emptying the tank in the loft. Then he followed Janice down to the first floor flat to make safe the electrical system. After that, he made his way down to the basement, which housed the boiler, and switched that off, finally returning to his own flat to contact the letting agency to inform them about the leak.

Predictably, there was nobody there, it being Sunday. A recorded message told him that office hours were nine-thirty to four thirty, Monday to Friday and nine-thirty to one on Saturday.

He went to his desk, which was in the alcove to the left of the chimney breast in the main room, in search of an emergency number. Opening the drawer, he discovered that this too had been affected by the water descending from above and all his meticulously stored paperwork was damp. He took it all out carefully and carried it into the kitchen, which appeared unaffected by the flood. He spread out the contents of the drawer on the working surface and table: driving licence, passport, utility bills, birth certificate, building society passbooks and bank statements were all limp and soggy. He carefully pulled apart the pages of his rental agreement, taking care not to tear them, and peered down, looking for contact details, but the only phone number listed was the one he had just rung. What should he do now? The landlord ought to be informed and someone ought to decide on urgent repairs to the hot water system – not to mention his ceiling.

In the end, he went back downstairs and knocked on Janice's door. After a few minutes she appeared, wrapped in a towel, her hair wet from the shower.

'There's no hot water!' she complained. 'I've just been getting frostbite in the shower!'

Paul explained, as patiently as he could, that he was running off all the hot water to empty the header tank and prevent more water coming into his flat. Until the tank could be fixed, the residents would have to make do with cold water. Janice looked aghast. Clearly, she had never experienced life without hot and cold running water available at all times.

She led him into her lounge and left him there while she got dressed. Then, after much rummaging in drawers and thumbing through notebooks, she held out a scrap of paper with a telephone number on it.

'That's the landlord's mobile number,' she said. 'I prised it out of him last year after I had trouble with mould growing on the wall in the bedroom.'

Paul rang the number and the landlord agreed, with rather bad grace, to come over later that day to survey the damage and decide what was to be done. By the time he arrived at three o'clock that afternoon, there was a reception party waiting for him in the ground floor hallway, comprising: Paul, Janice, Janice's best friend Christa, Andy and Julie, the couple who occupied the ground floor flat, and Ben from the basement. They huddled morosely on the stairs, wrapped in coats to fend off the chill that had descended on the house now that the heating had been off for several hours.

Janice repeatedly declared that she was not staying if there was going to be no hot water and no lights in her flat. Christa assured her that she could come and stay with her for as long as she liked. Ben silently sent and received texts on his mobile phone. Andy and Julie sat holding hands and whispering to one another. Paul, whose flat had suffered the greatest damage in the incident, sat in silence wondering whether he would do better going back upstairs to try to work out a way of drying out his valuable paperwork.

The calm demeanour of the landlord, when he did eventually arrive, was in marked contrast to that of his tenants. He insisted on being shown up to the loft to see the offending water tank, and into Paul's flat to inspect the damage to the ceiling. Eventually he was satisfied and he came back down and addressed the assembled company.

He would have to get a builder and a plumber in to assess what needed to be done, but that would not be possible until Monday. Meanwhile the hot water system would have to remain off. He saw no reason why they should not all stay on in their flats until the work had been done. It was only September, so the central heating was hardly necessary; but if it got colder, he would see what he could do about lending them some electric heaters, or perhaps portable gas heaters. He was sorry that they were being inconvenienced, but this was an incident that could not have been predicted and everyone would just have to be patient while the problem was fixed.

Unsurprisingly, the tenants were far from impressed by this speech, but he brushed aside their protests and departed, leaving them standing in a dissatisfied group in the hall. Janice immediately declared her intention of going to stay with Christa until her electric lighting, heating and hot water were restored. She did not intend to suffer any more cold showers! Christa loudly agreed with her that the landlord's attitude was completely unreasonable in this respect. They disappeared upstairs to collect Janice's things.

After several frantic phone calls, Julie announced that they would be moving in with her parents that afternoon. She and Andy went back into their flat to start packing. Ben also returned to his flat. He said nothing, but that evening Paul saw him setting off up the road with a large rucksack on his back, evidently planning to sleep elsewhere that night.

Paul was left as the only occupant of the house. That night, as he washed in water that he had warmed in a kettle, and changed into his pyjamas in the chilly bedroom, he wondered whether he too ought to seek alternative accommodation; but hotels were expensive and he had no handy friends or relations whom he could ask to put him up. He resolved to stay. At least then he could keep an eye on the workmen and prevent them from doing further damage to his models. He fell into a fitful sleep, dreaming of earthquakes and tidal waves.

CHAPTER 18

Paul was late for work the following day, something which was almost unheard of and which made him very angry with himself. He prided himself on being well-organised and reliable. He slipped into the back of the room, where Peter was already engaged in running through the facts of the case with the small team of officers who were involved in the investigation, and started hastily tying his tie, which he had merely draped around his neck as he left the flat.

'So, it's looking increasingly likely that it was suicide,' Peter concluded. 'We just have a few loose ends to tie up regarding the drug that he took before he went into the river, but essentially we seem to be looking at a young man with a history of depression who, for whatever reason, decided to end it all. So there's not really a lot more to be done. Andrews: I'd like you to finish writing up your report on the river search and then help Philipson with collating the house-to house interviews. Once you've got the file in order, report to DI Hopkins. She needs some more manpower for an Assault and Grievous Bodily Harm, which came in on Saturday.'

The other two officers left the room and Peter turned to Paul.

'I'm sorry I'm late sir; it won't happen again.'

'Was there any particular reason?' Peter asked mildly, noticing that Paul was less well-groomed than usual, with his longish brown curly hair tousled and unkempt, his tie untidily knotted and two small pieces of tissue sticking to his cheek where it appeared he must have cut himself shaving.

'Not really. I just got behind and then, once I was running late, everything seemed to take longer than usual – you know how it is.'

'Late night, last night?' Peter suggested, wondering whether his subordinate might at last have started to develop some sort of social life.

'No sir, not exactly.' Paul hesitated and then decided to tell Peter all about it. He explained about the flood in the flat and the difficulties associated with living without hot water or heating.

'And to top it all,' he ended, 'when I tried to make myself some toast this morning it fused the ring main, so now I can't even heat water in the kettle or use my electric shaver. But don't worry, I'll be sure and leave more time in the morning in future.'

Peter shook his head.

'We can't have you living like that,' he said decidedly. 'Why don't you come and stay with us for a few days, until you landlord gets things fixed? You can have Hannah's old room.'

'That's very generous of you sir,' Paul said hesitantly, torn between two contradictory thoughts. It would be very nice indeed to have a night's sleep unaccompanied by the constant sound of water dripping from the ceiling into a bucket. It would also be pleasant to experience once more the luxury of washing in warm water and shaving with an electric shaver. On the other hand, however, surely it was inappropriate for him to stay at the home of his commanding officer, especially when that home was a two-up-two-down terraced house shared with his wife who had not been consulted about the offer.

'But I couldn't impose on you and your wife like that,' he concluded. 'I'll be fine, don't you worry. I'll soon get myself organised and I don't suppose it'll be for long anyway.'

'Don't you believe it!' Peter replied bitterly. 'It sounds like you've got a typical Oxford landlord, out to fleece the tenants for everything he can get. How old on earth is that hot water system of yours? Nobody with any sense has been installing the old-fashioned sort with a cold-water tank in the loft for the last twenty-odd years! If he'd put in a modern system and kept it properly maintained you wouldn't be in this fix. He ought to be paying for you to stay in a hotel while he makes the flat habitable again.'

Paul said nothing. He was starting to feel the same embarrassment that Eddie had experienced when faced with Peter's diatribe on racial discrimination. He began to wish that he had never mentioned the situation at his flat and hoped that Peter would not take it into his head to approach the landlord on his behalf.

'It's not just in Oxford either,' Peter continued. 'It's universities that attract them: lots of students and young academics needing somewhere to stay without much money and no experience. It was the same in Leeds when my daughter, Hannah, was a student. One of the houses that she had a room in was a death trap, and she and her friends were paying through the nose for it. There should be better enforcement of the safety regulations and landlords ought to be made to take their responsibilities for repairs more seriously.'

'It's really not so bad as all that sir,' Paul said earnestly, when Peter paused for breath. 'If you could just spare me for a few minutes at lunch time to go and get a battery powered shaver, I'll be absolutely fine."

'Nonsense!' Peter declared, refusing to drop the subject. 'You can't possibly carry on living in that flat. 'Isn't there someone else you could stay with? What about your parents? Do they live locally?'

'Reading. It would be too much of a trek, and besides, they don't have the room. It wouldn't be fair to ask them to put me up. Really sir, I'll be-'

'I know!' Peter interrupted. 'I've got a friend who'd be delighted to give you a room for a few days – or weeks, if it comes to that – a police widow with a young daughter. It's just the two of them in a five bedroomed house in Headington. She lets rooms to students, but she hasn't got any at the moment, so she'd be glad of the company. And she can bill your landlord for the rent.'

'I'd rather pay her myself,' Paul argued, forgetting that he had intended to refuse all offers of accommodation and persevere in his determination to rough it in his own flat. 'I wouldn't want her to be out of pocket.'

'Don't you worry on that score,' Peter grinned. 'Nobody says "no" to Our Bernie. Take it from me: if your landlord tries anything on with her he'll soon be retreating back under whatever stone it was he crawled out from, licking his wounds and wishing he'd treated you properly in the first place!'

'A bit of a tough cookie, then?'

'Born and raised on the mean streets of Toxteth. She eats the likes of your landlord for breakfast.'

'I'll be a bit nervous of meeting such a formidable lady!' Paul replied, only half joking. He began to wonder what sort of person Peter was proposing he should move in with and what might happen if he were to annoy her in any way.

'Don't you worry,' Peter repeated. 'She's nothing if not loyal and once she's taken you under her wing it'll be a matter of pride to her to see you're treated right. I'll ring her right away and fix it up.'

'Thank you sir,' Paul mumbled. He still had misgivings about the proposal, but decided that there was nothing to be gained by continuing to fight against Peter's determined efforts to find suitable accommodation for him. He sat in silence contemplating the situation, while Peter rang Bernie and made the arrangements. He had never seen Peter in this mood before. Usually he was easy-going and preferred to stay out of his colleagues' personal lives. He wondered why he was suddenly taking such a keen interest in his sergeant's welfare.

Bernie agreed at once to take Paul in, and she and Peter arranged that he would deliver him to the house in Headington that evening after work. The conversation would have been brief if it were not for Lucy, who heard Bernie saying Peter's name and demanded to speak to him. Peter was unable to refuse a request from his beloved goddaughter and it was only Bernie's insistence that Lucy must allow him to get back to his important police work that brought the call to an end. He turned to Paul.

'There you are: it's all fixed up. I'll drive you over and introduce you to Our Bernie this evening and you can move into her spare room right away.'

'Thank you sir. And sir? Is that the same Lucy as the little girl with your son in the Park the other day?'

'That's right. I'd forgotten you knew about that. My wife and I are Lucy's godparents. Her father was Detective Superintendent Richard Paige. Perhaps you've heard of him?'

'Vaguely. Wasn't he killed in the line of duty a couple of years back? I remember my old boss taking half a day off work to go to the funeral. Apparently he'd worked with him years ago and wanted to pay his respects.'

'That's right. He fell off a roof while in pursuit of a suspect. Tragic really – it was only a few weeks before he was due to retire.'

'And with a baby on the way too,' Paul commented, remembering the conversation in the pub the previous Thursday.

'You heard Lucy was born posthumously then?'

'It just happened to come up in conversation with some of the lads. A group of us were down the pub last week.'

'Don't tell me: Constable Fox was one of them, right? I suppose he was sounding off about my unfair treatment of his innocent mistake.'

'No. Actually, sir, I think he wanted to stick up for you, but it was difficult for him with Adams being there-'

'Adams!' Peter grunted angrily. 'I hope you don't make a habit of hanging around with him and his cronies.'

'No sir. He was just there with the others when I arrived and he forced Fox to tell him about the incident in the park and then, when Fox mentioned that the little girl was Paige's daughter, Adams made some rather crude remarks about how unlikely it was that someone as old as Paige could have fathered a child. That's all. When I saw Adams there, I wished I hadn't gone,' Paul continued, anxious to assure Peter that he did not share Adams' views, and also keen not to let slip the insinuations that had been made about Peter's own sexuality and his relationship with the Paige family. 'But then afterwards I managed to get Fox on his own and give him a bit of advice about choosing his company more wisely in future. He's a good lad sir, but rather easily led, I think.'

'Yes, well, that's enough of that anyway. We'd better get back to the Robert White case. As I was telling the others, his parents told me that he has a history of depression, which, together with the note, makes suicide by far the most likely scenario. Whether the depression was the only cause or whether drugs were a contributing factor, we'll probably never know. But if the tablets you found at his flat turn out to be Rohypnol, as I expect they will, then it looks likely that he took them himself, either intending to end it all with an overdose or to make it easier to psych himself up to jumping in the river.'

'So what next, sir?'

'I've arranged to take the parents to the mortuary this morning. While I do that, I'd like you to chase up those lab results on the tablets you found. Then, this afternoon, I've organised for them to meet Gemma at the flat so they can take away Robert's things. I think we had better both be there, because I've a nasty feeling there may be trouble. The father in particular is inclined to blame Gemma for making Robert unhappy and I'm afraid that even the mother is likely to want to know how it was that she didn't do anything to stop him.'

CHAPTER 19

Peter's fears about the emotional state of Bernard and Samantha White proved unfounded. Rested after their journey, they remained admirably calm when viewing their son's body and later they managed to maintain a cool and rather distant politeness when speaking to Gemma. Peter saw them into a taxi and then went back to Gemma's flat, where he found her in animated conversation with Paul, who jumped hastily to his feet on Peter's return, conscious that he must avoid appearing to be on terms of friendship with someone who was still a witness in an ongoing investigation. The two police officers said their goodbyes to Gemma and then left, driving first to Paul's flat to collect essential items and then setting off for Bernie's home on the outskirts of the city.

'You and Gemma seemed to be having an interesting chat,' Peter commented as they drove up Headington Hill. 'Remembering old times, was it?'

'Yes.' Paul replied shortly. He was still unsure about admitting to a desire to revive his friendship with Gemma.

The drove on in silence, then Paul plucked up courage to ask for Peter's opinion on something that had been puzzling him ever since Gemma had reminded him about the bully who had tormented him during his time in care.

'There was this boy in the home,' he began. 'His name was Leroy King, but everyone called him Bongo. Gemma reckons that was because he was black and someone once told him to go back to Bongo-Bongo land.'

Peter's arms tensed and his hands gripped the wheel more firmly as he listened to this account of casual racism in the care home, but he said nothing. Seeing this reaction, Paul hurried on to explain what he wanted to know.

'What I don't understand is why he – Bongo – encouraged it. I mean he actually insisted on being called Bongo; he wouldn't answer to his real name. At the time, I didn't realise where it had come from, but now Gemma's told me and it just doesn't make sense!'

Peter had attended a good number of training courses on 'policing a multicultural society', 'equality and diversity' and 'interacting with minority communities'. In the aftermath of the Macpherson report, which had labelled the Metropolitan Police 'institutionally racist' every police service in the UK had taken steps to ensure that its members could not have that accusation levelled against them and Peter had been seen as an obvious champion for promoting racial harmony, much to his annoyance. He had also made it his business, after the first occasion when Hannah was teased at school for her colour, to read up on the psychology of bullying and racial abuse. He thought for a few moments before answering.

'I think,' he said at last, 'that it's probably a case of him wanting to get in first with the insulting nickname to show he doesn't care. It's sort of, "you can't hurt me by calling me that, because I'm doing it myself," if that makes sense.'

'I suppose so. You mean, if he asked people to call him Bongo then that was one less derogatory name they could use against him.'

'Something like that: and it also shows that he's a good sport and can take a bit of so-called harmless banter.'

'He was pretty unpleasant to the other kids,' Paul went on. 'You'd have thought he'd have sympathised.'

'Just another defence mechanism: you can't hurt me; I'm the big strong guy who makes everyone else feel small.'

'He certainly did that,' Paul agreed, bringing the conversation to an end. For the next few minutes, they drove on in silence.

'You'll like Our Bernie,' Peter told Paul, as they crossed the ring road into the residential area on the far side. 'She's what people call a rough diamond, but there's nobody I'd like better on my side in a tight corner!'

'Why do you keep calling her Our Bernie?' Paul asked. 'I mean – what's she really called?'

'*Everyone* calls her Our Bernie,' Peter answered, smiling at Paul's confusion.

'But I can't very well go up to a woman I've never met and say "hello Our Bernie" can I? What should *I* call her? Mrs Paige?'

'Not if you value your life! Our Bernie doesn't believe in standing on ceremony. And I don't suppose anyone has ever addressed her as Mrs Paige in her life – unless Richard did in secret. Now there's a thought! I wouldn't put it past him, you know – like a Jane Austen character or something. I must ask Our Bernie about that sometime.' He chuckled to himself.

'So what *do* I call her?' Paul persisted.

'If you insist on being formal then the correct way to address her is "Dr Fazakerley" but she won't thank you for it.'

'Fazakerley being her maiden name?'

'That's right. It wasn't convenient for her to change to Paige when she got married. She'd been Bernadette Fazakerley for so long that it would have been far too complicated to change everything – degree certificates, learned publications, all that sort of thing – so she just stuck with her old name. Richard didn't mind: he knew better then to expect her to conform to the social norms.'

'So Bernie is short for Bernadette,' Paul said thoughtfully, 'but why do you keep saying *Our* Bernie?'

'Haven't you ever met anyone from "oop North"?' Peter asked, teasingly.

'What do you mean?' Paul was still puzzled.

'You'll see soon enough. Now here we are,' Peter replied, turning off the road into a long, curving drive, which led up to a large detached house, built in an L-shape. Lettering carved into one of the stone gateposts declared that the house was named *Llanwrda*, which struck Paul as a strange choice for a dwelling in suburban Oxford. He wondered how it was pronounced. There seemed to be too many consonants and too few vowels.

Peter pulled up in front of the door, which was on the inside corner of the L, and got out. He stepped up to ring the bell, leaving Paul to get his belongings out of the car and join him on the doorstep.

It was not long before the door opened and Paul got his first view of his new temporary landlady. He was not sure what he had been expecting, but this was certainly not it. She was of average height, or perhaps slightly smaller, and medium build. Her hair – what there was of it – was mousey brown, greying at the temples and cropped shorter than any woman's hair that he had seen before. Her eyes were a nondescript bluish grey colour behind metal-rimmed glasses. She was dressed in bottle green trousers and a chunky sweater.

'Peter!' she cried, in a tone of such evident delight that for a moment Paul wondered if there could be any truth in Adams' story that there was some sort of romantic relationship between them. He quickly pushed any such thoughts to the back of his mind as he realised that she was now addressing him.

'And you must be Paul,' she said, holding out her hand towards him, 'looking for an ark to protect you from the floods! Come inside both of you. We were just saying it was about time you got here.'

'Very pleased to meet you, Dr Fazakerley,' Paul mumbled as he shook Bernie's hand. She raised her eyebrows at being addressed in this way, but said nothing. She merely smiled at them both, opening the door wide and standing aside to let them in.

The moment he set foot inside the house Paul became aware of a commotion going on around his knees. He looked down and saw a tousled mop of curly golden hair, beneath which he identified the small girl whom he had seen briefly in the park a few days ago. She was clinging to Peter's legs and begging him to pick her up, which he did, hugging her to him and planting a kiss on her cheek.

'Now Lucy,' her mother said seriously, 'Peter hasn't come to see you. He's here to introduce a guest who's going to be staying with is for a while. Say "hello" to Paul.'

Lucy looked at Paul with serious blue eyes. Held in Peter's arms she was able to look him in the eye and she did so with an expression on her face that suggested she was sizing him up and was unsure whether she liked what she saw.

'Hello Paul,' she said obediently.

'Hello Lucy.' Paul replied. He had no experience of young children and was unsure how he ought to speak to her. It suddenly occurred to him that he probably ought to have brought her a present of some sort. Too late for that now, but he would make a note to give her something as a "thank you" when he left. He ought to get something for Bernie too, he supposed.

'Now Lucy,' Bernie continued, 'why don't you take our Peter into the living room and play with him while I show Paul up to his room?'

'Peter and Paul!' Lucy shouted triumphantly. 'Two little dickie birds,' she added with a giggle, as if that explained her sudden delight.

Paul looked at Peter, wondering if he could throw any light on this sudden pronouncement. He was smiling and looking at Bernie who returned the smile. Then she notice Paul's bewilderment and took pity on him.

'Poor Paul doesn't know what you're talking about, Lucy love.'

'Two little dickie birds,' Lucy chanted obligingly, 'sitting on a wall. One named Peter and one named Paul. Fly away Peter. Fly away Paul. Come back Peter. Come back Paul.'

'Well now Lucy,' Peter said. 'This little dickie bird is going to have to fly away home very soon. Your godmother Angie will have my guts for garters if I'm late for her special ackee and salt fish dinner! I can give you five minutes and then that's your lot.'

'Guts for garters!' Lucy repeated, enjoying the alliteration. 'Guts for garters!'

'You're going to regret ever having said that, our Peter,' Bernie laughed. 'First rule of toddlers: the only expressions they learn first time they hear them are the ones that are going to drive you up the wall after you've heard them non-stop for the next fortnight!'

She turned to Paul and looked down at the two bags he had set down in the hall.

'Come with me. Is that all you've brought?'

Nodding, Paul picked up the bags and waited while Bernie opened the safety gate at the bottom of the long staircase. He followed her upstairs and Peter carefully closed the stair gate behind them.

'What do you think of the ducks?' she asked, seeing him looking at the three plaster ducks hanging on the wall over the stairs. 'I found them in a charity shop and put them there to annoy Richard. He thought they were naff, but I told him they reminded me of my working class roots!'

They reached the top of the stairs and, while waiting as Bernie opened a second safety gate, Paul got a glimpse of the extensive back garden through a window ahead of them.

'The "bathroom with separate WC" as the estate agents say, is on the right, just at the top of the stairs' Bernie said, pointing. 'The rooms are all labelled to avoid guests accidentally barging in where they're not supposed to be.'

Paul looked and saw two doors opening off the landing, each with hand-painted ceramic plaques decorated with humorous cartoons illustrative of their functions.

'A friend of mine painted them for me,' Bernie explained. 'Now, my room is behind you, across the head of the stairs from the toilet.

Paul turned and saw that this door bore a lurid black and red plaque depicting a doorway, over which were the words: *Abandon hope all ye who enter here!*

'Our Lucy's bedroom is next to the bathroom,' Bernie continued, waving towards a half-open door on which the name *Lucy* appeared in red on the side of a bright green tank engine, 'and then that's my study,' she added, indicating the next room, labelled *Silence! Genius at work*.

'Your room is opposite Lucy's. We put guests there because it's the only one with a washbasin in it. These days it would probably have an en suite, but nothing much has been done to the house since Richard's grandfather built it before the First World War. The other front bedroom is a graveyard for all the things the family no longer used but were too good to throw away. I keep planning to give it a proper clear out, but it's more like an archaeological dig than normal room tidying in there!'

Paul looked towards the room in question and saw that it bore the inscription *The Dump*. Bernie meanwhile went ahead into the guest room, continuing to talk as she went. Paul began to find her strong accent grating on his nerves and felt a desire to laugh at it. Surely, nobody was really that Scouse! He discovered later that, Bernie was indeed putting on an exaggerated Liverpool accent for the benefit of the newcomer and that, according to the occasion, she altered her pronunciation for effect between that of a comedy Liverpudlian through various gradations to something that could only be distinguished from standard English by its short a's and long u's.

'Our Lucy tends to be an early riser,' Bernie was saying, 'which has the advantage for you that we'll almost certainly be out of the bathroom in the morning before you get up. So, if you want a bath or a shower to start the day, you don't need to worry that you'll be in our way. The down side is that she usually comes into my bedroom at the crack of dawn and frequently makes a row about it. If we're disturbing you, just bang on the wall. Your room and mine are back to back and the sound does travel I'm afraid.'

'I'm sure that won't be necessary, Dr Fazakerley,' Paul answered, rather bemused by the catalogue of instructions and explanations, but feeling that some sort of response was necessary.

'And you can stop all that Dr Fazakerley nonsense. My name's Bernie, alright?'

'Right you are,' Paul agreed nervously, still not sure what was expected of him.

'And now I'll leave you to get on while I go and rescue our Peter from our Lucy's clutches.'

'And send him on his way back to our Angie?' Paul suggested mischievously, surprising himself by his own temerity.

'Less of your lip, young Godwin!' Bernie retorted, smiling broadly. 'Peter never warned me you were such a cheeky devil. Tea's in the kitchen in about half an hour – don't be late!'

CHAPTER 20

Bernie excused herself after putting Lucy to bed, and retired to her study to work, leaving Paul sitting alone in the living room. He stared round, wondering whether to stay there or to go up to his own room. Bernie had seemed to be expecting to find him downstairs when she finished her lecture-preparation, but what was he expected to do meanwhile?

He looked down at his feet. The floor looked as if a bomb had exploded above it. Winding round the furniture was a plastic railway track, its locomotives and carriages lying higgledy-piggledy on their sides as if a major rail crash had taken place. In between the curves and branches of the complex layout were piles of what looked to Paul like giant Lego bricks, some single, others joined in blocks of various shapes. A large plastic bucket lay on its side with an assortment of plastic shapes – cylinders, cuboids and triangular prisms – spilling out. In a corner of the room, a tea party seemed to be taking place, with toy animals arranged in a circle around a checked tea-towel on which lay plastic cups and plates. In amongst everything else there were children's books, some lying in piles, others propped open to make tunnels for the toy trains to go through.

Paul decided to help out by trying to bring order to this chaos. Looking round again, he saw that the large dresser had a paper label on one of its doors: Lucy's toys. He

148

opened it and looked inside. It was about half full, but there would be room for the shape-sorter bucket and the dolls' tea set. Then he spotted, under the window that overlooked the front garden, a large, open wooden box, which, although almost empty, turned out to contain the remaining pieces of plastic railway track. Paul got down on his knees and began the task of tidying the room.

He was just placing the last of the books on the low bookcase under the side window when Bernie came in.

'Wow!' she exclaimed. 'You've been busy. There are parts of that carpet I haven't seen since Christmas! Are you sure you want to go back to your lodgings after the floods subside? Can't I persuade you to stay on here as housekeeper? How does free board and lodging and generous pocket money grab you?'

'Just filling in the idle moment,' Paul answered, grinning up from his sitting position on the floor. 'Hand me those and I'll put them away with the rest.'

Bernie passed him the small pile of books that she had brought down from Lucy's room.

'Hairy Maclary from Donaldson's Dairy,' Paul read out from the cover of one of the books. 'I heard you reading that one to Lucy when I passed her bedroom earlier. It sounded as if you were both having a good time.'

'Of course: bedtime story time is one of the highlights of the day. Didn't you have bedtime stories when you were a kid?'

'My family wasn't that organised. I didn't really have bedtime, never mind bedtime stories,' Paul said ruefully. He finished arranging the books on the shelf and stood up. Then he reached out and picked up a small object from the marble mantle-piece that surrounded the large fireplace. He held it out to Bernie.

'I found this in one of the trucks. Lucy must have been taking it for a ride'.

Bernie looked down at the shiny silver medal, which he had placed in her hand. It had a ribbon attached to it made up of blue and silver stripes with thinner red stripes in the silver ones.

'Thanks,' she said reaching up to the top shelf of the huge dresser, which stood next to the fireplace, and placing the medal next to a calendar plate for the year 1959. 'I thought I'd put it out of her reach, but she must be taller than I thought – or else found something to stand on.'

'Your husband's?' Paul asked. He had never seen a Queen's Police Medal before and he was curious to know what Detective Superintendent Paige had done to deserve it. Peter Johns had not mentioned this when talking about his old friend. 'Was it for the incident that killed him?'

'Hardly!' Bernie said scornfully. 'If he hadn't died, he'd probably been reprimanded for reckless behaviour and taking unnecessary risks – at least he certainly ought to have been. No, this was miles earlier when he was just a very young PC. Everyone had forgotten all about it – including Richard as far as I can tell. That's why it was lying around here for Lucy to pick up. I'd been trying to clean it up a bit. It was in a right state when I found it down the back of a drawer.'

'So, what was it for?' Paul asked. 'I mean you don't get one of those for nothing. It says "for gallantry" on the back: that must mean something pretty special, mustn't it?'

'Mmm. But it was such a long time ago. Most of the people who might have remembered are dead or moved away and Richard never let on a whisper about it when he was alive. I had the dickens of a job piecing together what it was all about.'

'But you did? Tell me about it.' Paul said eagerly.

'Yes, alright,' Bernie said, looking at her watch. 'I'll fish out the newspaper cuttings and things to show you – but not right now: Peter will be expecting you at the station bright-eyed and bushy-tailed first thing tomorrow and, as I told you before, Lucy will be getting me up at the crack of dawn; so it's time we were both hitting the hay.'

She started towards the door, intending to go upstairs but then she turned and smiled, remembering what Paul had said earlier about his childhood home life.

'Tell you what,' she said with a grin, 'you be a good boy and get yourself ready for bed and I'll pop in, in, say, twenty minutes, and tell you a bed time story. How's that?'

'That would be very nice,' Paul managed to stammer out, taken aback and not sure how to react. 'I'll look forward to it.'

It was only about a quarter of an hour later when Paul heard a knock at his door. He had changed into his pyjamas before washing and brushing his teeth at the basin in his room and he was now engaged in hanging up his jacket in the large old-fashioned wardrobe. He hastily got into bed and called out to Bernie to come in.

The door opened and there she was, dressed in navy blue pyjamas under a red dressing gown emblazoned with the arms of Liverpool football club. Her feet were clad in tartan carpet slippers, which looked very much the worse for wear. She was carrying a large red ring binder and a box file. She sat down on the edge of the bed and put them down next to her. Then she picked up the ring binder and held it up so that Paul could see the gold lettering on the front: Detective Superintendent Richard Paige 1939 – 1999.

'After Richard died,' she explained, 'I started collecting stuff about his life to show to Lucy when she's older. I want her to know that she's got a father, even though she won't ever be able to meet him.'

She opened the box file and took out of it the medal that Paul had seen earlier and handed it to him.

'I've collected together some bits and pieces here: this medal, his boy scout badge, his warrant card …'

'Shouldn't you have given that back?'

'I suppose perhaps I should,' Bernie shrugged. 'Nobody's ever asked for it. I don't suppose they will now, after nearly three years.'

She closed the box and picked up the ring binder.

'Peter Johns got the ball rolling by asking his colleagues to write down their memories of Richard; and Eileen Brookes – the Chief Super's secretary – put them all together in this folder. And she found some photos and things and made a sort of *This is Your Life* book. I've been trying to fill in the gaps so Lucy will be able to get an idea what her father was like, but it's hard-going getting stuff from his childhood and early career. You see, I didn't meet Richard until he was in his mid-fifties, so I feel I hardly know him myself.'

'I suppose, with his background, old Peter would be keen on the idea of helping your little girl to know her father,' Paul suggested.

'What do you mean, his background?' Bernie asked sharply.

'Well, growing up in care, he'd understand what it's like not to know who your parents are or what they were like.'

'Who told you about that?' demanded Bernie, sounding unexpectedly aggressive.

'Peter told me himself. Why? What does it matter?'

'That's alright then,' Bernie conceded. 'Sorry. Peter doesn't usually talk about it and I was afraid you'd been listening to police gossip. You shouldn't believe everything you hear; and there are some people who seem to think that growing up in a children's home is something to be ashamed of.'

'Yes, Peter warned me about that.'

'What do you mean – warned you?'

'That's how we came to be talking about it,' Paul explained. 'I had to tell him about me being taken into care for a while when I was a kid, because that's where I met Gemma Markham. Her boyfriend was Robert White, the corpse in the Thames that we've been investigating the last few days,' he went on, seeing Bernie's puzzled expression. 'Peter needed to know how I came to know her.'

'And he still let you stay on the case? Peter's usually

very strict about conflicts of interest.'

'Well, I only knew her for a few months and it was years ago; so I suppose he thought it didn't matter. And it isn't as if there's any question of her being responsible for his death or anything. She's just a witness, that's all.'

'I think if your girlfriend died a sudden and violent death you'd probably consider yourself more than just a witness,' Bernie observed. 'You'd better watch out that you don't step out of line in your dealings with this Gemma. My guess is that Peter has decided you're less of a liability staying on the case, where he can keep an eye on you, than being off it and therefore feeling free to consort with her and maybe let slip information that isn't supposed to be in the public domain. Don't underestimate our Peter – he's a lot more astute than people give him credit for. Richard always said he was one of his best men, even though most people put him down as rather a plodder.'

There was a pause while Paul took in this unexpectedly long speech. Then Bernie shook herself and opened the folder to reveal plastic wallets containing handwritten pages, each signed by one of her husband's former colleagues. She turned the pages until she came to one that contained a newspaper cutting with a picture of a young-looking police constable in uniform standing awkwardly, holding up something in his hand.

'You wanted to know what Richard got his police medal for,' she said, turning the binder round so that Paul could see the text the right way up. 'It took a lot of digging through the archives, but eventually I found this article. Here he is just after the ceremony. I suppose they made him pose for the press in order to get the publicity for the force.'

'Police constable decorated for heroic bid to save child from flood,' Paul read aloud. 'Constable Richard Paige was awarded the Queen's Police Medal for Gallantry for his bravery in plunging into the swollen river last year in an attempt to rescue eight-year-old Susan Cartwright who had fallen into the Isis while playing with the family dog on Christ Church Meadow.'

He looked up at Bernie. 'So he was saving a child from the river!'

'Not saving,' Bernie corrected him. 'See how it says "an attempt to rescue": the child was dead when he got her out. Here's the report about the incident.'

She turned the page and pointed at another headline.

'Mystery man pulls child's body from the flood,' he read. 'The Cartwright family of Cardigan Street, Jericho are appealing for the young man who risked his life trying to save their daughter to come forward. The mysterious youth plunged into the swollen river last Thursday after their young daughter, Susan (aged 8), fell in while trying to save the family's beloved Jack Russell, Cindy, who had been swept off her feet by the water. He managed to reach the child and bring her back to land, but despite administering the kiss of life, neither he nor the ambulance crew who were soon on the scene, were able to revive her. Enid Cartwright described what took place when a family walk in Christ Church Meadow with her three young children turned into a tragic nightmare.'

'You see?' Bernie pointed out. 'He got the girl out, but she'd already drowned. The family were grateful though, because at least they had a body to bury. She could have been washed away and never found – like the dog. It's all there further down.'

'Patrons of the nearby Head of the River pub rushed to help,' Paul read on. 'They threw a life belt to the young hero and pulled him and his precious burden ashore, but Susan had already succumbed to the raging torrent. The youth slipped away unnoticed as soon as the ambulance arrived and nobody knows who he is. We can only speculate that he was a student from the university and perhaps should have been at his studies instead of out running in the meadow.'

'The Head of the River!' he repeated as if to himself.

'That's by Folly Bridge, where Robert White went in last week. And the river was running very high then too. I wonder if there's any possibility that he was trying to rescue someone or something from the river …'

'Who? Or what?' Bernie asked sceptically. 'Nobody else went into the river that night and there haven't been any other bodies washed up or missing persons reported, have there?'

'There was a dead dog found in the river not far from where he landed up. That's what I was thinking: could it have been like it says here? Where a dog falls in and someone goes in after it to try to pull it out. Or he could have imagined there was someone in the river. It was dark and raining: he could easily have thought he saw something when there was nothing there really.'

'But isn't it much more likely that he either fell in by accident or jumped in with the intention of drowning himself?' Bernie argued.

'The thing is, it doesn't look much like an accident, and I was thinking his parents might find it easier to think that he might have been a hero, rather than a suicide.'

'Well, I think it's a very kind thought, but that's all it is. You don't have a shred of evidence, do you? If I was this Robert's parents, I wouldn't be convinced.'

'No, I suppose not,' Paul said slowly, reluctant to let go of the idea.

'And is it really the parents that you're thinking of?' Bernie asked. 'Or could it be Gemma that you're worrying about? Do you think she blames herself for what he did?'

'I don't know,' Paul sighed. 'Sometimes I think she maybe didn't care that much about him and then sometimes she seems really cut up about it all. But anyway, I interrupted you. You were telling me about your husband. I suppose he saw the piece in the paper and came forward to tell them who he was?'

'No, but he did sneak along to the funeral and leave a bunch of flowers on the grave. He didn't speak to anyone, but he was in his uniform, and when the mother said she thought she recognised him, someone took down his number and talked to their own local Bobby and tracked him down that way. And that's how he came to get the medal, I suppose.'

'You must be very proud of him.'

'It's difficult to say,' Bernie said, frowning as if thinking hard. 'It's difficult to associate that with the Richard I knew so many years later. But I'd like Lucy to be proud of him. If she has to grow up without a father, at least she can know that she did have one and that he was … well … I don't know … worthy of admiration, I suppose.'

'I'd say she has a very good substitute father in old Peter,' Paul said, feeling rather awkward at having apparently touched a raw nerve. 'He and Lucy appear to have a very good relationship.'

'And what exactly might you be implying by that?' asked Bernie, suddenly on the defensive again.

'Nothing. They just seem very close, that's all.'

'There are those,' Bernie said menacingly, 'who have suggested that there might be more to it than that. You wouldn't happen to have heard anything like that would you?'

'Well actually,' Paul admitted, realising that he would never get away with a lie while under Bernie's steely gaze, 'I did hear Sergeant Adams' version of events the other night in the pub but I didn't take any notice of him.'

'And by his version of events, you mean the one that makes Peter into Lucy's biological father and Richard into what Adams no doubt terms a raging poofdah?'

'That about sums it up,' Paul agreed, 'but I didn't believe a word of it. I know Peter and Adams don't get on and I know Adams-'

'Adams has had it in for Peter ever since he joined the force,' Bernie broke in. 'It was the way Peter handled Adams' bullying of him that first impressed Richard and made him choose him for his team.'

'Really?' Paul thought for a few moments. 'You know, somehow I can't picture old Peter being bullied. He's so … I don't know … so solid I suppose, and unflappable. I can't see how a bully would get any fun out of it.'

'But you're forgetting that Adams and he go back a long way – right back to when Peter was a green young constable. Adams is just a couple of years older than him and had been there for about nine months when Peter arrived. He's very popular with a certain sort of person and he'd got a group of cronies around him, which Peter didn't fit into. And then, when Richard spotted Peter and took him under his wing and off into CID, Adams was jealous that he'd been passed over. I suppose then he teased him to show it didn't make any difference that he was the DI's chosen favourite, he could still be picked on for anything from having red hair to not having any parents.'

'Or for having a black wife?' Paul suggested.

'Yes – that too. So now you see why Peter doesn't talk about his private life at work … which makes you extraordinarily privileged and makes me a big-mouth telling you all these things. So you'd better keep them all under your hat – I don't want to be responsible for spreading any more gossip around the place.'

'You can rely on me to keep it to myself,' Paul assured her, 'but what I don't get is how you know so much. You've never even met Adams, have you?'

'No, but Richard told me all about him. He made no secret that he wanted him out of the force. He thought he was setting a bad example to the younger men and could cause reputational damage if some of the things he said got into the press. But as I said, there was something about him that made him curiously attractive to some people – including some of the senior officers, who like a man who isn't afraid of calling a spade a "bloody shovel" – and he never stepped out of line quite far enough to pin anything on him.'

'And I suppose Peter must have told you about this

nonsense about him being Lucy's father?'

'Oh no – I don't think our Peter knows about that. You won't tell him, will you?' Bernie asked anxiously. 'I don't want him to think he might be damaging my reputation by letting people see him and Lucy together or anything daft like that.'

'So how did you get to hear about it?' asked Paul, puzzled.

'Remember I told you Eileen went round collecting stories about Richard for Lucy's book? Well, Adams made a great joke of it, telling her she'd been taken in if she thought Richard was really capable of fathering a child, and reiterating his old theory that Richard and Peter were an item. And then, he came up with the idea that Peter must be the father, rather than Richard. I don't suppose he believes a word of it himself – he just likes making trouble for people like Richard and Peter who don't find his behaviour amusing. Anyway, Eileen told me what he'd said, just so as it wouldn't come as a shock if it got round to me by some other route. I never told Peter though. I didn't even tell Angie until much later. I was afraid they'd be worried that it would worry me – though I couldn't care less myself what silly rumours Adams and his like may be spreading. Nobody that's worth bothering about is going to believe a word of it.'

After this lengthy speech, they sat in silence for a few moments. Then Bernie picked up the box file and got up to go.

'I'd better be saying goodnight,' she said, holding out her hand for the ring binder, which Paul still had open in front of him. 'I shouldn't really have told you any of those things about Adams and Peter,' she went on. 'It's not for me to be telling you about the private life of your boss or poisoning your mind against a fellow officer. So mind you don't let on to anyone about it.'

'Don't worry, I can be discrete,' Paul promised her. 'Thank you for the bedtime story. I think getting this folder together for Lucy is a really good idea – can I have a read of it sometime?'

'Of course. You can keep it now if you like, and give it back when you've finished with it. Just make sure you keep it safe – which means out of Lucy's reach. She's into everything with her sticky fingers, which reminds me: keep your door closed so she can't come in and start rummaging through your things.'

'Maybe you'd better have it back,' Paul said, suddenly feeling a great weight of responsibility for the safekeeping of what were, he reflected, irreplaceable manuscripts. 'I'm not sure I can trust myself not to spill something on it or something.'

'If you're worried, I've got photocopies you can have a look at instead – or, tell you what! How's about another bedtime story another night?'

'Yes, please,' Paul said, trying to sound like an eager infant. 'I'd like that.'

'Right you are then – you can have the second instalment of "The Life and Times of Detective Superintendent Paige" tomorrow. Now, it's late; I really must go. Lie down like a good lad and I'll tuck you in!'

CHAPTER 21

Tuesday was a day of tying off loose ends. The Robert White case was essentially complete: it would be for the coroner's inquest to decide whether he had deliberately thrown himself off Folly Bridge or if he could have fallen accidentally after climbing on to the parapet, perhaps under the influence of the drug that he had taken. There was no evidence of foul play and consequently no need for the police team to continue the investigation, but this all had to be documented and filed and reports sent to the relevant authorities.

After several telephone calls, with a mixture of threats and cajolery, Paul eventually managed to obtain written confirmation from the overworked laboratory staff that the Rohypnol in White's bloodstream almost certainly came from the tablets found in his own bathroom cabinet, which, according to Gemma, belonged to him.

'So it looks as if he took the tablets himself,' Paul observed to Peter, showing him the lab report. 'Whether to help him to sleep or with the intention of taking his own life, who can say?'

'And, assuming he was intent on suicide,' added Peter, 'who can say whether he thought he'd taken an overdose or just took it to make it easier for him to get up the nerve to throw himself off the bridge?' He sighed. 'However you look at it, it's pretty grim for the parents.'

'And for Gemma,' Paul pointed out.

'Yes, and for Gemma,' Peter agreed. 'Now I think I'll get on to the coroner and press for the body to be released for burial and for the inquest to be opened ASAP. Then at least they can be doing something instead of just hanging around.'

By mid-morning, when the Whites arrived at the police station, bringing details of the doctor in Melbourne who had treated Robert for depression when he was a boy, Peter was able to tell them that the inquest would be formally opened and adjourned the next day, after which the body would be released to them. Therefore, they were now free to start making the funeral arrangements. He explained to them that they would need to apply for permission if they wanted to take his body back to Australia, but that it was quite straightforward and he could find the forms for them if that was their choice.

'No,' Samantha White said firmly. 'We've discussed it and we're sure Robert wouldn't want us to waste the resources flying his body back to Melbourne. We've been having a look on the web and we've found a nice place that does "green burials" not too far from here. We'll have a small funeral here for his English friends and then a memorial service at our church after we get home. I'm sure that's what Robert would have wanted: he was very concerned about not increasing our carbon footprint. Now, speaking of funerals, we don't know anyone here so I was wondering if your minister – the one we met on Sunday – would do the honours? We'd like a short church service before he's buried – nothing grand, just something simple. Do you think she'd be willing?'

Peter assured them that Denise would be delighted to take the service and gave them her telephone number and the address of the manse. They left, looking almost cheerful, as they headed off to make the arrangements. Having something positive to do made it so much easier to keep their minds off the nagging thoughts about why their son had taken his own life and what they ought to have done to prevent it.

Shortly after noon, there was a telephone call from the waiter at the Head of the River saying that the older of the two men who had visited the pub the previous Wednesday was back. Peter, who in his own mind had already dismissed the theory that White had survived the night and drowned the following afternoon after eating a second meal of gammon and pineapple, sent Paul off to investigate.

When Paul arrived, the waiter took him behind the screen that shielded the door into the kitchen from the view of customers in the dining area. Then, with ostentatious care not to be seen, he pointed out the man. Paul peered round the screen at a table for two where a man in his forties was in conversation with a woman of about the same age. They were both dressed in business suits and Paul noticed a briefcase lying under the table, close to the man's feet. He thanked the waiter briefly and walked over to the table.

'Excuse me,' he said, addressing the man. 'I'm detective sergeant Paul Godwin. I wonder if I might have a few words?'

The man looked up in surprise and then leaned over to the next table and pulled over a chair and motioned to Paul to sit down. His companion watched without speaking. The conversation did not take long. The man gave his name as Victor Barrington. He worked for an executive recruitment agency and often lunched here with people whom he was head-hunting for senior positions with his client companies. The man with whom he had been seen the previous week was one Charles Penrose. He had his business card here.

Paul took the card in his hand and read it. Sure enough, it said, 'Charles Penrose, software engineer,' and had the address of a company in Reading and a mobile telephone number.

And here was Barrington's own card, with the agency

address and his secretary's phone number on it. She would confirm the appointment with Mr Penrose the previous Wednesday and could show him the receipt for the meal if he cared to call in on her.

Paul thanked Mr Barrington, apologised for having interrupted his lunch and left. For form's sake, he called in at the agency on the way back to the police station and obtained corroboration of Barrington's story, but he had not had any doubts that it was true. He wondered whether the waiter had really believed that Penrose was Robert White or if he had merely been unable to resist spinning a story in order to share in the excitement of a police investigation. Oh well! At least that was one more piece of the jigsaw puzzle in place. One more uncertainty had been removed.

The only possible explanation of the facts appeared to be that, for whatever reason, the previous Tuesday night Robert White had taken a tranquilising drug and then, instead of joining his girlfriend in bed, had gone out into the rain and wandered down to Folly Bridge. There he had climbed on to the wall and then, either by accident or design, had fallen into the river, striking his head on the stone pillar as he did so.

His suicide note, together with his childhood history of depression, suggested that his actions were deliberate, but who could tell what was really going on inside his mind that night? Didn't depressed people often consider suicide and then not go through with it? Perhaps he intended his actions to be just a gesture, a cry for help? Maybe he expected someone to come along and pull him back from the brink? Or maybe he was confident of being able to swim strongly enough to come out of the river alive? Or could it even have been an act of heroism? Could Robert have plunged into the swollen river in an attempt to rescue some real or imaginary victim of the flood? Bernie had been sceptical, but Paul clung fondly to that possibility and decided to suggest it to Gemma the next time he saw her.

He had his opportunity the next day when he and Peter attended the opening of the inquest. Gemma was there, looking rather white and scared, dressed in a bottle green coat over a black dress. She crept into the court just as the proceedings were beginning and sat down next to Samantha White, who gave her a weak smile. Bernard White glanced past his wife to see what the disturbance was and frowned when he recognised Gemma.

After the short session was over, everyone started filing out of the courtroom. As they spilled out into the lobby, Peter hurried across to the Whites and started talking to them. Paul noticed that there was a woman in a clerical collar with them who seemed to know Peter. That must be Denise, the minister from Peter's church, he supposed. He walked casually across the room to where Gemma was standing awkwardly, looking round as if uncertain what to do next.

'Can I give you a lift home?' he asked.

'Thanks, but I think I'd rather get some fresh air and then I suppose I'd better get back to work. Marcus has been very kind letting me come, but I can tell he's getting fed up with me taking time off and I'll need another half day at least to go to the funeral.'

'OK, if you're sure,' Paul said, disappointed not to have an opportunity to prolong their conversation. Then he had an idea. 'If you want fresh air, how about a quick walk in the park and I'll drop you off at the salon afterwards.'

'OK, you're on!' Gemma agreed, seeming to brighten up at the suggestion. 'If you're sure your boss won't mind.'

'Don't you worry,' Paul assured her, looking towards where Peter was still engrossed in conversation with the Whites. 'Inspector Johns sees taking care of bereaved relatives as all part of the job.'

'But I'm not a relative,' Gemma pointed out, as they walked down the steps into the cool October air, 'as Rob's parents are keen to remind me. His mum's not so bad, I suppose, but his dad seems to think I drove Rob to suicide.'

'I don't suppose he really thinks that,' Paul tried to reassure her. 'He's just upset and looking for someone to blame.'

'And they've completely taken over organising his funeral and all that,' Gemma went on. 'They're insisting on a church service – although I told them Robert didn't believe in that sort of thing anymore – and then going out to some sort of "woodland burial ground" place miles away. I don't even know how I'm going to get there.'

'I expect you'll be invited to go in the funeral car with Mr and Mrs White,' Paul said. After all, there won't be any other family. And if not,' he went on hopefully, 'you can come with us. DI Johns and I are sure to be there to pay our respects on behalf of the police service. That's another thing that he sees as part of the job.'

'He seems very nice,' Gemma suggested. 'Not like I expected a police inspector to be.'

'I'm sorry you don't think policemen are nice,' Paul joked. 'I'll have to try to show you what a kind and thoughtful lot we are!'

'I didn't mean you!' Gemma protested. 'I just meant – well I'm not sure what I meant. I suppose I just expected a police inspector to be a tough guy barking out questions and trying to trip people up all the time.'

'Anyway, I didn't come here to talk about DI Johns,' Paul said, remembering his plan to try to soften the blow by suggesting that Robert White could have had a heroic motive for jumping into the river. 'How are you? It must be very lonely for you in the flat on your own.'

'Yes,' Gemma admitted. 'And it seems sort of empty now that all his things have gone. I don't know whether I'm glad his parents took everything, because they'd have kept reminding me that he's gone, or sorry not to have anything to remember him by.'

'Didn't they leave you anything?' Paul demanded, shocked at the Whites' callousness.

'Well, of course I've got photos and the presents he gave me, but they took away all his books and clothes and everything. I suppose the thing I notice most is the maps. Did you see on the wall, there were two maps? They were from the project he did for his degree: something to do with erosion in the outback. I didn't really take a lot of interest, but the maps were pretty.'

'He cared a lot about things, didn't he?' Paul said, taking the opportunity to turn the conversation towards Robert's state of mind when he died. 'It makes you think it must have been some sort of accident that killed him – I mean if he wanted to save the world, he wouldn't be likely to take his own life would he?'

'His father thinks I made him so unhappy that he wanted to kill himself,' Gemma blurted out.

'His father wasn't there, was he? He's just unhappy himself and trying to make sense of what happened and …,' Paul tried to think of a way of diverting Gemma from her indignation at Bernard White's unfairness. Then he remembered Peter's words about the parents of a suicide holding themselves responsible. 'I expect he's really blaming himself and it makes it a bit easier for him if he can convince himself that it was partly your fault.'

CHAPTER 22

As Paul had expected, Peter attended Robert White's funeral and invited Paul to come with him. Paul was surprised at the number of people in the church, considering that Robert was in a foreign land where he had no family and few friends. He recognised Mr and Mrs White and Claire Chiao, Professor Baxter and Dr Abbott from the Geography department, but most of the congregation was unknown to him. Peter introduced him to his wife, Angela, who was one of a group of people from the church who were greeting people at the door, handing out orders of service and showing them to their seats. She smiled at him and told him that she had heard a lot about him. Paul gathered that a good number of the regulars from the church had decided to turn out to swell the numbers and support the parents of this young man who had died so far from home.

Gemma had arrived early and was sitting alone near the front of the church when Paul arrived. He hurried down the aisle and sat down next to her. She smiled gratefully at him and whispered that the Whites had not invited her to go to the burial ground in their car so she would be grateful if he would allow her to take him up on his offer of a lift. Paul, while indignant at the Whites' treatment of Gemma, was secretly pleased to have the opportunity to be of service and to spend some time alone with her. Peter and Angela, it seemed, were included in the party who would travel in the limousine provided by the funeral directors. Paul wondered at this and it crossed his mind that DI Johns might have allowed himself to become more personally involved in this case than was strictly appropriate.

The group of mourners at the woodland burial ground was much smaller than the congregation at the church service. It comprised only Robert's parents, Peter and Angie Johns, and Gemma accompanied by Paul. After the ceremony was over, the two parties separated again and Paul drove Gemma back to her flat. Peter watched thoughtfully from his seat in the official funeral car, unsure whether he was pleased or disturbed to see his sergeant taking such assiduous care of this young woman, whom everyone else appeared to have forgotten about in their concern for the deceased's grieving parents. He had a nagging feeling that Paul was more emotionally involved than he had admitted and that this could cause trouble in the future.

'Where to?' the driver asked, breaking into Peter's thoughts.

'Inspector?' Samantha White asked. 'We need to go back to the hotel, but what about you and your wife?'

'The hotel will do fine,' Peter assured her. 'We can make our own way home from there.'

'If you're sure,' Samantha said dubiously. Then, when neither Peter nor Angie said anything further, she called to the driver, 'take us back to our hotel – where you picked us up earlier.'

'Will we see you again before you go back to Australia?' Angie asked, breaking the long silence that had descended on them as they drove back towards Oxford. 'If you're still here on Sunday, we'd be pleased if you came to church with us again.'

'I don't think so,' Samantha White answered. We're booked on a Saturday flight. We want to get back home as soon as possible. We need to see our daughter and tell her about everything. She'll be disappointed not to have been here for the funeral …'

'Yes; of course.' Angie reflected on how she would approach the task of explaining to Hannah if Eddie were to kill himself. Like most siblings, they rarely seemed to get on together, but she had no doubt that her daughter would be devastated if anything were to happen to her brother. 'She'll need you both with her.'

'I suppose you'll be back for the inquest?' she resumed, after another long silence.

'Just try to keep us away!' Bernard growled, speaking for the first time. 'Whenever it is, whatever it takes, we'll be there.'

'What happens now?' asked Gemma, as Paul's car pulled out on to the main road. 'I mean: is it all over? What about the inquest? It was adjourned, wasn't it? What exactly does that mean?'

Paul gathered his thoughts before replying. In all the suspicious death cases that he had investigated, he had never before thought beyond the role of the police. Now he suddenly realised that, for the friends and relatives of the victim, things did not stop there.

'Well,' he said slowly, 'the police investigation's over. DI Johns will send a report to the coroner and the coroner will decide what happens next. The inquest will probably be in a few months' time, and then I suppose it will all be over.'

'Why does it take so long?' Gemma wanted to know. 'I thought you said your Inspector Johns was happy that it was suicide; what else is there to do?'

'It's not a matter of what the police think,' Paul explained patiently. 'We just investigate to find the facts. It's up to the inquest to decide what happened and produce a verdict on the cause of death. The police report is just part of the evidence that the coroner will be looking at. And anyway,' he added, hoping to give Gemma some sort of comfort, 'our investigation doesn't actually prove that it was suicide, it could have been an accident.'

'I see,' Gemma said, sounding rather dissatisfied, 'but why can't that all happen right away? Why do you say it could be months before the inquest?'

'I suppose the coroner will need time to get other things – medical reports, for example – and then the inquest will have to be scheduled for a time when the coroner and the court are free. I know it sounds callous, but Robert's death isn't the only one that he'll be looking into at the moment and it's a matter of fitting everything in. There may be other inquests that are more urgent or where the families have already been waiting for longer.'

They drove on in silence for several minutes. Then Gemma said suddenly:

'So where does that leave you and me?'

'Sorry?'

'Well, you said you had to keep our relationship on a purely professional level for as long as the police investigation was going on. Can we be friends again now? Or do we have to wait until the inquest is over?'

'Would you like us to be friends?' Paul stammered out, taken aback by Gemma's direct approach and unsure what to say.

'Well, I think it would be a pity to lose contact again when we've only just met for the first time after all these years. And …,' Gemma paused for a moment, 'I don't really have anyone else I can talk to.'

'I'd like us to be friends too,' Paul said, hardly able to believe what was happening, 'if you're sure … I mean, I wouldn't like you to think I'm trying to rush in and set myself up as some sort of replacement for Robert so soon after his death. I do realise that you're only talking about friendship, not … well … you know.'

'Yes. I know you understand. It'll be like the old days: the two of us against the world!' Gemma smiled and ruffled Paul's hair playfully.

CHAPTER 23

Paul's enforced residence with Bernie turned out to be longer than he had expected. The builder, who looked at the damage to the ceilings in his living room and bedroom, declared that the plaster would all have to come off and be replaced – but not until the plumbing had been repaired and the rooms dried out. The plumber, who looked at the heating and hot water system, tut-tutted and then declared that it would be madness simply to repair the leak: the radiators were furred up with lime scale, the boiler was on its last legs, the pipework was inefficient and in poor condition. He recommended a new 'combi' boiler, which would bring the house up to current standards and save the occupants a fortune in fuel bills. The electrician, who was brought in to stop the lights fusing in Janice's flat, condemned the wiring as unsafe and insisted that he could not issue an electrical safety certificate unless the house was re-wired throughout. All in all, the work that would be needed to bring the flats up to a satisfactory condition for the tenants to return would take a matter of months, rather than weeks.

The landlord sighed and scratched his head and punched numbers into his calculator, but in the end, he decided that the work would have to be done if the value of his property were not to be severely diminished. He told the builder and the plumber and the electrician to get on with the job and he told the tenants that they could choose whether to move out permanently or to find temporary accommodation, with a view to moving back in, in two or three months' time. Bernie seemed perfectly happy for him to stay, so Paul opted to retain his lease on the flat and planned to go back as soon as the work was completed.

Lucy was delighted with the prolongation of Paul's visit. She regarded all adults as having been placed upon the earth principally for the purpose of entertaining her, and Paul soon found himself being presented with books and felt pens and other toys in the expectation that he would play with her. He had never had any dealings with children before and was surprised at the degree of satisfaction that he felt when she clapped her hands in delight as together they fitted the last piece into a jigsaw puzzle or demanded that he read a well-loved book 'one more time'. No wonder Peter Johns was so fond of his little goddaughter!

At first, Bernie tried to discourage her daughter from making demands on Paul's time. However, once she was convinced that he genuinely enjoyed playing with her and was not simply being polite, she left the two of them to work out their own rules of engagement, merely instructing Paul to feel free to hand Lucy back to her own charge if she became too demanding.

At Bernie's insistence, when the landlord told Paul that he must move everything out of his flat so as to give a free rein to the builder, plumber and electrician to knock the place about as they saw fit, he hired a van and brought a lifetime's accumulation of possessions to the house in Headington.

'I'm afraid there's more than I thought,' he said apologetically, as Bernie helped him to carry in the boxes and bags and, with some difficulty, the baseboard for Paul's railway layout, 'but don't worry, I'll keep everything in my room out of your way.'

'Don't be daft! We've plenty of storage space. You take everything you don't need on a day-to-day basis upstairs to the attic. There are a couple of bedrooms up there that we don't use any more. You can dump everything in one of those.'

So-saying, Bernie led the way upstairs and then up a further flight to the floor above.

'This house is just ridiculously big for the two of us,' she continued as they turned at the top of the stairs on to a narrow landing, lit from a skylight in the roof. 'When Richard's grandfather had it built – that was before the First World War – they had servants who slept up in the attic, but we don't come up here at all anymore.'

She led the way into a large room with a sloping ceiling that met the wall along one side only about four feet from the floor. It was sparsely furnished with an old iron bedstead under the window, a small wardrobe in one corner and a chest of drawers next to it. Along one wall, about a dozen old-fashioned trunks were piled up and there were several tea chests standing in the middle of the room. Bernie moved these back against the wall.

'I keep trying to find time to go through all this lot,' she said apologetically, gesturing vaguely in the direction of the pile of trunks. 'I don't know what's in any of these. I've got it in mind, when Lucy's old enough to be safe on the stairs, to turn one of the rooms into a playroom for her – well away from the rest of the house so she can make as much noise as she likes. Meanwhile, feel free to rummage – I'll be grateful if you can tell me if there's anything in here that might help me in pursuit of my investigation into Superintendent Paige and what made him tick!'

Paul said nothing, privately determined that nothing would induce him to do anything so intrusive as to start rummaging in the Paige family archives, which he presumed was what the various boxes and cases contained. He put down the box that he was carrying and went back down the steep attic stairs for more.

Thus it was that, in between investigating crimes and entertaining Lucy, Paul was able to fill his time with the painstaking job of restoring his model railway to its former glory. He set up the layout in the attic room, balancing the board on four tea chests, and set to work stripping away the sodden papier-mâché and repairing the damaged buildings. After a few days in the airing cupboard and application of oil to the moving parts, the rolling stock was back in working order and he was able to connect the new transformer that he had bought and test them out.

He was so engrossed in checking that everything was as it should be that he did not notice the sound of small feet on the bare floor and jumped with surprise when a small hand tugged at his trousers. Looking down he saw Lucy, staring in delight at the moving trains. Somehow, the gate at the bottom of the attic stairs had been left unfastened and, attracted by the sounds from above, she had climbed up to see what was going on.

'Oh Lucy!' Paul exclaimed, 'your mum's going to have words with me about this. Whatever are you doing here?'

'Watching the trains,' Lucy said, as if Paul must be very dense not to have realised this self-evident fact.

'But you're not allowed up here, are you?' Paul pointed out. 'And it must be my fault the gate was open.'

Lucy considered this for a few seconds. Then she smiled.

'Mam doesn't know,' she said with an air of satisfaction. Then, putting her finger to her lips, she added, 'I won't tell, if you don't.'

'Now I wonder who taught you to be devious and deceitful like that,' Paul commented, surprised that a two-year-old should display such a well-developed understanding of the adult world of intrigue.

'Eddie,' Lucy answered promptly, not at all put off her stride by the long words, which Paul had been confident would pass harmlessly over her head. 'He says there are lots of things it's better for the grown-ups not to know about.'

'But then I'm one of the grown-ups, aren't I? So I'm

sorry, but I'd better take you back down to your Mum and apologise for not shutting the gate properly.'

'No!' Lucy shouted, 'I want to watch the trains!'

She pulled away from the hand that he had put out to take hold of her and ran across the room, colliding with a door in the low wall that ran along one side of the room, where the ceiling sloped down. The door came open as her weight released the spring catch and the next moment she had disappeared inside the under-eaves cupboard.

Paul flung the door wide open and bent down to peer inside. Beyond the immediate vicinity of the opening, the storage area was dark and Paul only caught a glimpse of Lucy's feet as she crawled away, before she disappeared into the gloom. He called anxiously to her to come back, conscious that in all likelihood, the floorboards did not extend to the edge of the roof and she might crawl off the edge and fall through the first floor ceiling. Getting no response apart from a giggle, he stood up again and reached for the torch that he had been using to check the wiring on the underside of the railway layout board. Then he knelt down again and shone the light round inside the cupboard.

The first thing he saw was a wooden rocking horse. It was standing close to the entrance where the ceiling was high enough to accommodate it. Its paint was peeling and it was covered with dust, but Paul could see that it had once been a dapple grey with flaring nostrils and brown eyes. Its bedraggled black mane was hanging half off and its tail looked as if the mice had been chewing it. He swung the torch round and at last spotted Lucy sitting, with a merry grin on her face, in front of what looked like a small oak tree. Behind that, there was an expanse of blue, dotted with what looked like white clouds.

'Come on out,' Paul pleaded with Lucy. 'I really will be in serious trouble if I let you get lost in here.'

A few hours later, after Lucy had been put to bed, Paul brought Bernie up to the attic room.

'There's something I'd like you to see,' he explained, opening the door and pointing to a pile of plywood sheets, which lay in the centre of the room. 'I found it under the eaves when Lucy got in the cupboard this afternoon.'

'What is it?' Bernie asked, peering at the gaily-painted pieces of wood. 'This looks like the sky, and this looks like a woodland scene, and these look like curtains,' she added, picking up a rail from which hung two pieces of purple velvet.

'It's a toy theatre,' Paul explained. 'I think it's all there, but one or two pieces are broken, so I haven't managed to put it all together yet. Once I've fixed it, the sides simply slot together and the stage fits in at the bottom and those curtains attach along the front. All these,' he waved his hand towards the wooden sheets painted with trees, hills and other landscapes, 'are all different backdrops to make the scenery.'

'Wow!' Bernie exclaimed, moving some of the sheets aside to see the ones below, 'there's masses of it. I wonder who it belonged to. How old do you reckon it is?'

'Dunno,' Paul shrugged. 'There's a rocking horse in there that looks as if it could be Edwardian or even Victorian, so this could go back as far as that too. Or then again, it could be a lot more recent. I don't know how you'd tell.'

'Richard's father was one of three brothers,' Bernie mused. 'If this really does date back to before the war then it could have been theirs – or it could have been Richard's, I suppose.'

'Even if it belonged to his father originally, you'd think Richard must have played with it,' Paul pointed out. 'I mean: what's the point of keeping it safe if you don't pass it on to the next generation? Didn't he say anything about it? If it'd been mine, I wouldn't have left it mouldering away up here.'

'No, Richard never spoke about his childhood. To be honest, I find it difficult to imagine him ever having been a boy.'

'I'd like to restore it,' Paul mused. 'If you don't mind, that is – for Lucy,' he added hastily lest Bernie might get the impression that he was trying to take possession of the little theatre.

'Could you? I mean would you? Really?' Bernie asked eagerly. 'But wouldn't it take a long time? And you've got your own things to fix already,' she added, pointing to the railway layout which still looked as if a bomb had hit it.'

'Well, it won't all be done by next week,' Paul admitted with a smile, 'but I've got plenty of free time. It's not as if I've got a house to run and a family to look after – I don't even have to cook my own meals at the moment!'

'Hmmph! In my experience policemen never have plenty of free time,' Bernie observed. 'But if you don't mind …'

'I'd love it,' Paul assured her. 'I've always enjoyed models: railways, boats, farmyards, anything like that. I suppose the psychologists would say it's a sign of insecurity: wanting to create a world where I'm in control!'

'Alright – you're on!' Bernie agreed, 'but you must let me pay for the materials. I don't want you being out of pocket on our Lucy's account.'

CHAPTER 24

After that, Paul's life settled down into a routine – disturbed, of course, on numerous occasions by the demands of his police work – whereby he would spend an hour or two each evening up in the attic, working to restore the toy theatre. He found a collection of dusty and dishevelled puppets in the cupboard: Robin Hood and the remains of his Merry Men, a few pirates and, to Paul's great delight, a policeman whom he privately named Constable Paige and secretly planned to make into a representation of Lucy's father as a young man, before he joined CID.

On Friday evenings, Paul allowed himself the luxury of calling on Gemma at her flat. He told himself that this was an act of friendship prompted by sympathy for her recent bereavement, but in his heart he knew that he was hoping that, after a reasonable period of time had passed, she might allow him to take Robert White's place and that they might have a long-term future together.

One Friday night he was surprised to hear voices from the living room as he entered the hall after an evening with Gemma. He had never before known Bernie to have visitors so late in the evening, and there had been no car parked outside in which they could have arrived. He had hardly begun to take off his coat when the door opened and Bernie's face appeared round it.

'Come in here, Paul!' she called to him. 'You've got a

visitor!'

Paul hastily hung up his coat on one of the hooks attached to the wall of the hall and hurried into the living room to find out who it could be who was calling on him so late at night and at this address. How many people were there, he wondered, who knew where he was staying?

'Paul, darling!'

Paul stared in disbelief as his mother greeted him, putting her arms around his shoulders and planting a kiss on his cheek. She was a tall woman in her fifties with wavy black-dyed hair showing its grey roots, brown eyes hidden behind thick glasses a large mouth, made even more conspicuous by the liberal application of red lipstick, and a rather prominent nose. Paul noticed an angry purple bruise on her left cheek. He shuddered slightly as he detected the smell of alcohol on her breath and hoped that Bernie would not have noticed it.

'Why didn't you give us your new address?' she demanded, pouting like a spoilt child. 'If one of the workmen hadn't known it, I'd never have found you.'

'You could have rung me,' Paul said reproachfully, silently cursing himself for having left a forwarding address with the builder, who had offered to re-direct any post that arrived for him. 'You know my mobile number.'

'I would have done, only my phone's dead, and I had to find you – I couldn't think of anywhere else to go!'

'What on earth do you mean?' Paul asked, wondering what this was all about and trying desperately to think of a way of persuading his mother to leave. 'Why do you need to go anywhere?'

'I've left your father,' she said dramatically. 'I had no choice. His behaviour was intolerable. I just had to get out.'

'I'll contact the local Women's Refuge,' Paul said quickly, seeing a way out of his difficulty. 'And if they don't have a place, there are other hostels you can try.'

'Don't be silly, Paul,' Bernie intervened. 'Your mother's

staying here for the night. It's all arranged. I've put her in the room next to yours. It's in a bit of a mess, but we've put clean sheets on the bed and cleared out some space in the wardrobe. Then, in the morning, we can talk about what to do next.'

'No Bernie,' Paul tried to argue, 'we can't have you putting up perfect strangers at the drop of a hat like this. Don't you worry: I'll find-'

'She's not a stranger; she's your mother,' Bernie said firmly, 'and I've invited her to stay. So stop arguing and sit down the both of you while I go and make a brew. Is tea OK for you, Rowena, or would you prefer some cocoa, as it's bedtime?'

'Well, I was really hoping for something stronger,' Mrs Godwin answered, looking round in search of a drinks cabinet or some other sign of alcoholic refreshment. She eyed the large dresser suspiciously, thinking that it would have been the perfect place to keep a decanter of sherry.

'I'm sorry,' Bernie answered, not sounding in the least sorry. 'This is a dry house, I'm afraid. My mother was in the Salvation Army and I was brought up strictly T-T. I'll put the kettle on and we can all have some of the "cup that cheers but does not inebriate" as she used to be fond of saying.'

'Oh!' Paul's mother sounded completely taken aback as if the idea of a house where alcohol was simply not to be found had never occurred to her before. 'Never mind!' she went on, after Bernie had left for the kitchen, 'I saw an off-licence from the taxi when I was on my way here. It's not far. You can run me there can't you Paul?'

'No. I absolutely could not,' Paul hissed angrily, putting his face to her ear and speaking very low to be sure that Bernie could not hear. 'What do you think you're doing, coming here and insinuating yourself into Dr Fazakerley's house like this? If you had any decency at all you'd ask me to take you to a hostel right now and leave her alone.'

'Now that's no way to talk to your mother,' Rowena

Godwin said reproachfully. 'And dear Bernie would be terribly upset if you continue to try to push me out. She was very insistent that I should stay. She understands, you see.'

'I think that's extremely unlikely!' Paul muttered, keeping his voice low with difficulty while his instinct was to shout at his mother to go away and leave them alone.

'Oh well! Never mind,' his mother went on, ignoring him. 'I suppose I'll have to rely on my reserves.'

So saying, she picked up her handbag from where it lay on the settee and drew out of it a small bottle of gin. Paul stared at her for a second then snatched it from her hand and pocketed it. At that moment, Bernie reappeared carrying a tray containing three mugs, a milk jug and a teapot. She put it down on the coffee table and busied herself with pouring out, kneeling on the floor to do so. Then she looked round at Paul and his mother who were both still standing. Under her gaze, they collapsed on to the large settee and sat next to one another in silence as she passed them mugs of strong tea.

While they drank, Mrs Godwin spoke in a surprisingly cheerful way about the enormities of her husband's behaviour, which had driven her to flee the family home. Paul maintained an angry silence, seething inwardly and willing her to stop talking and go away. When addressed directly he answered in monosyllables or by nodding or shaking his head. Bernie at first tried to bring him into the conversation, but then gave up and sat pondering what could have gone on to create such antipathy between Paul and his mother.

After what seemed to Paul like several hours, but which was in fact only a matter of twenty minutes, Rowena Godwin got up and declared her intention of going to bed. Paul sprang up and opened the door for her. Then he picked up the tray and insisted on carrying it out to the kitchen for Bernie, who followed protesting indignantly that she was quite capable and did not need any help.

Once they were both in the kitchen, Paul put down the tray and closed the door firmly behind them.

'Bernie,' he said earnestly, 'you must listen to me. You've made a big mistake. I know you think you're helping, but really, there's nothing you can do. She's just-'

'She's your mother,' Bernie interrupted. 'And she needs help. You must have seen that bruise on her face. She's running away from an impossible situation. I don't understand why you're so hostile.'

'It's all just a story,' Paul argued, trying to think of a way of explaining the situation to Bernie, who had clearly taken at face value everything that his mother had told her about her home life. 'It may be that Dad gave her that bruise, but it's just as likely that she walked into a door while she was too plastered to know what she was doing. And if it comes to domestic violence, believe me, she can give as good as she gets – if not more!'

'Oh Paul! Can't you see? Whatever may have gone on in the past – and I suppose you know better than me about that – you must see that she needs our help now. She's run away with nothing, apart from a few clothes thrown into a suitcase: no home, no money, no credit cards. I even had to pay for the taxi that brought her here.'

'You lent her money?'

'No – I just paid off the taxi man. What else could I have done?'

'That's exactly what I'm saying,' Paul said with mounting frustration. 'Can't you see how she's using you? She's waltzed in here with some trumped up story-'

'That bruise is hardly trumped up,' Bernie retorted. 'I just can't understand why you aren't more sympathetic.'

'I know her,' Paul insisted, coming close and looking Bernie in the eye. 'Believe me, you can't help her – not unless she starts being willing to help herself. Listen! You remember I told you I was put into care for a few months when I was thirteen?'

'Mmm,' Bernie nodded.

'Well, I wasn't being completely honest with you when I said it was because my mum was ill. She was in a rehab centre drying out – at least that was the idea, but it didn't last long. She's her own worst enemy and being kind to her and allowing her to get away with it only makes things worse in the long run.'

'Oh,' said Bernie in a small voice, not really knowing how to react to this unexpected revelation. This was something completely beyond her experience. 'And what about your dad?' she said at last. 'Is he violent towards her? Or was she making that up?'

'Oh, I've seen him hit her often enough,' Paul admitted. 'The two of them are as bad as each other when they've had a few – and then they get all remorseful after they start to sober up. This is first time she's actually taken the plunge and run away. I expect she'll be off back to him in the morning – especially now that you've dropped the bombshell that this house is dry!'

He smiled in spite of himself at this thought and then looked at his watch.

'We'd better get off to bed,' he said. 'It could be a busy time for me in the morning, getting Mum sorted out. Now promise me you will *not* give her any money. She'll only spend it on booze. I'll see to it she's looked after OK – right?'

Bernie nodded, but still looked dissatisfied. Paul racked his brains to think of a way of lightening the atmosphere. He knew that she had acted with the best of intentions but really, what did she think she was doing inviting a perfect stranger to stay for an indeterminate length of time? He did not want to go to bed still angry with Bernie, but nevertheless he *was* angry. Why could she not have sent his mother packing? Or, at least, rung him to get him to come back from Gemma's to deal with her? It was too late now to find her a place in a hostel – that would have to wait for the morning.

'I suppose it's too late for a bedtime story?' he said at

last, hoping that this cheeky request might restore the easy-going relationship that he had enjoyed with Bernie up to now.

'Don't you think, under the circumstances, that's something you should be asking from your mother, rather than me?' Bernie asked mildly, but with a twinkle in her eye that showed that she appreciated his efforts to restore normality.

'I told you – my family doesn't do bedtime stories.'

'We've exhausted the Red Book: so what had you in mind? Don't you think maybe it's time for *you* to tell *me* a story – the story of your life?'

'I'm not sure I'm ready for that yet – perhaps later, after this is all over.'

'I'll look forward to it. Meanwhile, I think it would probably be best to "pass" on the bedtime story tonight. I'm not sure what your mother would think if she sees me coming out of your room in my dressing gown after you're supposed to be tucked up in bed! I know you think I'm foolish and naïve, but I'm quite well aware of the expectations that people have when it comes to handsome young men and widows of a certain age.'

'You're not of a certain age,' Paul objected.

'I think you'll find that I am,' Bernie smiled, 'or at least I would be if I were to allow myself to be seen in a compromising position with your mother's only son – I assume you are the only one?'

'Yup,' Paul admitted, grinning in spite of his continuing anxiety. 'The one and only.'

'Which is why, I'm quite sure she would not be amused at the thought that you were being preyed upon by an older woman,' Bernie said, heading for the stairs. 'So goodnight: see you in the morning.'

'Good night Mrs Robinson,' Paul responded, speaking softly so as not to be overheard. 'Thank you for the warning!'

CHAPTER 25

Bernie lay awake pondering on what she had learned about Paul's family. She struggled to imagine what it must have been like for him growing up with two violent alcoholic parents. This was something completely outside her own experience. Life in seventies Liverpool with a disabled mother and a father working – or often not working – in the docks, had not been particularly easy, but she had always felt safe and secure. Paul's home life must have been very different. No wonder it was what he had described as 'disorganised'. That was probably a euphemism for something much worse. Had he, too, been subjected to domestic violence, she wondered. That would certainly explain his apparent antipathy towards his mother. Or was that more to do with embarrassment at having been forced to air his family's dirty linen in front of a comparative stranger – and one who was, moreover, friendly with his boss?

Did Peter know about Paul's background? Bernie doubted it: he was not one to pry into people's affairs and it was unlikely that Paul would have volunteered the information. Peter probably assumed – as Bernie had done – that Paul's mother had suffered from some serious physical illness, which made it necessary for him to go into temporary care. How had Paul felt about that? Bernie had imagined him being distraught at being separated from his parents, but what if it had actually come as a relief to him? Maybe, in Gemma, he had found a mother figure to take the place of the one he needed but had never had.

Now what? Paul seemed determined to send his mother packing the next day, but might not staying here with Bernie and her family be just what she needed to kick the drink habit and get her back on to the straight and narrow? She would be kept away from others who were drinking socially, would be safe from her husband's assaults and would have space to sit back and think through what she was going to do with her life. She had been very taken with Lucy – as almost all adults were – when she met her briefly that evening, before Bernie spirited her away to bed. Spending time with her and enjoying her unquestioning affection would be like therapy.

On the other hand, what if Paul's father were to come after her? If he were violent, his wife might not be the only person who got hurt. And was Paul right in saying that his mother, too, was violent at times? For Lucy's sake, did Bernie have a responsibility to send her away from the house?

Then again, perhaps most unsettling of all was the thought that the outside world might imagine something unsavoury about her own relationship with Paul. For some time she had realised that she was starting to adopt a maternal attitude towards him, but it was only the thought of Rowena's possible reaction to seeing them together that had suggested to her that there was any danger of their innocent behaviour being misconstrued. Paul's ready understanding of the potential problem and his reference to the predatory Mrs Robinson from 'The Graduate' made her uneasy. Was he expecting more from her than she intended to give? However, on the other hand, he had Gemma, who was apparently becoming a more and more important part of his life. Everything was very confusing!

In the adjoining bedroom, Paul was also finding it hard to get to sleep. He was angry. In spite of his determination not to be, he was still angry with Bernie for having invited his mother to stay. He was also angry with himself for not handling the situation better. He was angry with his father for having caused his mother to leave home and seek refuge with him. Most of all, he was angry with his mother for coming here and disrupting his comfortable routine.

He had planned to spend some time this weekend renovating the old rocking horse that he had found in the under-eaves cupboard in the attic, as a surprise present for Lucy. He had already restored its tail and had intended to start the process of re-painting its body, a task that would take some time if he were to reproduce the dapple-grey pattern of the original. Now he would have to fritter away most of Saturday looking for somewhere that would take in his mother and then transporting her there.

He sighed and turned over, trying to get comfortable. The bedclothes followed him round creating a gap at his back, which soon started feeling cold in the chill of the autumn night. It reminded him that Bernie had not paid her usual visit to tell him a story and tuck him in as if he were a little boy. Would that game have to stop now? Now that they had both acknowledged that although innocent, it could be misinterpreted. Why could his own mother not have been more like Bernie when he was growing up? He had watched her with Lucy and it had made him realise how much he had missed out.

It was not so much that his mother had never shown love towards him: on the contrary, she was sometimes embarrassingly affectionate. The thing that had made life hard was her unpredictability and her mood swings. He never knew what to expect or how to win her approval. Acts that caused her to bestow hugs and kisses on him one day would provoke screams and slaps the next – or worse, send her into paroxysms of sobbing. He had learned to stay away from her as much as possible, retreating into his own bedroom where he could create his own worlds in miniature in which things happened according to rules and where he was the one who made those rules. At least, that was what he had done until the building society had foreclosed on the mortgage and they had lost the house. The new rented place on the Blackbird Leys estate – the first of many, as the family kept moving to keep ahead of a sequence of disgruntled landlords and their demands for unpaid rent – had only one bedroom and he had been relegated to sleeping on a sofa bed in the lounge.

What right had she coming here now, disrupting his life, knowing that he had no choice but to help her? She was his mother, after all: he could hardly just turn her out into the street – even if it were not for Bernie, who would certainly prevent him doing such a thing. Bernie would insist that he owed it to his mother to look after her in her hour of need. Did he owe her anything? He supposed that they must have had some good times together when he was a child, although he found it difficult to recall what they had been. At any rate, she had seen to his basic needs: he had never gone hungry or unclad. He had even had quite liberal pocket money – on and off, depending on the state of his parents debts – and little parental control over what he spent it on.

The next morning Bernie was woken as usual by Lucy, who came bursting into her bedroom declaring at the top of her voice that it was time to get up. Bernie accepted the inevitable and got out of bed, telling her daughter to keep her voice down and remember that they had guests staying who would probably prefer to sleep on until it was time for breakfast. Ignoring her, Lucy climbed on to the bed and amused herself by bouncing up and down on it as if it were a trampoline, while Bernie got dressed. Then they both went to Lucy's room to dress her – a process that took longer than it needed to have done because of the many distractions that interrupted the process. By the time they were both washed and dressed and ready to go downstairs, Bernie could hear sounds from Paul's room suggesting that he too was getting up.

A few minutes later, Bernie was on her way to the front

door to collect the milk from the step ready for breakfast. She stopped short and stared as she noticed that all was not as she had expected it to be. She was certain that the previous night she had double-locked the door as usual and fastened the burglar chain. She was all the more certain about this because the conversation with Paul in the kitchen had driven the usual routine from her mind and she had come down specially to lock up after changing into her pyjamas. Now, the chain was dangling loose, suggesting that someone had gone out through the front door that morning. Bernie tried the catch and found that it opened without the need for a key. Yes, certainly someone had opened the door since she had locked it the previous night.

But, who? And why? It was mid-November and the mornings were dark and cold. It was hardly likely that anyone would be attracted out for an early morning walk. Paul, she knew, had no interest in sport of any kind, so it was implausible in the extreme that he might have had a sudden urge to take up jogging. In any case, she could hear him moving around in his room, which was above the front door. If he was the one who had gone out, he must have come back in again without disturbing her or Lucy on either occasion.

She opened the door and peered out. Not only was it cold and dark, but fog had descended during the night, making it all the more uninviting out there for anyone seeking the great outdoors for mere pleasure. It looked as if Rowena Godwin must have left in the night. Bernie turned to go upstairs to look for her, but then she stopped and checked first in the drawer of the hall-stand where she kept a key to the front door, so as to be sure of being able to escape in case of fire. The key was still there but the small supply of cash, which she had left in the drawer in readiness for paying the milkman when he returned later that morning with his weekly bill, was gone.

Bernie headed upstairs and tapped on Rowena's

bedroom door, gently at first and then louder. She called out to her, but there was no reply. She was just opening the door a crack to peep in when Paul appeared, tousle-headed and pulling on his sweater as he asked her what was up.

'I think your mother must have gone out,' Bernie explained, opening the door fully and fumbling for the light switch. Paul followed her in and looked round the room. The duvet was lying half off the big old-fashioned bed. On the sheet next to it lay an empty vodka bottle. Apart from those, there was no evidence that the room had been occupied.

'Her case is gone,' Bernie commented, 'unless she put it away somewhere.'

She peered under the bed, thinking that her guest might have stowed the suitcase there, but she was interrupted in her investigations by Lucy's plaintive voice in the hall, calling to her and rattling the stair gate.

'Alright, love, I'm coming!' Bernie called to her. Then she turned to Paul. 'Where do you think she's gone?'

'Based on past experience,' Paul answered with a shrug, 'the nearest off-licence – except she didn't have any money.'

'Well … the milk money's gone from the hall drawer,' Bernie told him, feeling strangely reluctant to reveal his mother's dishonesty.

'Ma-am!' Lucy wailed again from downstairs.

Bernie hurried down and carried her daughter upstairs to join Paul in *The Dump*. Lucy looked around with delight at being in a room that was normally out of bounds to her.

'I suppose the first thing to do,' Bernie said, 'is to find out whether she *has* taken her things with her and gone or if she may just be taking an early morning stroll.'

She started opening doors and drawers, looking for the missing suitcase or any of Rowena's clothes hanging in the wardrobe or any other sign that she was still in residence. Lucy joined in with a will, pulling out drawers and peering into them. There was a crash as she pulled too hard at a drawer in the massive oak dressing table and it fell to the floor. Paul rushed to help, anxious that she might have hurt herself as she sat down 'plop' on the floor with the drawer on top of her. Fortunately, she appeared undamaged, but she gazed round anxiously at the adults, wondering whether she was going to be in trouble for breaking the furniture.

'Don't worry love,' Bernie reassured her, picking up the drawer and showing Lucy that it fitted back into the dressing table quite easily. 'There's no harm done.'

Paul bent down to pick up the contents of the drawer, which had spilled out on the floor.

'What are these?' he asked Bernie, holding out two small, hinged boxes.

'Just some old rings,' she answered without showing much interest. 'I think they must have belonged to Richard's grandmother.'

Paul was about to put the boxes back in the drawer, but something prompted him to check inside first. Both boxes were empty. Paul showed them to Bernie with a meaningful expression on his face.

'They must be different ones,' she said at once. 'I expect these empty ones were out of sight at the back of the drawer. The rings must be here somewhere.'

She took the drawer back out of the dressing table and put it down on the bed so that she could look through the contents easily. Paul leaned past her and snatched up a larger, dark blue box, with the initials DMP in gold on the top. He turned it over briefly to inspect a label on the bottom before opening it. It bore the name of the same exclusive London jeweller as had been on the two ring boxes. The inside was cushioned silk with a semi-circular indentation suggesting that whatever was usually stored there was missing.

'What was in here?' he asked Bernie. 'And it's no good telling me it must already have been empty, because I won't believe you.'

'It was a necklace,' Bernie answered, looking rather uncomfortable. 'Perhaps it fell out of the box when the draw fell out. It could be loose in the drawer now – or on the floor. Lucy love – have a look round on the floor and see if you can find anything, especially any more of these little boxes or anything sparkly, like bits of glass.'

Lucy obediently started crawling around the carpet, peering under the bed and feeling under the dressing table. She found another small jewellery box and an expensive-looking fountain pen.

'Good girl!' Bernie praised her. 'Put them up here on the bed and then carry on looking.'

Paul opened the box and showed Bernie that this too was empty.

'What was in this one?' he asked.

'I think it was a pair of earrings. I can't really remember. Does it matter?'

'Of course it matters!' Paul said in exasperated tone. 'You need to make a list of everything that's gone so you can report it to the police.'

'You *are* the police.'

'I can hardly investigate my own mother for theft!'

'Of course not – and I can't report your mother for theft either.'

'You've got to. You can't just ignore it.'

'We can't be sure she took the things,' Bernie argued. 'Maybe I was wrong about what was in this drawer – or maybe she just moved them – or … Lucy? Come here a minute!'

Lucy pulled herself up to a standing position by grasping the bed and came over to her mother. She stood looking up into her face.

'Now Lucy,' Bernie said seriously. 'I want you to tell me something, and I promise you won't be in trouble about anything so long as you tell the truth. Do you understand?'

'Yes,' Lucy nodded vigorously.

'OK. Now I want you to tell me if you've ever been in this room before and if you've ever looked inside any of the drawers before.'

'No.' Lucy said solemnly, shaking her head. 'Never.'

'You're sure?'

'Yes.'

'OK. That's alright then.'

'Come on Bernie!' Paul said with rising frustration. 'You've got to face it. My mother took the rings and the necklace and the earrings and quite possibly other things too. And you've got to report them to the police. If they get after her right away, they may be able to find her before she has a chance to turn them into cash – which is what she'll be wanting to do. Cash and then alcohol.'

'You don't think she may simply have got them out to look at and then put them away in the wrong drawer?' Bernie suggested, fully aware how unconvincing that suggestion sounded but determined to try to find a way of exonerating Paul's mother.

'No. I don't,' Paul said firmly. 'And now, if you don't phone the police, I will.'

'OK, you phone them,' Bernie conceded, 'but to report a missing person, not a theft. I'm not going to allow your mother to be dragged through the courts just because of a few pieces of old jewellery. They probably aren't even worth anything much.'

'That's not the point, is it? The thing is, we've got to find her-'

'Yes – I quite agree. But not in order to prosecute her for stealing a few worthless trinkets. It was my fault for leaving them there. After all, I knew she was feeling pretty desperate.'

'Stop trying to make excuses for her. She knew what she was doing. Now I'm calling the police whether you like it or-'

'Hang on! Don't be in such a hurry. I'll call Peter – he'll

know how to find your mother without having to report her for stealing.'

'You can't do that. He's not on duty this weekend.'

'All the better. Then he won't have to log it as an official crime report.'

'But-'

'It's no good Paul. It's *my* possessions that have walked and a guest in *my* house who seems to have walked off with them; and if I decide to confide in my best friend, Angie, and her husband and don't think it's something to bother our overworked police force with, that's none of your business. If you want to enlist the help of the police to find your mother before anything unpleasant happens to her then that's up to you, but it's no good trying to get me to press charges for stealing, because I'm not going to.'

With that, Bernie got up, picked up Lucy and clattered downstairs to the telephone in the hall. A minute later, Paul heard her voice on the phone explaining what had happened to an incredulous Angie. He followed her down and they had breakfast together in the kitchen, trying to make ordinary conversation despite the whirl of different thoughts and feelings with which each of them was contending. They were both relieved when a ring at the door announced the arrival of Peter and Angie.

Lucy was ecstatic to see her godparents on a day that she had been expecting to spend with only her mother for company. She hurled herself at Peter, who swept her up in his arms and kissed her before handing her over to his wife.

'Sorry Lucy,' he apologised, 'I can't play with you just now. You run along with Angie like a good girl and I'll see you later on.'

After some loud protests, which threatened to turn into a full-blown tantrum, Lucy was persuaded to accept that her favourite grown up had important business to transact with Paul, which could not be delayed, and she trotted off happily hand-in-hand with her godmother. Peter turned to

Paul.

'Have you any idea where your mum's gone now? Have you checked that she's not just gone home?'

'I rang Dad just now. He hasn't seen her since yesterday morning. She had no money and no transport of her own, so I don't see how she could get back to Reading – at least not until she'd turned some of the jewellery into cash. I'd say that would be what would be uppermost in her mind.'

'She did have some money,' Bernie contributed, reluctant to accuse Paul's mother of further dishonesty but wanting Peter to have the facts. 'At least – the milk money was gone from the hall drawer. It was only one week's worth, so it wouldn't finance a taxi to Reading, but it would probably get her to anywhere she wanted to go within Oxford.'

'OK,' Peter thought for a moment. 'Assuming that she didn't set off on foot, she probably rang for a taxi to take her to somewhere where she could sell the stuff she'd taken. Does your phone store the last number dialled?'

'Yes,' Bernie answered. 'You just press "re-dial". But I rang you this morning, remember? So that'll be the number it's got in it at the moment.'

Peter withdrew the hand that he had stretched out towards the telephone and frowned. Then he turned to Paul again.

'OK Paul – tell me what you think she would do next?'

'Well, if she was at home, I'd lay bets on her heading straight off to her friendly neighbourhood pawnbroker, but she doesn't know Oxford, so she wouldn't know where to go to find one.'

'But she could look it up easily enough,' Peter said, brightening up and taking hold of a copy of Yellow Pages, which lay on the hall-stand next to the telephone. Now we're getting somewhere.'

He leafed through the pages and soon found what he was looking for. He held out the book to Paul and pointed down at the page. There were three pawnbrokers listed in the Oxford area.

'All in Cowley,' Paul commented.

'What do you expect?' Bernie asked. 'Plenty of potential customers and the only part of Oxford without a whole load of middle class whingers moaning about it lowering the tone of the neighbourhood and the value of their properties!'

'It's still early,' Peter said, looking at his watch. 'If we get over there right away, we may be able to intercept her before she has a chance to pawn the loot. We need a photo of her and preferably photos of the things that she's taken.'

'I'm afraid I don't have any pictures more recent than when I was in Primary school,' Paul said apologetically.

'I took one of her playing with Lucy yesterday.' Bernie said eagerly. 'It's on my phone. I'll download it on to the computer and print you out a copy.'

'And what about the rings and necklace and stuff?' Peter called after her as she headed upstairs to her study. 'Presumably you must have descriptions and valuations for the insurance.'

'Not that I know of,' Bernie called back over her shoulder. 'I've always ticked the box that there aren't any single items worth more than whatever; and I don't remember the contents policy that I inherited from Richard saying any different. I don't suppose they're worth anything much.'

'Bouwmeester and Merryweather stuff is never not worth anything much,' Paul intervened decidedly. 'Their pieces are all top of the range.'

'Who're they when they're at home?' Bernie asked, continuing upstairs and heading for the study.' I've never heard of them.'

'They're a really top-notch Bond Street Jeweller – a very old firm, but they've been taken over by one of the big multi-nationals now. Bouwmeester owned South

African diamond mines and Merryweather had aristocratic connections. Before the war they were one of the most fashionable jewellers in Europe.'

'You seem to know a lot about it,' Bernie commented. 'I never had you down as a connoisseur of ladies jewellery – or are you interested in diamond mining?'

'My mother's engagement ring was from Bouwmeester and Merryweather,' Paul admitted, going red with embarrassment and hoping that Peter, who was bringing up the rear, would not notice his discomfiture. 'She got me to dispose of it for her, and the bloke I sold it to insisted on giving me a history lesson. He was very impressed: I don't think he saw many of them.'

'If you don't have proper descriptions, can you at least tell me what they looked like?' Peter asked. 'We need to know what we're looking for.'

'The wedding ring's just a plain gold band, but it's got an inscription on the inside, which is how I knew it belonged to Richard's grandmother. It had a date that matched to her marriage certificate: 1905. The engagement ring was a solitaire diamond. It just looked pretty ordinary to me. Then the earrings were gold with red centres.'

'And the necklace?' Paul asked. 'It looked as if it must have been pretty impressive.'

'I don't see how you can tell just by the box,' Bernie grumbled. 'That presumably belonged to Richard's Grandmother too, judging by the initials on the lid: Dorothy Maud Paige. It was sparkly – like pieces of broken glass – a semi-circle on the inside and what I suppose you'd called scalloped on the outside, and there were some blue bits – they were bigger and arranged in a pattern.'

'Diamonds and sapphires,' Paul opined.

'I shouldn't think so: there were so many of them: four or five rows with, I don't know, maybe twenty stones in each. I mean, if they were real diamonds it'd be worth a fortune wouldn't it?'

'Yes,' agreed Paul, 'that's what I've been trying to tell you. Gold rings, ruby earrings and a diamond and sapphire necklace: you're definitely talking five figures there, maybe more.'

'Well I hope your wrong,' Bernie said, fumbling in a drawer in search of the cable for connecting her camera to her computer. 'I was only keeping them because they were a link to Richard's family and I thought Lucy might like dressing up in them when she's a bit older. If they're really valuable, I'll have to get rid of them: it would be too much of a risk having stuff like that lying around in the house. I expect it's only the boxes that were made by Thingummy and Whatshisname. I can't believe that real people wear diamond necklaces and ruby earrings.'

'Get me the boxes,' Peter instructed. 'Then we can match them up to the contents if we manage to find them.'

Paul disappeared into the spare bedroom, returning shortly with the jewellery boxes. He handed them to Peter who studied them briefly before putting them down on the desk next to the computer. Bernie meanwhile printed five copies of the photograph she had taken of Rowena Godwin with Lucy on her lap and handed them to Peter. Then she rummaged in a drawer and found a plastic carrier bag into which she put the boxes.

'There you are,' she said. 'Now you can walk the streets without looking as if you've just done a jewel heist.'

CHAPTER 26

'Is our Bernie really as unworldly as she makes out?' Paul asked as Peter drove them both round the ring road in the direction of Cowley, in the quest to reach the pawnbrokers before Paul's mother did, 'or is it just a pose?'

'Oh there is a bit of putting on an act about it,' Peter laughed, 'but I wouldn't say she's trying to appear unworldly – more showing off her contempt for ostentatious wealth. She likes to imagine that she's still close to her working class roots. And she doesn't believe in the idea of women adorning themselves so as to appear more attractive.'

'I was meaning: do you think she really believes that stuff about the necklace and things being just worthless trinkets?'

'Well that was probably mostly to make you feel better about your mother having taken them,' Peter replied. 'That and feeling stupid for not having got them properly insured. Not that the insurance would have paid out anyway, seeing as there wasn't a break-in.'

He pulled up outside the first of the pawnbrokers' shops.

'You wait in the car,' he instructed. 'I'll handle this.'

'No – let me. It's my mother.'

'But I know these guys,' Peter argued. 'Not through personal experience,' he added hastily, 'although it was sometimes a close-run thing back when the kids were

199

young and I was still just a sergeant. My salary seemed to go nowhere and I don't know how we'd have survived if we hadn't had Bernie giving us free childcare so that Angie could go back to work. What I meant was: this is my neighbourhood and it's useful to keep in with the local businesses – especially the ones that may get to know about criminal activity. These wouldn't be the first stolen goods that have ended up here.'

'Then wouldn't it be useful experience for me to be introduced to the proprietors?' Paul suggested, reluctant to be side-lined.

Peter hesitated for a moment, then he nodded and they both got out of the car and went into the shop. The manager greeted Peter cheerfully by name and answered his questions with no apparent reluctance. He did not recognise the photograph of Rowena Godwin and was confident that no woman had been in that morning with any jewellery to pawn. He kept the picture and promised that, if she were to turn up later, he would ring Peter and attempt to keep her talking for long enough for him to get back there to speak to her.

One of the staff at the second shop recognised the photograph at once and confirmed that the woman in it had pawned two gold rings that morning.

'She was sitting on the doorstep when I got here to open up,' he told them. 'I wasn't sure about doing business with her, because I wondered if she was sleeping rough but she had a story that sounded genuine enough: forced out of home by a violent husband and wanting to raise some money to tide her over until she could get set up on her own. She had a trolley suitcase with her and she said she'd run away with just the clothes she stood up in and what she managed to throw into the case before she left. Were they stolen then?'

'Yes, I'm afraid so,' Peter answered. 'But we'd better make sure.'

He repeated the description that Bernie had given him

of the two rings. The man nodded.

'A solitaire diamond and a plain gold band – that sounds like them. I didn't notice the engraving, but I'll fetch them and you can have a look.'

A few minutes later Peter and Paul were back in the car on their way to the third, and last, pawnshop, with the rings safely in Peter's pocket. The pawnbroker had gratefully accepted Peter's offer to reimburse him the money that he had given Paul's mother and willingly agreed to let him know if she were to come in again.

'You must let me pay,' Paul insisted, 'I can't have you paying my mother's debts.'

'We can settle up later,' Peter muttered. 'Let's just concentrate on finding your mother before anything happens to her. If I know Our Bernie, she won't be remotely interested in the fact that we've recovered her property if we have to admit that your Mum could be lying in an alcoholic stupor in a gutter somewhere.'

The third pawnbroker had the most interesting story to tell.

'You've just missed her,' he told them. 'She was in about half an hour ago with this big diamond necklace. I had a look at it, thinking it must be just costume jewellery, but when I saw the hallmark I realised it was the genuine article. It must have been worth tens, maybe hundreds, of thousands – well out of my league. I told her she'd need to find a specialist if she wanted to pawn that. I asked her where she got it from and she said it had been in her family for years. It looked old, so I believed her. If I'd thought it was stolen I'd have reported it, wouldn't I?' he added defensively. 'Anyway, I didn't take it, did I?'

'OK Joe. Nobody's blaming you,' Peter assured him. 'You know my number. Just keep a look out, will you, and let me know if she turns up again.'

They went outside and stood looking up and down the street wondering what to do next. Paul spotted an off licence and set off across the street towards it. Peter followed.

'If I know Mum,' Paul said, 'once she got some cash she won't have left it long before buying something to drink. She feels insecure without a bottle somewhere about her.'

He was right: the shop assistant in the off licence confirmed that the woman in the photograph had purchased a bottle of gin and a bottle of vodka earlier that morning. She hadn't seen which way the woman had gone after she left, but she remembered her having said something about being on the way to the station. She had a trolley case with her, so presumably she was going away to stay somewhere. In fact, the assistant thought she had said that the vodka was a present for a friend whom she was visiting.

Peter and Paul retreated to the car to talk over what to do next. The story about catching a train might just have been a way of explaining away the presence of the suitcase. Perhaps the shop assistant had commented on it or looked suspiciously at it. On the other hand it might be that Paul's mother was genuinely planning to travel by rail, perhaps going back home to Reading. The station was some distance from here but, now that she had money, she could have taken a bus or a taxi. Should they drive to the station in the hope of getting there before her or stay in this neighbourhood in case she was still in the vicinity?

A call on Peter's phone settled the question for them. It was the first pawnbroker, reporting that the woman in the photograph was in his shop now negotiating a loan against a diamond and sapphire necklace, which she said had belonged to an aunt who had left it to her in her will. His assistant was taking her through the formalities while he rang Peter from the office at the back of the shop. Could Peter get over there right away? They would not be able to draw the process out very much longer.

Five minutes later, Peter and Paul entered the shop and stood on either side of Rowena Godwin, who was sitting in a chair waiting for the assistant to 'check with the boss' that all the paperwork was in order. She looked up and smiled at her son.

'You didn't need to come,' she said. 'I'll be alright now. Your landlady was very kind allowing me to borrow some of her things to tide me over until I get back on my feet.'

'This is Detective Inspector Johns,' Paul replied coldly. 'He needs to have a word with you, but first he'd better take charge of that necklace you were showing off just now and then there are the earrings – do you still have them?'

They left a few minute later, with Paul holding firmly on to his mother's arm, Peter having pocketed the necklace and earrings. Peter slipped a ten-pound note into the manager's hand as he went out and suggested in a low voice that it would be as well if none of what had taken place went any further. The manager nodded knowingly and gave his assistant a warning look.

They drove to a hostel that specialised in housing women who had been subjected to domestic violence. Paul was again surprised to see that Peter was apparently well known to the staff and spoke to several of them by name. He was in luck they told him: one of their residents was moving out to her own rented flat today and her room would be free for Mrs Godwin. Paul went with his mother to see the room and to meet some of the other residents, while Peter had a serious talk with the warden about the precautions that needed to be taken to keep her off the drink and away from other people's valuables. The warden pulled a face when she heard about the theft from Bernie's house, but nonetheless agreed to take Rowena in and to say nothing to her about it.

'I think she genuinely did only plan to borrow the items,' Peter explained. 'I'm sure she intended to give them back, but I rather doubt that she'd ever have managed to get the cash together to do it. Anyway Di, see what you can do with her and if it gets too much, give me a ring and

I'll see if I can find somewhere else for her.'

'I'll do my best,' Diane Berry sighed, 'but, for a policeman, you have a surprising degree of faith in human nature. I won't be the least surprised if we're calling you out in your professional capacity before long.'

Paul knocked on the warden's office door and came in, looking around rather nervously.

'I can't tell you how grateful I am to you for taking my mother in,' he began.

'It's what we're here for,' Diane said, cutting across him, embarrassed by his earnest thanks. 'And I know Peter wouldn't have brought her if there wasn't a genuine reason.'

'Well, we'd better be getting off,' Peter said, getting up. 'Our Bernie will be wondering what's become of us!'

'I'd better ring Dad and let him know she's safe,' Paul said as they got in the car. 'They've always fought, but he does genuinely care for her.'

As Peter drove away, Paul punched numbers into his phone and waited for his father to answer. Then, after a brief conversation, he turned to Peter again.

'He never really settled down after leaving the army,' he explained. 'He was used to having everything decided for him – working to rules – everyone doing what they were told. As for Mum – well she took to drinking while he was in the forces because she couldn't cope with him being away so much. But then, when he came out and was back for good, she couldn't cope with having him around the place all the time. That's when he started knocking her about and she started getting into a rage and throwing things at him. They neither of them mean anything by it. I bet they'll be back together again in a few weeks.'

'And you were piggy-in-the-middle, I suppose?' Peter murmured attempting to sound interested but not as if he were trying to force confidences.

'I kept out of the way as much as I could – and then got out of it as soon as I left school.'

'Well, I think I have to warn you,' Peter said, with mock seriousness, 'that this will only increase Our Bernie's level of maternal concern for your well-being. I assume you realise that you have already become "our Paul"?'

'I didn't know, but I'm not surprised,' Paul answered with a grin. 'Don't worry – I can handle it.'

'It's a brave man who claims to be able to handle Our Bernie,' Peter declared.

'I meant I can handle the situation,' Paul responded. 'Actually I quite like having Bernie as a mother – she's a lot less work than my real one!'

CHAPTER 27

Two weeks later, Paul gave Bernie the opportunity to display her abilities to offer parental advice. She returned to the living room after putting Lucy to bed to find Paul sitting in one of the easy chairs staring into space.

'Penny for your thoughts!' she said brightly, sitting down in the other chair.

'Bernie?' Paul began, looking up. 'Bernie, I'd like to know what you think: about Gemma.'

He stopped, unsure how to go on. Bernie looked back at him in silence, trying to appear encouraging.

'I know it's only a couple of months since Robert died, but I'd like ...' he trailed off again, unable to put what he wanted to say into words. Bernie still did not speak, so he took another breath and tried again.

'Do you think...? I mean, how soon do you think...? Tell me, Bernie,' he said at last, 'if your boyfriend had topped himself, how long would it be before you'd be ready to have someone else ask you out for a date? A proper date, I mean. I mean, we've been seeing each other as friends ever since the case was closed, as you know, but ...'

'And what makes you ask me?' Bernie asked, 'Did our Peter put you up to it?'

'No,' Paul said in a puzzled tone. 'I never mentioned it to him. What makes you think that?'

'I just thought he might have pointed you in my

direction as an Expert in the Field,' Bernie said enigmatically.

'I just thought, being a woman you might have a better idea how Gemma's feeling right now.'

'I'd say that's a ridiculous simplification. Everyone takes these things differently. Being a man or a woman doesn't really have much to do with it.'

'Oh,' Paul said, feeling rather deflated.

'I just so happens,' Bernie went on kindly, noticing his discomfiture, 'that I do happen to know a bit about that sort of thing, but it's not as simple as: you ought to wait precisely n months or x years. I think this is something to be tackled as a Bedtime Story. Would that do?'

A few hours later Paul was sitting up in bed waiting for Bernie. She came in, clad in her usual red dressing gown over yellow pyjamas. She sat down on the bed and looked at him.

'So you'd like a story about a girl whose boyfriend kills himself?' she said with a rather sad smile. 'I think I can manage that.'

'I want to be fair to Gemma,' Paul said earnestly. 'I don't want to rush her, but I don't want to deceive her either. I mean: it's not fair if she thinks we're just friends and doesn't realise that I'm wanting more from our relationship; but I know it's too soon for her to be thinking about that sort of thing yet.'

'Well, here goes,' Bernie answered. 'For what it's worth here's a true story of someone who was in a rather similar situation to your Gemma. But you must remember: everyone's different. Gemma may feel completely differently about what's happened.'

She paused to gather her thoughts before taking a deep breath and starting her narrative.

'Once upon a time, in the great city of Liverpool, there lived a girl by the name of Bernadette Catherine Fazakerley. Her father worked in the docks and her mother had been a nurse, but was now incapacitated by motor neurone disease. She attended a convent school by day and she generally stayed at home in the evenings to look after her mother. Not being at liberty to go out as much as her friends, she became sufficiently studious to attract the attention of Sister Teresa, one of the teachers. Sister Teresa became determined that Bernadette would be the pupil who showed the world that good catholic working class girls from The North were just as good as upper class protestants from posh boarding schools in deepest southern England!

'And so it came to pass that young Bernadette – who, I might add, was far from being a good catholic girl, seeing as she played in the Salvation Army band and from time to time entertained thoughts of becoming an officer – was awarded a scholarship at one of the few Oxford colleges in those day which admitted women. Sister Teresa was ecstatic and Bernadette's parents were proud and everything seemed to be going along very nicely, except that, a few months before term was due to start, Bernadette's mother died.'

'How dreadful!' Paul commented, taken aback at this sudden revelation and feeling that he ought to say something.

'Young Bernadette was all for throwing up the scholarship and trying for place at Liverpool University instead,' Bernie continued, ignoring him. 'She had this crazy idea that her father needed her around to look after him, which was bonkers, because he'd been looking after all three of them for the last fifteen years so he was hardly likely to suddenly become incapable now. Eventually, with much persuasion from her father and his extensive family – he was the youngest of thirteen kids – she agreed to go to Oxford, on the grounds that it would have disappointed her mother to think that she had given up such a great opportunity.'

She paused briefly to collect her thoughts.

'So she came up to Oxford, determined to do well as a

sort of tribute to her mother,' Bernie continued, 'but at first she didn't seem to fit in very well. The other girls on her corridor all seemed to be members of the Pony Club and the Young Conservatives; the tutors smiled indulgently at her accent; nobody knew what she meant when she tried to buy a barm cake...'

'What *is* a barm cake?' Paul asked to fill the pause that followed.

'Just a big bread roll. They have something similar in Manchester, but it's a bit flatter and they call them muffins; and in Newcastle they have stotties, which are bigger and flatter still. Anyway, young Bernadette was just starting to wonder whether it had all been a big mistake and she'd better bolt back home after all, when she met a lad called Stephen who was having much the same experience himself. He was doing maths too and he was from the North as well. In fact, he was from so far north that he didn't consider Liverpool was in the north at all!'

Bernie pointed up at a framed cartoon hanging on the wall of the bedroom. It depicted a mother zebra bending down to speak to her foal. A speech bubble contained the words: 'It's no good, son, we can't afford to buy you a West Ham strip, you'll just have to support Newcastle like the rest of the family!'

'Steve's father was a welder in the shipyards and his mum worked in a shop, she went on. 'He was feeling like a fish out of water too. He was sharing a set of rooms with an old-Etonian who was a leading light in the Officers Training Corps and was hoping to follow his papa into the diplomatic service. So Stephen and Bernadette formed an alliance against the rest of the world and gradually they discovered that actually there were quite a lot of other undergraduates whose parents had ordinary jobs and who hadn't attended one of the better Public Schools. And they also discovered that speaking with a posh accent and having been to boarding school didn't automatically prevent you being a nice person.

'By the end of the second year they'd decided that they wanted to stay together, so they announced their engagement. Everyone around them seemed pleased for them and everything appeared to be working out just right. They both managed to secure grants to stay on in Oxford to study for a DPhil, so they made plans to get married shortly after Finals – in the Methodist Church in the centre of Oxford which they'd both been going to since the first year.'

'So what happened?' Paul asked, although he had a good idea what must be coming next.

'Two weeks before the wedding was due to take place Steve jumped to his death from the top of the Engineering Tower.'

For perhaps two minutes neither of them spoke. Then Bernie gave a sigh and took up the story again.

'He didn't leave a note, so we could never be sure why he did it, but the general consensus was that he must have been worried he'd messed up in the exams – which he hadn't, by the way – and couldn't face the idea that he'd let everyone down. It was absolutely awful for his parents, because they blamed themselves for making such a fuss of him over getting his scholarship. They were so proud of him, you see, and they thought that he knew that and was afraid of disappointing them.'

'It must have been pretty awful for you too,' Paul said sincerely. 'All your plans dashed – just like that! How on earth did you cope?'

'Like they say, life must go on,' Bernie replied ruefully. 'I suppose I carried on, on autopilot for a good while. The DPhil was all set up, so I got on with that. I switched to a different church – the one that Angie and Peter belong to – to avoid all the people who knew us both and would have been all over me with sympathy. And I spent a lot of time with Steve's parents. That was one of the good things that came out of the whole business. If Stephen and I had got married, they'd always have just been his parents and my in-laws. As it turned out, they're more like my own second Mum and Dad – especially after my own Dad died.'

'So is that why it was so long before you got married?' Paul asked, remembering why Bernie was telling him this story. 'Are you saying that it might be years and years before Gemma will be ready for another relationship?'

'Yes – and no,' Bernie said, smiling. 'Yes, losing Steve in that way made me wary of committing myself to any sort of permanent relationship, but if you think I mean you ought to back off and leave Gemma to get to the stage where she's ready to start looking for someone to replace Robert then you're wrong there.'

'So what *are* you saying?' Paul asked, puzzled.

'First of all – and I have to keep saying this – everyone's different, so the way I felt isn't the same as the way Gemma's feeling now,' Bernie said emphatically. 'And secondly, just because it took me the best part of fifteen years before I allowed myself to risk any sort of emotional entanglement, it doesn't mean that it might not have been better if someone had taken the bull by the horns and forced me to have another go.'

'How do you mean?'

'It wasn't just that I was afraid that if I allowed myself to fall in love again I'd get hurt,' Bernie explained. 'You have to understand what it's like when someone close to you kills themselves. I was carrying around this great weight of guilt – and so were Steve's parents (that's one of the things that brought us together) – because I hadn't seen it coming and done something to stop it. So I didn't believe that I was worthy of being loved. Does that make any sort of sense?'

'I suppose so,' Paul said slowly. 'So do you think Gemma might want to protect me from falling in love with her? I'm afraid it's a bit late for that!'

'I don't know – I can only tell you how I felt back then. Gemma's older and has had a completely different life history, so she may see things totally differently. It's not the first sudden death she's experienced, for one thing; and she probably hasn't lived all her life with the idea being drummed into her that suicide is a mortal sin. I'm just pointing out to you the possibilities. The thing is: I don't know whether everything would have worked out differently if someone had come along, after Stephen died, who was brave enough to tell me to snap out of it and get on with life and have another go. My natural instinct was to give up on the idea of marriage and a family and all that and just concentrate on my job and the church and all sorts of non-personal things. And I probably made it difficult for anyone who might have wanted to get close to me. It could be that, even if that is the way Gemma's feeling right now, it would be good for her to have someone who wants to make a commitment to her. Do you see what I'm getting at?'

'You mean, you wish Richard – or someone like him – had come along sooner?'

'I'm not sure I'd be comfortable with putting it quite as strongly as that,' Bernie answered, 'but you're getting the idea. The thing is, despite everything, I do find it difficult to say that I wish my life had been any different from what it was. It's mug's game playing "what if?" For example, if I'd married Stephen then maybe I'd have had all the things I was expecting when I was twenty. Like two or three kids – but not Lucy of course – and a stable home and maybe the two of us working together at the university. But then I wouldn't have got to know Angie and her kids, and I probably would never have met Richard, and I certainly wouldn't have been able to marry him and Lucy would never have been born – and I would never have got to know you either! And if, after Steve died, someone had come along and jolted me out of my conviction that any sort of intimate relationship was not for me then I might still have managed to miss out on Richard and Lucy. So I really can't wish for things to have been different…'

'So are you saying everything always works out for the best in the end?'

'No – not exactly. I think I'm saying it's no good trying to make comparisons. I mean, you can't arrange all the possible permutations in rank order and say: that's the best and that's only second best and that alternative is not so good at all.'

'You mean marrying Stephen would have been one good thing but marrying Richard was good too?'

'Something like that. And Stephen killing himself was a bad thing, even though if it hadn't happened there are all sorts of good things that wouldn't have been able to happen. If you take the line that "things always work out for the best in the end" to its logical conclusion then you wouldn't bother trying to do the right thing, because it wouldn't really matter, would it? It has to be possible to get it wrong and really make things worse than they could have been or everything's all a bit pointless. Does that make sense?'

'I'm not sure,' Paul said cautiously. This sort of philosophical argument was new to him and he felt somewhat out of his depth. 'So, getting back to me and Gemma: how long do you think I ought to leave it before I ask her out on a proper date?'

Bernie considered the question for a few moments.

'I think,' she said slowly, 'that on balance it's always best to be honest with people. If that's the way you feel about her then it's not fair stringing her along with the idea that you are just old friends chatting about old times. And then you've got to hope she'll be equally honest with you about how she feels about it.'

'And if she says she could never love anyone else after Robert?'

'Then you have to decide whether you're going to accept that at face value and either break off diplomatic relations altogether or try to carry on with some sort of platonic relationship, or …,' Bernie paused and looked

Paul intently in the eyes. 'Or you bide your time and wait to see if she still feels like that in two years or five years or twenty-five years, depending on how long you're prepared to wait. But then you've got to ask yourself: is Gemma so special compared with anyone else that it justifies putting your life on hold while you wait until she's ready to move on from Robert?'

'I think she is,' Paul said quietly. 'I think I've been in love with her since we were in the home together. I don't think I'll ever love anyone else the way I love Gemma.'

They sat for a minute in silence. Then Paul spoke again.

'I nearly committed suicide once.'

'Why was that?' Bernie asked in surprise.

''It was while I was in care. I was being bullied quite badly by some of the other boys and I couldn't see any other way out. I thought: either I stay here until I leave school, with Stuart and Ian Bottinger kicking me all the time just for the fun of it and Bongo King calling me names and laughing at me; or I get sent back to Mum and Dad in their pokey little flat, where there's no space to do my homework and nowhere to get away from their endless rowing, and I have to keep covering up for them with their employers and Social Services. Either way, it just didn't seem worth going on.'

'That's awful!'

'I had it all planned,' Paul continued. 'There was a road quite near the care home which went over the railway: Godstow Lane; do you know it?'

'Vaguely.'

'Anyway, my plan was to jump off the bridge just as a train was coming through, so that it would go right over me without having time to stop.'

'What a dreadful way to kill yourself.'

'Do you think so? I thought it would be quite quick.'

'I meant for everyone else,' Bernie explained, becoming more animated as she warmed to the subject. 'Suicide really is a very selfish thing to do. It's the people who are left behind that suffer: all the people who would have tried to help if they'd known that there was something wrong; all the friends and family who didn't get a chance even to say goodbye; and in this case there would have been all the people on the train who saw it happen and the driver, who might very well be traumatised for life and never be able to work again. And then,' she continued, trying to introduce a somewhat lighter note to the conversation, 'there's all the inconvenience you would have caused to thousands of other rail passengers. They always have to close the line for hours when there's a fatality. It was really a most inconsiderate thing for you to have decided to do!'

There was another long silence.

'Anyway,' Bernie said at last. 'I'm really glad you changed you mind. What was it that stopped you carrying out your plan?'

'Gemma,' Paul replied simply. 'She talked me out of it. She persuaded me that things wouldn't always be the way they were and that it was up to me to make them better. I suppose, with her losing both her parents like that, she thought my problems were pretty small compared with hers. Anyway, she saved my life and I suppose that was when I fell in love with her.'

'And are you sure it's not the fifteen-year-old Gemma who gave you a reason not to kill yourself that you're in love with now?' Bernie asked anxiously. 'You're neither of you the same people you were then. You do realise that, don't you?'

'Yes, of course. I've grown up a lot since then – I was only thirteen after all – and Gemma's, well Gemma's not the tough girl defending me against the world any longer. I've get more to offer her now – if only she's ready to accept it. Thank you for telling me about you and Stephen. I think I'll be able to get up the courage to talk to Gemma now.'

'Pleased to be of service,' Bernie said casually. 'And now, it's time for lights out. Lie down and I'll tuck you in.'

Paul lay back obediently and Bernie pulled the bedclothes up round him before kissing him lightly on the cheek and then leaving the room, switching off the light as she did so. He lay there smiling to himself imagining what he was going to say when he met Gemma the following evening.

CHAPTER 28

Paul was surprised and delighted at how easy it all was. Gemma greeted his tentative declaration of devotion with undisguised pleasure. Two and a half months after her lover's death, she pronounced herself ready to move on and thanked Paul both for his support in her grief and for his willingness to take her on despite her having so recently been living with another man. She confided to him that, thinking back over her time with Robert, she was coming to the conclusion that their relationship would never have succeeded in the longer term and that it was quite possible that he had planned his return to Australia at least in part as a way of ending it with minimal trouble for him.

'I can see now,' she said one evening as they sat together in her flat. 'Once he was back home, all he needed to do was to send me a text and that would have been it. He knew I couldn't afford to go over there after him, and anyway what would have been the point? He'd got bored with me and he didn't have the guts to tell me to my face.'

'I'm sure I could never get bored with you,' Paul assured her, putting his arm round her shoulder and drawing her closer to him. 'You're the most fascinating person I've ever met.'

Now that Paul no longer felt constrained by attempting to keep up the appearance of being merely a concerned friend, he began spending more and more of his time in Gemma's company. Peter stopped expecting to find him at Bernie's house when he made one of his frequent visits to see his goddaughter. Bernie got used to being told that there would be one fewer person at the evening meal. They both noticed a change in Paul's demeanour too: he seemed more relaxed and contented – perhaps more confident, and less anxious that he might not be performing well enough and that those around him were secretly criticising him.

'I think she's good for him,' Bernie confided in Peter. 'She's taken him out of himself a bit.'

'Yes,' Peter agreed. 'I just hope she can cope when it comes to meeting his parents! They're back together again – for the time being – but I can foresee that mother of his continuing to make trouble for Paul and you can't expect his girlfriend to take kindly to having a drunk suddenly descending on them the way she did with you.'

The project to restore the toy theatre suffered as a result of this new development in their relationship. As Paul began to spend more and more of his free time with Gemma, he found that it was as much as he could do to keep the renovation of the rocking horse on schedule in order to be ready to give it to Lucy at Christmas; the theatre remained in a state of disrepair. On one or two occasions, Gemma came and spent an evening with him at Bernie's home, but, perhaps understandably, she was reluctant to devote many hours to watching him carefully gluing the mane into place or painstakingly re-painting the pattern of spots on the dapple-grey's hind quarters.

He showed her the theatre and, at first, she was fascinated by the puppets and tried them each out by unwinding the strings and taking each of them for a walk around the loft room. However, after she had discovered that she lacked the skill to manipulate them to do more than simply walking around with a rather strange floating gait, she soon lost interest in Maid Marian, Long John

Silver and the others. So she and Paul spent most of their free time at her flat and when, about two weeks before Christmas, his own flat was pronounced by the landlord to be ready for him to move back into, the theatre was still lying around the room in pieces, very much as it had been when he first discovered it in October.

Bernie looked at it when she came up to help him move his possessions down from the attic and into the hire van that he was using to transport them back to his flat.

'Why don't you take it with you?' she asked him, seeing him eying it regretfully. 'It'll be years before Lucy's old enough to use it and in any case I don't have the skills to get it into working order. All this miniature stuff is your thing: you ought to have it.'

'If you really don't mind, I'd love to take it and finish mending it,' Paul answered eagerly. 'But it'd be for Lucy. I couldn't possibly keep it in the long term – not with it being Richard's and everything.'

'If that's the way you want it,' Bernie nodded. 'OK then – let's get it into the van.'

Bernie and Lucy were spending Christmas with Stephen's parents in Newcastle. As Bernie explained to Paul, they were the nearest thing that Lucy had to grandparents and they had welcomed her into their family as if she had been their own. So Paul and Gemma came over the day before they were due to make the journey 'up north' to give Lucy the, now fully restored, rocking horse.

Lucy's reaction to the gift more than met Paul's expectations. Her eyes lit up with delight when she saw it standing there, in the centre of the large living room. Paul and Peter had placed it there, staggering down with it from the attic while Bernie kept Lucy occupied in the kitchen. She ran over to it and stroked its tail before trying to climb up into the saddle. Peter stepped forward and lifted her on, signalling to Paul with his eyes to come over and join them.

'Paul will show you how to make it go,' Peter said, anxious not to steal the credit for the gift. 'He knows all about it because he fixed it.'

Paul started the horse rocking by giving it a gently push. Lucy smiled up at him and giggled. Then he showed her how to move her body in time with the rhythm of the horse's movements so that the rocking gradually became faster and more vigorous. She laughed again and shouted 'gee up!' loudly. Then suddenly she twisted her body round and grabbed hold of Paul round the waist in a wild attempt at a hug. Instinctively he took hold of her to prevent her from falling and found himself with her in his arms. He lifted her up to a more comfortable position with her weight resting on his hip and she immediately planted a wet kiss on his cheek.

'Dank you, Paul!'

Paul smiled back at Lucy and then looked round the room. Peter and Angela Johns were looking on with indulgent smiles on their faces, pleased to see their goddaughter so happy and pleased for Paul that his efforts had been appreciated. Bernie looked thoughtful and slightly amused. Gemma was watching Lucy's antics impassively, apparently rather bored and hoping it might be time to go home soon. Paul put Lucy down on the floor and went back to Gemma, putting his arm around her and wondering how to enable her to share in the magic of the moment. This was what it was all about, he thought, and perhaps one day he and Gemma would have their own children who would laugh in delight at his handiwork and give them both over-enthusiastic kisses of gratitude and affection.

Bernie continued to watch Gemma with interest. Her reaction to Lucy was exactly what she imagined her own would have been under the circumstances and at that stage in her life. She never ceased to be amazed at the way so many adults were immediately bewitched by Lucy's blue eyes, golden curls and easy smiles. It took Bernie much longer to become fond of other people's children – indeed, if she were honest, the only children she had ever managed feel any affinity for were Hannah and Edward Johns and her own daughter – and she could never understand why some people were able to declare in all honesty that they 'loved children' in the abstract. She was glad that Gemma has not felt the need to pretend to feelings that she did not have. That sort of honesty boded well for her future relationship with Paul, in Bernie's opinion.

Once the Christmas festivities were over, Paul's life fell into a routine in which his time was divided between work and spending time with Gemma, either at her flat or in his own. They occasionally went out together for a meal or to the cinema, but mostly they were content to enjoy one another's company in the privacy of their own homes. Paul enjoyed showing off his culinary skills, and Gemma, who viewed cooking as a chore rather than a pleasure, encouraged him with praise for each new dish that he prepared for them. He introduced her to his model railway and she showed polite interest in controlling the movements of the trains and planning a new branch line. His model castle, complete with jousting knights, she found more interesting – especially the crowds of onlookers watching the tournament, whose courtly clothes held a fascination for her.

'I never knew men could take an interest in clothes,' she observed, turning round a grand lady in her hands and inspecting the tiny stitches in the silk fabric of her dress. 'Did you sew this yourself?'

Paul nodded.

'I found this old sewing machine in a charity shop and I did it up and got it working again. That's good for the bigger stuff, but a lot of the more intricate bits – like attaching the lace round her wimple, for example – have to be done by hand. It's slow work, but up until now I was always grateful to have something to keep me busy at nights.'

'And now?' Gemma asked playfully.

'I've got my own full-sized beautiful princess, haven't I?'

By mid-January, evenings together often stretched into nights and it was not unusual for Paul to wake up to find himself in the bed which Gemma had so recently, it seemed to Paul, shared with Robert White in their central Oxford flat. He still felt like an intruder in that bedroom and preferred the occasions when she stayed with him. He was pleased, although surprised, when she proposed that she might move in permanently.

'I can't afford the Gloucester Green flat,' she explained. 'It was fine when Robert was paying half, but the rent's just too much for me on my own. And it isn't even as if,' she went on playfully,' I spend much time there anymore. I must be in your flat nearly as much as I am there.'

'If you really think you can stand sharing with me with nowhere to go to get away,' Paul said doubtfully, his heart racing with excitement at the idea that Gemma had actually taken the initiative to propose something that he had imagined he would have to wait months – perhaps even years – for. And you don't think it's too soon – after Robert, I mean? I wouldn't like you to feel I'm pushing you into something you're not ready for.'

'Oh Paul! I wish you could forget Robert – I almost have. He was just this guy who came into my life for a few months and then ... well he just got out of it again, didn't he? It seemed important at the time, but looking back ...'

'And what about me?' Paul asked. He often thought about the ease with which Gemma appeared to have come to terms with the loss of her previous boyfriend and was torn between relief that it did not appear to cast any sort of shadow over their current relationship and anxiety that this could be a sign that she was incapable of long-term commitment. 'Will you look back in a few years and say that our relationship seemed important at the time, but not anymore?'

Gemma smiled and put her arms round him hugging him tight and kissing him on his neck. She murmured in his ear.

'I think you're different. Haven't you already waited sixteen years for me?'

'Is it that long?'

'Mm-mm. In fact, it's coming up to seventeen years since we first met. I remember it was Saturday, February the third when the social worker brought you into Willowbank and introduced you to everyone.'

'You've got a good memory for dates,' Paul remarked. 'All I remember is that it must have been winter time because it was freezing cold in that room that I had to share with Stuart Bottinger when I first arrived. And I suppose it was after Christmas because it was over-indulgence during the festive period that finally convinced Mum to try going for rehab.'

'I kept a diary,' Gemma explained. 'I'll show you sometime, if you like. You can read what my first impressions of you were! We ought to celebrate our anniversary. Tell you what: how about I move in this coming Saturday and then you can cook us one of your specials on Monday, which is the actual day?'

'OK,' Paul answered, unable to think of anything to say that would be suitable for such a momentous occasion as this. Suddenly dreams that he had hardly dared to imagine seemed to be coming true without him even having to do anything to make them happen. 'Yes,' he went on, afraid that Gemma might interpret his silence as indicating reluctance on his part to go along with her proposal, 'I'll think of something that will make it a meal to remember. And now we'd better start thinking about how we're going to fit all your things into this flat.'

This last problem turned out to be much smaller than Paul had imagined. Gemma, it seemed, had accumulated very few possessions during her thirty-one years – or else most of them had been discarded along the way as she moved from home to Care to a sequence of rented flats and finally into the accommodation that she had shared with Robert White for a period of some two years. Apart from her clothes, most of which fitted easily into the large wardrobe in Paul's bedroom, alongside his spare suit and half a dozen shirts, she brought only a small box of personal effects. Paul watched as she stowed everything away tidily in cupboards and drawers. He wondered how anyone could travel so light through life, and compared Gemma's apparent unconcern for material possessions with his own need to create worlds for himself to be master of and his reluctance ever to throw away something that might provide a link back to a past that could never be revisited.

After that, their life together settled down to a comfortable routine. Paul wondered how he had ever been satisfied with his old solitary existence and felt more contented with life than he could remember ever having been before. Peter noticed the difference in the way he approached his work. Although he was now always eager to head for home at the end of his shift, he had a new energy and enthusiasm that drove him to succeed where others had failed. He was now the most valuable member of Peter's team and Peter regretfully – because he did not wish to lose him – wondered whether he ought to encourage him to start working towards promotion to inspector rank.

Shortly after Gemma moved in with Paul, the inquest into Robert White's death was reconvened. His parents flew in from Australia, despite having been told that it was likely to be a brief affair, in view of the police having concluded that there was no suspicion of foul play. Gemma at first decided not to attend, but Paul persuaded her that she ought to do so.

'You may regret it if you don't,' he argued, 'and Robert's parents are bound to assume you don't care about him.'

'I don't think I do, anymore,' Gemma murmured, 'but I suppose you're right. I wouldn't like people to say I wasn't upset that he died. It's just that it seems like a long time ago now. It's a pity to have to rake it all up again.'

'I'm afraid that's how the court system works,' Paul told her. 'We often feel the same about having to give evidence in a trial months after an investigation is over. Everything just takes a long time, because we have to be sure that all the evidence has been collected before things go to court.'

Gemma expressed the hope that they would be able to attend the inquest together, but Paul explained that he would be giving evidence as part of the police team and so it would not be appropriate for them to be seen as a couple. He also thought, but did not say, that it would not benefit either the Whites' opinion of Gemma or their peace of mind, for them to observe at first hand that their son's girlfriend had so soon switched her affections to another man.

So that Gemma would not need to repeat her lonely experience at the first hearing, Paul persuaded Bernie to accompany her to the full inquest. When he and Peter arrived to represent the police, he noticed that Mr and Mrs White were sitting in the company of Angela Johns. Clearly, Peter had adopted a similar approach in respect of providing support for the friends and relatives of the deceased. A young couple were sitting alongside them. Paul deduced, based on her resemblance to Samantha White, that the woman was Robert's sister, Marian. She and her husband sat together holding hands and looking round anxiously at the unfamiliar surroundings. By contrast, her parents appeared very calm and collected, sitting impassively and staring straight ahead as if determined not to make eye contact with anyone – perhaps particularly wanting to avoid giving any recognition to Gemma, who was sitting some distance away on the other side of the court and who appeared to be watching the White family closely.

The inquest was over surprisingly quickly. The coroner had clearly done his homework and kept the proceedings moving briskly. Both Peter and Paul gave brief evidence about the investigation into the death and this was followed by an appearance by Mike Carson, who confirmed that death had been by drowning and that the other injuries were consistent with having been caused by impact with the stonework of the bridge as Robert White fell into the river. Written evidence from the psychiatrist who had treated him as a child and expert testimony from a clinical psychologist united to present a picture of a young man who in all probability had suffered a recurrence of serious clinical depression, which had remained undiagnosed and hence untreated and had led to his deciding to take his own life. In the absence of any contrary evidence, and with the note that Robert had written to Gemma pointing in the same direction, a verdict of suicide was inevitable and swift.

CHAPTER 29

It must have been during the second half of March that Peter began to be uneasy about Paul. It had begun with the telephone calls. At first, it seemed touching that Gemma felt the need to ring Paul during her lunch break every day but, after a while, the calls became more frequent and Peter got the impression that Gemma was checking up on Paul, as if she did not trust him out of her sight. He could see that Paul was uncomfortable about the interruptions to his work and yet was not able to tell Gemma forcefully that she must stop.

Peter began to be conscious that, towards the end of each shift, Paul was clock-watching. Where previously he had been eagerly looking forward to returning to the arms of his truelove, now Peter got the impression that it was more a matter of being anxious not to annoy or upset her by being late. When Gemma's own working pattern allowed, she would often be outside the police station at the end of Paul's shift, waiting for him to emerge, and increasingly often, she would accompany him to the door when he arrived in the morning. It reminded Peter of some of the cases of stalking which he had known over the years, although it was more typically women who suffered at the hands of jealous and untrusting husbands and boyfriends.

He voiced his concerns to Angie one evening as they lay in bed together.

'What really bothers me,' he told her, 'is that it seems to be following exactly the same pattern that Robert White's colleagues at the university described about her relationship with him. They said that at first they thought she was good for him: helping him to get a better work-life balance, giving him something to go home for in the evenings, taking him out of himself. But then, later on, things started to change.'

'You're not suggesting she's likely to drive Paul to suicide are you?' Angie asked in tones of deep scepticism. 'He doesn't sound the type to me.'

'No, I didn't really mean that – although I don't think you can actually tell who might be getting near to the edge because people who are thinking of suicide bottle it all up and hide their feelings – I was more worried that she's expecting him to put her first, ahead of everything else and she's preventing him having any life apart from with her.'

'Isn't that just what people are like when they're in love? I can remember you being put out when I went for a night out with the girls from the ward instead of going to the pictures with you. That was before we were married of course. Once I'd got your ring on my finger I guess you decided you could relax a bit!'

'I know, but I let you go, didn't I? And I didn't make you pay for it afterwards by harping on about it all the time. And I'm sure I never forced you to let other people down just so as I could have you for myself,' Peter went on, becoming more vehement as he recounted the incident which had sparked off his resentment towards Gemma. 'There was this model railway exhibition on at the United Reformed Church in Headington last week. Paul promised Lucy he'd take her. Lucy used to love watching that layout he had set up in their attic, so she was really looking forward to it. Then, at the last minute, he rang Bernie to say he was too busy and he wouldn't be able to make it. Of course, Bernie assumed I'd pulled him in for some overtime and she wasn't exactly pleased with me; but that's not the worst. Lucy was so disappointed that Bernie took her to the exhibition herself – after all, it's not far from where they live – and what do you think? Paul was there with Gemma! Now, I don't have a problem with Gemma wanting to go with him, but why couldn't the two of them have taken Lucy – after he'd promised her he would?'

'Ah!' Angie said knowingly, 'now I see what's bugging you. You can't bear anyone to stand up your number one favourite goddaughter!'

'Don't you think it's important not to let people down?' Peter demanded, slightly put out that Angie did not appear to be viewing the offence with the gravity that it deserved. 'And Lucy's not three yet; she doesn't understand.'

'I agree that he ought to at least have been more honest about it,' Angie conceded calmly, 'but you can't blame Gemma for wanting her boyfriend to herself on their day off instead of spending the afternoon looking after someone else's toddler.'

'Not for wanting it, maybe, but she ought to know better than to force Paul to let Lucy down. Paul felt really bad about it – I could tell – but he still couldn't get up the courage to say "no" to Gemma.'

'It's not surprising he felt bad if he had his boss cross-examining him,' Angie observed mildly. 'How did you find out about it anyway? Bernie never said anything to me.'

'Paul told me himself. I merely asked him whether he and Lucy had had a good time – being the friendly, concerned commanding officer taking an interest in his subordinate – and he coloured up like a beetroot and told me all about it. He assumed Bernie had complained about his behaviour – which she would have had every right to do,' Peter added decidedly. 'He ought to know better; he does know better. It's just this Gemma getting at him, because she can't bear to let him go even for a moment. And I can't help thinking that it was probably the same with her last boyfriend too. I wish Paul would get out before he gets hurt.'

'Oh Peter!' Angie sighed. 'He's a grown man. You've got to let him make his own decisions. You're not his dad, you know. He's got his own parents to worry about that sort of thing.'

'Some parents! I've never met his dad but if his mother's anything to go by, he'd be a darned sight better off without them. I'll never get over the gall of the woman descending on him like that and insisting on being put up for the night and then absconding with a whole lot of irreplaceable heirlooms stolen from her host. I mean, I ask you!'

'Our Bernie's arranged to sell that necklace,' Angie said, hoping to divert the conversation away from Peter's over-anxiety about his sergeant's welfare. 'Did she tell you? She got it valued and it came out at over two hundred K, so she decided that, heirloom or no heirloom, she couldn't keep it in the house any longer. She's going to put the money away for Lucy to use as a deposit on a house or whatever when she grows up.'

'Never mind a deposit!' Peter exclaimed. 'That necklace must be worth nearly as much as our whole house.'

'That was my immediate reaction too,' Angie confessed. 'Bernie was ever so embarrassed about it. I don't think it had occurred to her that she would ever come into contact with people who owned that sort of thing. In a funny sort of way, I think it's driven a wedge between her and Richard, which doesn't make any sense but I can sort of see how she feels. His family must have been very well-to-do at one time.'

'Knowing Our Bernie, I'm surprised she doesn't feel obliged to give the money away,' Peter observed.

'I think she would if it wasn't that she feels obliged to respect the fact that it belonged to Richard and she doesn't feel entitled to deprive Lucy of anything that her father might have wanted her to have.'

'If he hadn't so carelessly got himself killed six months before she was born,' Peter said ruefully. 'If there's one thing in the whole of my life that I'd like to change it would be not getting to that crime scene before Richard took it into his head to chase our suspect across the roof.'

'I know,' Angie said soothingly, putting her arm around him and pushing him back on to the pillows so that she could kiss him on the lips. She was glad to have steered Peter back on to a well-trodden path and away from his preoccupation with his sergeant's well-being. 'We've been through that any number of times and you know perfectly well that there was no way you could have done anything different. Stuff happens and we just have to get on with it, don't we?'

'Mmm,' Peter murmured, hugging his wife tight and returning her kiss. 'Still,' he added, 'I've good mind to have a look at the files on Gemma Markham's parents' fatal accidents – just in case...'

CHAPTER 30

The following week Paul was on leave. He and Gemma were going away together to celebrate her thirty-second birthday. They were taking a package holiday to the Canary Islands, something that Paul only very vaguely remembered having done with his parents when he was very small, before his mother's drinking had destroyed all semblance to a normal family life. Gemma had been abroad with girlfriends a few times, but to the Mediterranean, so this would be new for her too. They both saw it as marking a new era in their ongoing relationship.

Peter took advantage of Paul's absence to search in the archive for the files on Gemma's parents' deaths, which he pored over during his lunch breaks, unsure whether he was hoping to find evidence that Gemma was somehow to blame or reassurance that she was definitely innocent.

It seemed clear that Roger Markham, Gemma's father, had been killed in a freak farming accident. The tractor that he had been driving had overturned as he manoeuvred it around a steep field, which he was ploughing with a view to planting winter wheat. He had ended up underneath the vehicle and was already crushed to death by the time his assistant, Adam West, and his wife, Patricia, were able to haul it off him. Six-year-old Gemma had been at school when the accident happened. There were no suggestions at all that there had been any foul play. The inquest had recorded a verdict of misadventure with some recommendations on ways of increasing safety around the use of tractors on steep gradients.

Peter turned to the second file. The record of the investigation into Patricia Markham's death was bulkier and Peter soon discovered that the possibility that it might not have been an accident had been considered in some detail. He looked for the name of the investigating officer: DI Charles Farrell. He was retired now, but Peter remembered him well. He had been almost exactly contemporary with Richard Paige, Bernie's husband, but had gained promotion more slowly, leaving the force as a Detective Chief Inspector the year Lucy was born. He was still living in the Oxford area and Peter was confident that he would be pleased to receive a visit to talk over old times. He made a mental note to ring and make an appointment to call round.

The pathologist's report gave the cause of death as a blow to the head following a fall down the stone steps of the cellar in the old farmhouse where Patricia and Gemma Markham were living. More interestingly, it also detailed a number of other injuries, which suggested that it was a lot more complicated than a simple fall to her death. Her right arm was not only broken but also swollen and twisted out of shape, as if she had tried to use it after the bone had been fractured. Torn fingernails and bloodied fingertips on her left hand suggested that she had scraped at some hard surface with her bare hands. Corresponding traces of blood on the inside of the cellar door indicated that she had found herself trapped inside and had injured her fingers in an effort to get out. This was also borne out by the bruising to her left hand where she had apparently hammered on the door in an attempt to attract attention.

Her collarbone and left wrist were broken: both things which the pathologist indicated probably happened during a second fall, since they would have made it extremely painful – and perhaps impossible – to scrape and bang at the door with sufficient force to rip the flesh of her fingers and tear her nails. The report concluded that, in the pathologist's opinion, the most likely explanation for Mrs Markham's injuries was that she had fallen twice: the first time breaking her right arm and then, after climbing back up the steps and attempting unsuccessfully to open the cellar door from the inside, a second time, breaking her wrist and collar bone and hitting her head. The head injury caused bleeding into the brain, which was the cause of death. The time of death was some time in the afternoon, probably between one and four.

Next, Peter read the statement that Gemma had given when she was interviewed by DI Farrell in the company of a young WPC and a Beverley Holmes, who was the local vicar's wife and the person to whom Gemma had turned when she was unable to find her mother on her return home from school. According to Gemma, she had left home as usual at about ten to eight in the morning and walked to the end of the farm track, where she picked up the school bus. When she left, her mother was in the kitchen, standing near the cellar door, which was open because she had just been down to collect a jar of chutney. (There was a note alongside the transcript of the interview, which said that a smashed jar of tomato chutney had been found near the foot of the cellar steps.)

When Gemma returned from school, sometime between four and half past, she could not find her mother. She called out and looked in the living rooms and the bedrooms. Then she went outside and looked for her in the henhouse and the barn and finally went down to the field where Adam West was supervising the cutting of silage. Adam called out to her, but she ignored him and set off across the fields to the vicarage. When asked why she did not stay to talk to West, she said that she did not like him and did not trust him to tell her where her mother was. She said that she went to the vicarage because she knew that her mother sometimes went there to talk to Mrs Holmes when she felt depressed about her husband's death. Had she seemed depressed, then, when Gemma left that morning? No – not particularly, but often it came on quite unexpectedly, if she got a letter addressed to her husband, for instance.

Beverley Holmes came back with Gemma and they searched the house for Patricia Markham without success. It was not until it started to get dark and the vicar's wife noticed light shining under the cellar door that they finally went down and found Gemma's mother lying at the foot of the flight of stone steps. Both Gemma and Beverley confirmed that the door was closed but unlocked. The key was in the lock on the outside of the door.

Peter turned over the papers in the file and came upon another statement. This was from Adam West. He confirmed that he had managed the farm, with Patricia Markham, since her husband's death and that he and she had planned to get married. He had been busy that day supervising the silage contractors and had not seen Pat since early in the morning, when he had agreed with her the work schedule for the day. It was early summer and he was taking advantage of the long days to get work done on the farm. He admitted to having come into the kitchen at lunchtime hoping to see her, but she had not been there. He assumed that she had gone over to the churchyard to visit her husband's grave, which was something she did most days, always choosing a time when Gemma was not around.

Peter sat and thought about this for a while. This was the same Adam West who had been present when Gemma's father had had his fatal accident. Was there any possibility that he was responsible for both deaths? Could he have killed Roger Markham in order to marry Patricia and then killed Patricia – why? In order to inherit the farm? But surely, he would have needed to have waited until they were married – unless she had already made a will in his favour in advance of the wedding? Hadn't Paul said something about Gemma suspecting West of being responsible for her mother's death?

He filed all these thoughts away in his mind and resolved to put them to Charles Farrell when they met.

CHAPTER 31

Charles Farrell and his wife, Rosemary, lived in a large semi-detached house in north Oxford. They had evidently been looking out for Peter's arrival, since they were both standing on the doorstep when he turned from carefully fastening the gate closed and started up the path towards the front door. Rosemary greeted him warmly and ushered him through the sitting room at the back of the house and into a conservatory, which was bright with multi-coloured flowers of many different kinds. She was small and energetic with medium-length grey hair held back by a wide band of blue and white material, which somehow made Peter think of pirates. She gestured towards four chairs grouped around a small table in amongst the foliage.

'Sit down both of you and I'll make a pot of tea – or would you prefer coffee?' she asked briskly.

'Tea would be very nice,' Peter assured her, choosing the seat furthest from the luxuriant plant growth that threatened to engulf unwary visitors.

"This is all Rosie's doing,' Charles told Peter, seeing him looking around at the abundant flora. 'She's got green fingers and no mistake! I don't even know the names of half the things she's got here. The only problem is trying to keep enough space free for us to sit. I often feel as if I need a machete to help me hack my way through the jungle to reach the back door!'

'It's very impressive,' Peter said. 'I feel as if I've been

transported to Kew gardens!'

It was not long before Rosemary Farrell returned with a tray, which she put down on the table in front of them.

'I'll leave you two boys to yourselves now,' she said. 'I know you won't want me in the way while you reminisce. There's plenty of tea in the pot and I've allowed three scones each for starters. If you run short of supplies, just give me a shout.'

'Thank you Mrs Farrell,' Peter said politely,' that looks like a magnificent spread. Are the scones home-made?'

'They are indeed, but it's Charles you've got to thank for them – and for the strawberry jam too,' Rosemary replied proudly. 'He's the cook in this family – and a very good one too.'

'But you grew the strawberries,' her husband protested, blushing at her praise of his culinary skills, 'so I reckon we both have to take responsibility for the jam.'

'It looks very good to me anyway,' Peter said diplomatically, helping himself to a scone and a generous portion of jam. 'If this is what retirement is like, I'm looking forward to it!'

'So, what can I do for you?' Charles asked when his wife had left them to their téte-à-téte.

'I was hoping you might be able to tell me more about a case you were involved in back in eighty-five: the death of a Mrs Patricia Markham on a farm out on Otmoor. Do you remember it?'

'I do indeed! Nasty business. As I recall, she fell down the cellar steps and injured herself, but that didn't actually kill her and then she climbed back up but, for some reason, she couldn't get out. I remember the pathologist's report was quite gruesome: he reckoned she may have been scrabbling at the door for several hours before she lost her footing again and fell to her death. They suppressed that at the inquest for the sake of the daughter.'

'Gemma?'

'Yes – that was the name. She was only a teenager and

she'd already lost her father in a farming accident some years previously, so everyone was keen to shield her from the worst.'

'It was Gemma I wanted to ask you about.'

Peter recounted the story of Robert White's death and then went on to explain about her new relationship with Paul.

'I'm probably just being paranoid,' he concluded, 'but now that I've seen the way she's trying to control Paul, I can't help wondering whether there's any chance she might have been responsible for Robert White's death – either by driving him to suicide or even …' he paused, uncertain whether to go on to voice his worst fears.

'Or even pushing him into the river herself?' Charles finished for him. 'Now it's funny you should say that, because I have to admit that I always did have my doubts about young Gemma. I kept them to myself because she was only fourteen and I didn't have any proof and it would have been a dreadful thing to ruin her whole life if I was wrong about it, but I must say I was always very uneasy about her story that the cellar door was unlocked when she got home that afternoon. It seemed so much more likely that her mother couldn't get out because someone had locked her in. And then there was her attitude to Adam West …'

'Her mother's lover?'

'That's right. But he was much more than that. Pat Markham and he were planning to get married – and Gemma didn't like the idea one bit! If he'd been the one taking a tumble down the cellar steps, I'd have been quite sure Gemma was responsible. She hated him with a passion.'

'Are you suggesting that she could have deliberately killed her mother to stop her marrying West? "If I can't have her then nobody's going to!" sort of thing?'

'Possibly,' Charles answered cautiously, 'or maybe they argued about it and Gemma pushed her mother down the cellar accidentally and then panicked and locked the door and went to school and tried to pretend nothing had happened.'

'But if the door was locked and that was why Gemma's mother couldn't get out then someone must have unlocked it again before the vicar's wife came along and found the body,' Peter objected.

'Exactly!' Charles said. 'And who else could that have been except Gemma?'

'What about Adam West? He admitted to having come into the kitchen during the day.'

'But the only fingerprints on the cellar door – and more importantly on the key to the cellar door – were Gemma's and Pat Markham's,' Charles pointed out. 'West's fingerprints were all over the rest of the house, mind you …'

'I saw,' Peter agreed, remembering the forensic report, which he had read carefully, 'including in Mrs Markham's bedroom.'

'But not in Gemma's room or even on the outside of her door,' Charles said firmly.

'So you'd rule out any possibility that Gemma's antagonism towards West was because he'd tried any funny business with her?' Peter asked.

'Absolutely I would! I got to know the community over there pretty well during the course of the investigation and one thing that everyone agreed on was that Adam West was a really nice chap. There wasn't a single person who would say a word against him.'

'Apart from Gemma,' Peter said drily. 'Maybe she saw a side of him nobody else did. I was wondering whether Mrs Markham could have made a will in his favour, in advance of the wedding, and he could've killed her in order to inherit.'

'Inherit what?' Charles asked scornfully. 'The Markham's didn't have two beans to rub together. They were tenant farmers with practically no capital of their own. After Roger's death, his wife continued to run the farm with the help of Adam West, and everyone agrees that if it hadn't been for him it would have gone under within a year. After she died, the landlord decided to merge the farm with one of his others to make a bigger holding and West was out of a job. So he had no motive at all to kill her.'

'But could he have assumed that he would be able to take over the farm?' Peter persisted, reluctant to give up on his pet theory.

'No. By all accounts, the landowner had been putting pressure on Pat Markham for years to give up the lease; there was no way he was going to allow West to stay on. Besides,' Charles added, 'he had a cast iron alibi for the whole day. The silage contractors swore blind that he'd never been out of their sight for more than a couple of minutes all day – including when he called in to see Pat Markham and she wasn't there. If you're looking for someone to blame, you're barking up the wrong tree trying to pin anything on Adam West. He left school at sixteen and went straight to work for Roger Markham – that was before he married Pat – and he stayed with them all the way through everything. He was pretty well running the place when Pat died.'

'So, do you buy the coroner's story that the door was unlocked all along and it was blind panic that prevented Patricia Markham finding her way out of the cellar?'

'Well, that was the outcome of the inquest, wasn't it?'

'That wasn't what I asked.'

'Look,' Charles said, staring directly into Peter's eyes, 'as far as I can see, the only alternative is that it was Gemma who unlocked the door – and by implication also Gemma who locked it in the first place. At first, I did try to take things further, but I got no support to put any resources into investigating what was seen as nothing but another tragic accident. And when I thought about it a bit more, I reckoned that, even if the kid was responsible, there was nothing to be gained by dragging her through the courts and probably not being able to make a conviction stick in the end. So I decided to let sleeping dogs lie and not rock the boat – to mix my metaphors magnificently. And you've got to remember that she was only fourteen.'

'But she's thirty-two now – or will be tomorrow – and she may have already been responsible, one way or another, for the death of one young man. And now she's got her claws into my sergeant, who deserves someone a whole lot better than the sort of young woman who locks her own mother in a cellar and leaves her to die.'

'I see,' Charles said slowly, watching Peter's face keenly. 'So what are you proposing to do about it?'

'I don't know,' Peter sighed. 'I wish I could find someone who really knows what makes Gemma tick. I don't want to believe that she's a killer, but I want to know what she's capable of and whether her relationship with Paul is likely to … to … oh I don't know … I just don't like the way she's changing him.'

'You never could maintain your objectivity, could you, Peter,' Charles observed.

'And you, as I remember, always used to say that as soon as you stopped feeling passionately about the people that we deal with and it all becomes just a job, you might as well give up policing,' Peter countered.

'I was talking about members of the public, not about trying to run our colleagues' lives for them.'

'I don't see how you can care about some people and not about the ones you work with day by day.'

Charles nodded and smiled, lapsing into silence as he addressed Peter's problem in his mind.

'I think you ought to speak to Beverley Holmes,' he said at last, after considering for a few moments. 'She knew Gemma better than anyone else, I think, and she knew her mother too. She's also very level-headed and not easily taken in. I believe she and her husband are still there in the parish. The last I heard he had been made Rural Dean, which I gather is one of those posts that come with no money, very little prestige and a vast amount of additional work. Anyway, as I said, call in at the vicarage and see what Beverley can tell you. If anyone knows what Gemma Markham's state of mind was, she will.'

CHAPTER 32

The vicarage of St Oswald's church was an old rambling house, set in large gardens, which were laid down largely to lawn and shrubs. Peter, having parked in the car park in front of the church, walked up the long drive towards the front door, wondering what to expect when he met Mrs Holmes and preparing in his mind how he would introduce the subject of Gemma Markham and her mother's death. He rang the bell and waited.

After a few moments, the door opened to reveal a tall, willowy woman with white hair hanging down her back in a long, tapering plait that reached her waist. She was wearing a long floral print skirt with bare legs and open-toed sandals. She smiled as she saw Peter.

'Detective Inspector Johns, I presume?'

'That's right,' Peter confirmed. 'It's good of you to see me.'

'Come in and tell me what this is all about,' Beverley Holmes urged. 'I found your telephone call quite intriguing. I hadn't realised that Gemma was involved in the suicide of that young man in Oxford last year. We quite lost touch with her after she was taken into care. The poor girl seems to have had her whole life dogged by tragedy. How is she now, do you know?'

'I'm not sure,' Peter said, following her inside and through a maze of dark passageways to a light, airy room furnished with an array of easy chairs in a variety of styles and colours. 'That's why I wanted to speak to you really. I'm afraid that her experiences may have left her with some sort of mental health issues, which make it difficult for her to have a normal relationship.'

'I see,' Beverley nodded, 'and you think that may have had a bearing on her boyfriend's suicide? Sit down – no, not there! We only use that chair when we have big meetings and there aren't enough to go round; the springs are coming through and it's very uncomfortable. Come over by the window; those two chairs are really quite bearable and new, by our standards, which means only in their second decade.'

Peter obediently took a seat next to the large window and gazed out across the lawn towards a rather dilapidated summerhouse, partially hidden by rhododendron bushes. He remained silent for a minute, gathering his thoughts. He had decided against telling Beverley about his suspicion that Gemma could have caused her mother's death, and to concentrate on trying to establish the girl's state of mind before and immediately after that event.

'She's got a new boyfriend now,' he went on, 'and it's someone I really wouldn't want to see getting hurt …'

'And you'd like to know whether he's in danger of going the same way as the last one,' Beverley finished for him. 'I understand completely, but I'm not sure how much I can do to help. It's a long time since I knew Gemma.'

'I know,' Peter said apologetically, 'but I think any problems she has are deep-rooted and go back to her childhood – to her father's death. I gather you knew the family as far back as that?'

'We did indeed. We know all the farming families. They're very loyal to the church: not very good at attending on a Sunday, because they're always so busy, but very loyal nonetheless. Gemma's father was a lovely man. Gemma and Pat both worshipped him. Pat had a breakdown after he died. If it hadn't been for Adam West, I'm quite sure she would have lost the farm. She just couldn't cope on her own. She married very young, you see, and depended completely on her husband to manage everything.'

'And how did that affect Gemma?' Peter asked. 'I mean: how did she cope with no father and a mother in a state of mental collapse?'

'On the face of it, not bad, but underneath there was a lot of anger.'

'Anger? With whom?' Peter asked, feeling rather puzzled. Did Gemma perhaps believe that her father's death was not, after all, an accident?

'With her father. You see, Pat Markham – foolishly in my opinion – didn't explain to her properly that he was dead. She told Gemma that her dad had gone to heaven. Well, she was only six and she took it completely literally. As far as she was concerned, he had gone off and left her in the lurch. It was completely absurd,' Beverley continued scornfully. 'I mean to say: the child had been brought up on a farm, for goodness sake! She understood about chickens being killed by foxes and pigs being sent off to be turned into bacon. But her mother thought she was being kind, shielding her from the truth; when in fact all it did was prevent her from being able to start the grieving process until much, much later.'

'So, do you think she went through life after that with a subconscious feeling that she couldn't trust anyone to stick by her?' Peter asked excitedly. 'That's just the feeling I've got about her relationship with Robert White and now with Paul. It's as if she doesn't dare let him out of her sight in case he runs off and leaves her.'

'You could well be right,' Beverley agreed. 'Certainly that sort of idea was probably at the bottom of her attitude towards Pat's plans to marry poor Adam West. I'm convinced that Gemma saw him as some sort of threat to her relationship with her mother and it may well be that it all stemmed from her insecurity after her father died. You know, she didn't even know he was buried in the churchyard until after Pat died and we opened up the grave for her to be buried with him? That was how I discovered that she'd never realised that he was actually dead.'

'Do you mean that, at the age of fourteen, she still imagined that he was alive somewhere?' Peter asked in astonishment.

'I almost think she did. Nobody ever talked about it to her, you see; so I suppose she kept that silly childish picture in her mind of him having run away somewhere wonderful and not taken her with him.'

'You said Gemma was angry with her father for leaving her; was she angry with her mother too?'

'At the thought that she was going to marry again? Yes, I think that's exactly how she felt: angry with her mother and with poor Adam too.'

'Angry enough to…?'

'To push her down the cellar steps and shut the door on her? I don't know. She did have quite a temper, but I don't really think she'd deliberately try to kill her own mother.'

'But could it have been an accident? I mean could she have lashed out and knocked her down without meaning to?'

'That I can't say. She told a very convincing story about leaving her mother alive and well in the kitchen when she went to school, and I'd be loath to accuse her of lying about that.'

Beverley paused and looked pensive. Peter judged that this was probably the first time she had considered this possibility.

'Look,' she went on eventually, 'if you really want to get inside Gemma Markham's head, the person you need to speak to is the psychologist who gave her counselling. If you give me a minute, I think I'll be able to hunt out her contact details. She does a lot of work with the Agricultural Chaplaincy – helping farming children. Did you know that the suicide rate among farmers is twice the national average? And of course the children are always the ones who suffer most.'

She got up and started rummaging in an overfull drawer in the large sideboard that stood along one wall of the room. Just as she pulled out a small black notebook with a look of triumph on her face, the doorbell rang.

'That'll be Adam,' she said, hastily stuffing papers back into the drawer and forcing it closed. 'I'll just let him in – won't be a tick!'

She left the room, returning a few minutes later, accompanied by a man in his fifties with red hair just starting to turn grey at the temples and a rather red face. He held out a large hand towards Peter as Beverley introduced them. Peter immediately warmed towards him, partly through the strange kinship felt among redheads, but mainly because the man exuded an air of openness and candour, an almost childlike innocence, which invited confidence.

'As I told you, Adam, Inspector Johns is investigating a suicide and it seems your Gemma is mixed up in it.'

'You've met Gemma?' Adam West asked eagerly. 'How is she?'

'She's well, as far as I can tell,' Peter answered, taken aback firstly by the fact that Beverley had seen fit to invite Adam West to join them without having told him and secondly by West's apparently genuine concern for the girl whom he had not seen for more than fifteen years. 'She's away in Tenerife at the moment celebrating her birthday with her latest boyfriend.'

'Not the one who committed suicide,' Beverley put in unnecessarily. 'This is a new one – a friend of the inspector's. I asked Adam to come,' she explained, turning to Peter, 'so that you could see for yourself what a decent chap he is – just in case you thought he was to blame for Pat's untimely demise.'

'I do blame myself,' Adam said earnestly. 'If I'd

thought to look in the cellar when I popped in at lunchtime we might have found her in time. The pathologist said she was probably still alive then.'

'Nonsense!' Beverley said briskly, and Peter got the impression that this was an argument that she had had with Adam many times previously. 'There was no way you could have known she was down there.'

She turned to Peter again and held out the notebook that she had extracted from the sideboard drawer.

'Here's that name and address I was telling you about. Her name's Rhoda Tebay. Gemma started having sessions with her when she was eight or nine and carried on until after she was taken into care. If anyone knows what goes on in her mind it'll be Rhoda.'

'You don't think Gemma drove the lad to kill himself do you?' Adam asked sharply.

'I don't know what to think,' Peter replied. 'That's what I'm trying to find out. At least,' he continued cautiously, disarmed by Adam's manner but still uncertain how much to reveal of his own thoughts, 'what I'm really interested in is whether or not she's any sort of danger to her current boyfriend. We can't do much about what happened in the past, but we might be able to stop it happening again.'

'Gemma could be difficult,' Adam said seriously, 'but you've got to remember what she'd been through. I wish she could have accepted me as her dad, but I can't blame her for thinking I was coming between her and her mum. If she made things hard for her boyfriend, it wasn't her fault; it's just how she was. It's just unfortunate if he couldn't cope.'

'I see,' Peter said slowly. 'And what advice would you have for any other young man who fell for her? Should he stick with it or get out before she becomes too "difficult" for him to handle?'

Adam did not answer, so Peter asked another question.

'Mrs Holmes has been telling me that Gemma saw her father's death as some sort of desertion and that made her anxious that her mother might desert her too. Is that how you see the situation just before Mrs Markham died? Is that why Gemma didn't want you to marry her mother?'

'I don't know; I really don't know,' Adam sighed. 'I've been over and over it in my mind, but I can't make sense of it. Gemma and I always got on very well. I'd been with the family since before she was born and I always thought she looked on me as a sort of uncle. But it all changed as soon as she got the idea that Pat and I might have something going between us. You're probably right when you say that she was afraid I was going to take her mother away from her – which couldn't have been further from the truth. I wanted to be a father to her, just as much as I wanted to be a husband for Pat!'

He looked round at Peter and Beverley with the air of a confused child. Peter was convinced, just as Beverley had been sure that he would be, that whatever else might have happened to cause Pat Markham to fall to her death, Adam West was not to blame.

CHAPTER 33

As Peter drove home, he mused on the unfairness of life. Take Adam West for example: what had he got out of his loyal service to the Markhams over nearly twenty years, man and boy? Redundancy, it seemed, and then several years of casual farm jobs until he finally managed to secure the tenancy of a local authority smallholding, which Beverley Holmes had made clear to Peter was the bottom rung of the farming ladder and something that most people took on far earlier in their careers. He must be about the same age as Peter himself, but he had none of the things that Peter had: no wife or children, no secure job – just eking out an existence on a piece of land too small to provide an adequate living.

Then there was Roger Markham, dying from an accident that nobody could have anticipated, the victim of a moment's loss of concentration while driving his tractor. And his wife: married at eighteen, a mother at twenty-one and a widow at thirty-six. And then there was Gemma. It was hardly surprising if she went through life thinking that the world was against her and that she needed to grab whatever happiness she could and then hold on to it like grim death.

Paul, too, had been the victim of a cruel fate it seemed to Peter. What had he done to deserve that awful mother of his? Small wonder then that he should cling to Gemma who, it appeared, was one of very few people who had shown him kindness. Perhaps Peter ought to leave them to get on with making a life together and stop interfering in something that was none of his business. But what if Gemma's possessiveness was more than that; what if she really did drive people to suicide or worse?

Peter pictured in his mind the events of that fateful day in May nearly eighteen years previously. Adam and Pat are both up early, making the most of the long hours of daylight. When Gemma comes down to breakfast, there they are chatting in the kitchen. Adam goes off to get on with the day's work and Gemma confronts her mother. Peter remembered his own daughter, Hannah's, behaviour as a young teenager and he could well imagine the conversation.

'What's he doing here?'

'Nothing: he just came in to tell me about the silage contractors.'

'I suppose he's been here all night!'

'No. You know he never stays overnight.'

'You're *so* unfair! You wouldn't like it if I expected to have one of my boyfriends around at this time in the morning.'

'Oh Gemma! You know it's not like that. Adam just came in to check where they should start with the silage.'

'Not that what you think matters! You let him run the farm as if he owned it. If Dad was still here-'

'Yes, but he's not, is he? And we've got to learn to get on without him. And Adam is the person who makes that possible. Anyway, I can't stand here all day; I've got work to do. Have your breakfast while I go down and get a fresh jar of chutney out of the cellar. The men all like to have it on their sandwiches at lunchtime.'

So, down she goes, wondering all the time how she can persuade Gemma to accept her marriage to Adam. But when she gets back up to the top of the stairs, there's Gemma waiting for her, still keen to make her mother regret her decision to marry Adam.

'You mean,' she says menacingly, barring the way out of the cellar, '*Adam* likes your chutney. You do everything he says, don't you? It's so unfair!'

And she steps forward to look her mother closer in the eye and Pat Markham steps back instinctively and misses her footing and goes crashing down the stone steps into the cellar. Gemma stands stunned for a moment before following her part way down. In the dim light of the single bulb she can make out her mother's body lying motionless. Convinced that she has killed her, she panics and races back up into the kitchen and slams the door closed to shut out the horrible scene. Out of habit – or perhaps to deter other people from going down into the cellar – she turns the key in the lock before setting off for school, trying to act as if nothing had happened.

Down in the cellar, Pat regains consciousness and clambers up the stairs. It's hard going because of the pain in her right arm, but she manages to get to the top. She takes hold of the handle with her left hand and turns it, expecting the door to swing open easily. It seems to be jammed, so she pushes harder, but nothing happens. She bangs on the door as hard as she can and shouts out, hoping that someone will hear her and come to let her out. Still nothing. She can't work out what can be wrong. She scratches at the edge of the door, hoping somehow to force it away from the frame, thinking that it must have swollen and got stuck somehow. Eventually she slides down into a sitting position on the top step, exhausted after her exertions.

I few hours later, in comes Adam West, accompanied by one of the silage contractors. They all have a free run of the utility room adjoining the kitchen for washing and making cups of tea and so on. Adam pops his head round the door of the kitchen expecting to see Pat preparing her own lunch. When he sees she isn't there, he goes through to the door into the hall and calls out, but she doesn't answer and he concludes that she must have gone out.

Within two minutes or less, he's back in the utility room with the men.

Faint with pain from her broken arm and tired out after her efforts to attract attention, Pat is unaware of his presence in the kitchen and she doesn't hear him shouting out for her. Or perhaps by the time he comes in for his lunch she has already fallen again, striking her head on the stone steps as she does so. Whatever the exact sequence of events, by mid-afternoon she is lying unconscious at the bottom of the cellar steps with bleeding in her brain that is going to kill her within a few hours. Is she still alive when Gemma returns home from school? Who can tell? The pathology report suggests that it is possible, but time of death is always uncertain and that is all irrelevant now, because Gemma does not tell anyone that her mother is in the cellar and so she is not found for several more hours.

Could it be that Gemma had successfully blotted out from her memory the events of the morning? Or did she deliberately avoid suggesting the cellar as a possible place that her mother could be? She must have turned the key in the lock before going for help, which suggested some degree of calculation on her part.

Peter frowned to himself. That key was the key to the whole puzzle, he decided, and He had failed to ask the key question about it, which was: how was the cellar door normally left? Did the family keep it locked and with the key in the lock, or locked but with the key put away somewhere else, or unlocked, with or without the key in the lock? When Gemma locked the door after her mother's fall, was she simply restoring normality, or was it a positive decision to lock her in and lock other people out? Moreover, there was another question that nobody appeared to have asked: was the key in the lock when Adam West came in at lunchtime? He probably would not have noticed, but it was a question that ought to have been put to him.

Peter sighed. Despite all his efforts, he seemed to have

made very little progress. He still felt vaguely uneasy about Gemma's influence on Paul, but there was really nothing concrete to indicate that she was necessarily anything other than a victim of a sequence of tragic events. Even if Robert White's suicide was caused by her possessiveness, she could hardly be held completely to blame. After all, he had a history of depression that he had chosen not to tell her about, and her anxiety that he might leave her was understandable, given her previous experiences. Perhaps it was just an unfortunate pairing between two incompatible people.

And yet ... and yet ...

CHAPTER 34

When Paul returned from his holiday he appeared to be much happier than before and less anxious about his work interfering with his home-life. It seemed, too, that their time away together had helped Gemma to feel more secure and not any longer to need the reassurance of constantly checking up on where he was and what he was doing. After several weeks, during which the old keen-as-mustard always-anxious-to-please Paul seemed to have returned, Peter decided that he had been wrong to suspect Gemma of more than a natural clinginess as a result of having fallen in love. On the few occasions when he met her, she seemed like a perfectly ordinary young woman and he felt a pang of guilt at having suspected that she might have driven her previous boyfriend to take his own life. The piece of paper on which he had copied down her psychologist's telephone number lay unread in his wallet.

By the second half of April, however, as Peter prepared to celebrate his wife's birthday with a meal out, he was once again starting to have doubts about Gemma's influence on his sergeant. She had resumed the daily telephone calls during his working hours and seemed to manage to be around wherever his work happened to take him if she was not at work herself. Peter grumbled to Angie that he wondered if he ought to try to get her to join the force, she was obviously so good at trailing people! He noticed a change in Paul's demeanour too: he was clearly embarrassed by Gemma's constant attentions, but did not like – perhaps did not dare would be a better way of putting it – to ask her to desist.

As he finished a filing job (which Paul had failed to complete after receiving a call from Gemma on her mobile to say that she was waiting outside for him and hadn't his shift finished ten minutes ago?) preparatory to heading home for Angie's birthday celebration, Peter did his best to set aside his worries about Paul and to concentrate on giving Angie a good time.

Angie had booked a table for them at a restaurant that Peter had never been to before. It was popular with students, having the reputation for good food at cheaper than average prices. Angie had been recommended it by a colleague who told her that she could not do better for 'well-cooked food that hasn't been messed about'.

In true Oxford fashion, they decided to cycle to the restaurant. As they approached Folly Bridge, Peter called over his shoulder to his wife:

'Hey Angie! What was the name of the place again?'

'The Rabbit Hole,' she called back. 'It's just beyond the bridge, on the right. You can't miss it.'

They chained their bikes together outside the building and Peter held the door open for his wife to go in.

'I'd forgotten until now,' he remarked. 'This is where Gemma Markham and Robert White had their last meal together the night he killed himself.'

'Well just try and forget about it again,' Angie replied, pretending to be annoyed with him for bringing his work into the conversation, 'or you may find yourself having similar thoughts before the evening's out!'

Luckily, Trinity term did not begin until the following Sunday, so there were very few students in evidence and Peter and Angie were looking forward to a quiet meal. They were greeted as they entered by a softly spoken young man with an Australian accent who informed them that his name was Luke. He showed them to a table and handed them each a menu. In the easy way that she had with strangers, Angie fell into conversation with him and had soon extracted the following information: he was from Melbourne; he had been over in England since last July, working his way through a gap year before taking up his place as a medical student at the University of Adelaide; his parents were both doctors, as was his older sister; he admired the NHS very much and thought that nurses like Angie were wonderful people; he had planned to travel, but he'd met a girl in Oxford and decided to stay put and spend his whole year abroad working in the Rabbit Hole, which, he assured them, was a much more interesting job than people imagined.

Peter listened with amusement, wishing that he were as effective at persuading witnesses to be forthcoming about every detail of their lives. He wondered whether Luke had been working the night Robert White had visited the restaurant with Gemma. He was about to ask, when it occurred to him that he really ought to be putting all such thoughts aside and allowing his wife to enjoy her meal, free from discussions of dead bodies and police investigations. Still, it would have been interesting to know.

Over the difficult task of deciding which dessert to choose from the all-too-delicious-looking array of naughty-but-nice confections, Angie persuaded Luke to reveal that he was hoping to become a psychiatrist and to specialise in forensic psychiatry.

'Now that's a branch of medicine that my husband probably knows more about that I do,' Angie told him. 'He's a police officer.'

'Are you really?' Luke asked politely. 'That must be an interesting job. Do you get many mental cases in your work?'

'More than we'd like,' Peter admitted grimly, 'and we could certainly do with more psychiatrists and psychologists to help us deal with them – and more places in mental hospitals. We get criticised for keeping people with mental illnesses in police cells – and God help us if they injure themselves in any way while they're there – but very often there's nowhere else to send them to prevent them being a danger to themselves as well as other people.'

'It's only anecdotal,' Angie put in, 'but looking around there seems to be more mental illness being diagnosed these days than, say twenty years ago – especially depression.'

'I'd say that's got a lot to do with people being more willing to admit to it,' Peter said. 'Twenty years ago, for example, you'd never have got a police constable taking time off work for depression – and he'd have got short shrift from his sergeant if he tried. People were just expected to pull themselves together and get on with the job.'

'Do you think we've become more compassionate and understanding these days?' Luke asked with interest.

'I don't know. Maybe: but there are a lot of senior officers who go through the motions, because they have to, but underneath see it as a lot of nonsense. I think it's a difficult balance to get right. If you give people permission to suffer from "work-related stress" you open yourself up to all sorts of abuse of the system – and also to people who genuinely think they're ill when they just need to show a bit of old-fashioned backbone – but I think we lost a lot of good officers under the old regime. I've known a few who left the service rather than admit that they couldn't cope.'

'And more generally in society?' Luke asked. 'I mean, have you seen a reduction in crime as a result of more people with mental health problems being willing to seek treatment?'

'No, I wouldn't say so,' Peter said, shaking his head. 'What I'd really like to see is fewer suicide cases – particularly in young people – but if there has been a change it hasn't been noticeable to the copper on the ground picking up the pieces – literally sometimes!'

'Talking of suicide,' Luke said eagerly. 'You don't happen to have been involved in a case last autumn, were you – a drowning?'

'I may have been,' Peter answered cautiously. 'Why do you ask?'

'It was only that the victim ate here the night he died and he was an Australian – from Melbourne in fact – so I took an interest.'

'I was the investigating officer in charge of the case,' Peter admitted. 'I hope you don't think we got it wrong!' he added, trying to sound light-hearted, but suddenly uneasy at the thought that perhaps he ought to have interviewed the staff at the restaurant in order to get an independent view of Robert White's mood immediately before his death. It had not seemed necessary at the time, but this young man seemed so observant and sensible that he very much regretted having placed so much reliance on Gemma's statements about her boyfriend's state of mind.'

'Well, I'm hardly in a position to say that, am I?' Luke responded with a smile, 'but I must say I was surprised when I read the inquest verdict. I really would not have put him down as a suicide risk – not based on what I saw of him that night. But of course, you'll have had a lot more to go on than that.'

'So, how would you describe him that night?' Peter asked. 'Not depressed, evidently: was he happy? Looking forward to the future? Or what would you say?'

'No – not happy, but then he'd hardly be that, would he? He was more …relieved, I'd say: glad to have got an unpleasant job over with and to be able to move on.'

'What do you mean?' Peter asked in puzzlement.

'Well,' Luke looked at them both with an expression of surprise on his face, 'he was dumping his girlfriend, wasn't he? That's what the meal here was all about.'

'That wasn't what she told us,' Peter said, baldly.

'You'd better sit down,' Angie said, pulling out the empty chair next to hers. 'I can see this may take some time. Don't worry: we'll square it with your boss,' she added, noticing Luke's anxious expression.

Luke sat down and turned back to Peter.

'I try not to eavesdrop on people's private conversations,' began, 'but sometimes you just can't help hearing. He was definitely telling her it was all over, and she wasn't happy about it. He was finding it difficult, but I'm convinced he was feeling happier once it was over and done with. I was amazed at the thought that he went off afterwards and threw himself in the river. To be honest, if either of them was going to commit suicide, my money would have been on the girl.'

'Really?' Peter asked with interest. 'Tell me more: how exactly did she take his announcement?'

'At first she was angry. Then she burst into tears. Then, after a few minutes, she seemed to get a hold on herself and she stopped crying and looked, well, sort of ... resigned, I supposed. But underneath, I think she was still very upset.'

'Did they finish their meal?'

'Oh yes! She insisted on carrying on with a dessert and then coffee and liqueurs to follow.'

'According to her, it was coffee for him and a liqueur for her,' said Peter, remembering. 'She said she was afraid that coffee might keep her awake.'

'Yes: you're probably right about that,' Luke agreed, 'but the coffee didn't look like it was having much effect keeping him awake by the time they left. I suppose it must have been the wine they had with the meal, but he definitely looked the worse for wear by then. It was odd really,' he went on, as if thinking through something for the first time, 'I thought she was the one putting it away, but he was leaning on her as they went out.'

'That's very interesting,' Peter said, sitting up very straight and thinking fast. 'When you say he appeared "the worse for wear" do you mean he was drunk or could it have been more like the effect of a drug of some sort – a sedative perhaps?'

'Yes. Now you mention it, that's just what it seemed like. Why?'

'As I expect you'd be able to find out if you read the right newspaper reports, so I'm not giving away any secrets by telling you now, the pathologist found Rohypnol in his blood stream, which we assumed he must have taken as a sleeping tablet after he got home; but what you've just told me makes me wonder about that.'

'You mean, perhaps he'd already taken it before he left here?'

Peter nodded.

'Yes: that's exactly what I'm starting to think. Not that it makes any difference to the final outcome,' he went on hastily. 'It's just annoying that we may well not have got the exact sequence of events right. Now, I'm going to plump for sticky toffee pudding – what about you Angie?'

After the meal, Peter and Angie cycled home in silence. Peter was thinking hard about what Luke had told him and worrying that the young Australian waiter might well be clever enough to put two and two together and deduce firstly that Gemma had probably spiked Robert's coffee with Rohypnol and secondly that, with the drug already starting to take effect when they left the restaurant, it was unlikely that he was going to set out again for a walk after reaching home.

'The obvious answer,' Peter said to Angie, as they got ready for bed that night, 'is that Gemma somehow managed to heave him over the side of the bridge on their way back from the Rabbit Hole, while he was too fuddled by the drug to resist.'

'But she's only a tiny little thing!' Angie protested. 'You're not telling me she lifted a grown man up on to the side of Folly Bridge, even if he was too far gone to resist. Believe me – I know all about lifting bodies and there's no way she could have managed it.'

'That's not the big problem,' Peter argued. 'Provided he

was still awake enough to manage it, she could easily have persuaded him to climb up there himself. Maybe she threatened to throw herself off because she couldn't bear to carry on living without him, and he climbed up to try to get her down. No. The big difficulty I've got is the witness who says she heard them both arriving back at their flat together. And that means that they must have gone out again after that – which seems incredibly unlikely, given his state after taking the drug and the fact that he had no reason to want to go out for a second time in the pouring rain. It just doesn't add up.'

'Well, I suggest you sleep on it,' Angie said decisively. 'Maybe you'll think of another explanation if you come to it again in the morning. Maybe even,' she added hopefully, 'one that doesn't involve anyone shoving anyone into the river!'

CHAPTER 35

'Thank you for agreeing to see me,' Peter said as he took a seat in Rhoda Tebay's small, well-kept house in Woodstock.

'You realise that my professional relationship with Gemma Markham is completely confidential,' she said, acknowledging his thanks with a slight inclination of the head. 'So I'm not sure that I can be a great deal of help to you.'

She spoke softly, with just a trace of a Cumbrian accent betraying her northern roots. She had dark hair and brown eyes that watched Peter intently, as if trying to work out why he had taken the trouble to come to speak to her about a girl whom she had not seen for fifteen years and a case that had been closed a similar length of time ago.

'I know, but I need to understand her better, and you are the one person that I've managed to find who spent a lot of time with her and may have got an idea what makes her tick.'

'It was a long time ago. Anything I am able to tell you may well only be misleading,' Rhoda said gently.

'I know. I realise I'm grasping at straws rather,' Peter admitted, 'but the thing is, I have a nasty suspicion that she may have killed two people and that she may be a danger to a third person – someone who happens to be a good friend of mine. So I really want to find out whether I'm barking up the wrong tree or whether I'm right and I need to stop her before something worse happens.'

'I see. And would the first person she's supposed to have killed be her own mother?'

'Yes. I've been looking at the files and that hypothesis seems completely consistent with the evidence – if you assume that Gemma herself was lying about her mother being alive and well and working in the kitchen when she left for school that morning.'

'And you know that the police considered the possibility that she had a hand in the accident at the time and decided not to pursue it?'

'Yes. And I've spoken to one of the officers involved. He said he didn't want to drop it, but he was being leaned on by more senior people who were keen not to waste police time investigating what was in all probability a tragic accident, even if the girl was involved somehow. Plus, he didn't want to blight the life of a fourteen-year-old girl if he'd got it wrong.'

'I see. So what exactly do you want from me?'

'I'd like to tell you a story and then I'd like you to tell me whether it resonates at all with what you know of Gemma Markham.'

'Fair enough. Tell on.'

'Well,' Peter began, thinking back over everything he had found out during the last few weeks, 'let's start back in the seventies with a little girl living an idyllic life with two loving parents in a beautiful old farmhouse in the country. One day she comes home from school to find her whole life turned upside down. Her mother has been taken ill and her father is gone. She doesn't know, but her father has been killed in a farming accident and her mother witnessed both the accident and his mangled body when it was pulled out from under the tractor. All she knows is that her parents aren't there and everyone is keeping some terrible secret from her! Do you think that might be how it would have seemed to Gemma?'

'Mmm,' Rhoda agreed,' that's probably a fairly good

summary of how her father's death came across in the early stages.'

'After a while, her mother gets better – or at least she comes back to the house and starts looking after Gemma again – and Gemma starts asking where her dad is. Nobody has the courage to explain to her properly, so they tell her that he's gone to heaven. Gemma is only six and she's never known anyone to die before – her grandparents were all dead before she was born – so she takes this literally and she thinks her father has gone away and deserted her. Maybe for a while she keeps expecting him to come back and, when he doesn't, she starts thinking that he must never have cared for her in the first place; or maybe she thinks she was naughty and drove him away. And, of course, her mother is still coming to terms with her own grief and not in a position to support Gemma or to explain things properly.'

'I didn't see Gemma until about eighteen months after her dad died,' Rhoda said as Peter paused for breath. 'You're quite right: nobody had managed to explain to her properly that her dad was dead and what that meant.'

'So that fixed the idea in Gemma's mind that people that she cared for couldn't be completely trusted, because any day they might go off and leave her. However, for a few years everything seemed to be OK. She had her mother, and the two of them became very close through sharing the loss of her father. Probably her Mum made a fuss of her and told her how much she relied on her. But then, having been a widow for seven years, Gemma's mother finds someone else. Adam West looks like the perfect stepfather for Gemma: he's been helping around the farm for years, he's fond of Gemma and in love with Mrs Markham. But all that Gemma can see is that he's become a threat to her and her relationship with her mother.'

'So why doesn't she attack Adam West?' Rhoda asked. 'You'd think she would want to kill him or drive him away rather than hurting her mother.'

'No, I think she blamed her mother more than Adam, because she felt it as a betrayal. First, her dad left her and now her mum was planning to leave her. Her mum, who had kept telling her how they must stick together now that Dad was gone, who made so much of how she relied on Gemma. I think she was full of pent-up anger towards her mother who had promised to stick by her, now that it was just the two of them, and now didn't seem to need her anymore.'

'And you think she was so angry that she got hold of her one morning and deliberately pushed her down the cellar steps?' Rhoda sounded sceptical.

'Not necessarily,' Peter said quickly. 'Actually I think it probably wasn't pre-meditated. I don't think Gemma set out to kill her mother, but when it happened she didn't do anything to save her.' He paused, picturing in his mind the scene on that Tuesday morning in nineteen eighty-five.

'Go on,' Rhoda urged.

'The way I see it, Gemma and her mother had an argument that morning, just before she set off for school. The cellar door was open – we think her mother had just been down to get some chutney – and they were standing in the kitchen by the entrance.

Gemma got angry and hit her mother and knocked her off balance and she fell down the cellar stairs. I don't know what was going through her mind after that. Maybe she thought her mother was already dead, or maybe she thought she was OK and decided to punish her by shutting her in the cellar while she went out. Whatever the reason, she closed the door and locked it and then went off to school as if nothing had happened.'

'And she spent the whole day at school behaving just as normal so that nobody suspected there was anything wrong?'

'But you have to remember that, for Gemma, being sullen and difficult and not talking to the other girls *was* normal. I've spoken to some of her classmates and they said that, since her Mum had started talking about marrying Adam, she'd withdrawn into a shell and wouldn't speak to anyone.'

'OK. So she gets through the day at school and comes home. Then what?'

'Hang on a bit. First, let's consider Pat Markham, Gemma's mother. She falls down the cellar steps, hits her head and breaks her arm. The jar of chutney smashes to pieces on the stone floor. She lies there for a while, too stunned to get up or even to call out. The cellar door slams shut and now she's in pitch darkness, lying at the bottom of the stairs, in pain from her broken arm and in shock at the thought that her own daughter has pushed her down. Her first thought is that the door must have swung closed by itself, so she calls out to Gemma to open it. When nothing happens, she realises that Gemma isn't going to help her.

'Slowly and painfully she drags herself up the steps and eventually manages to reach the door. She pulls herself up so that she can reach the knob, but the door won't open. After a while, it dawns on her that Gemma must have locked it. Now she's really starting to panic. If Gemma has gone out then it could be hours before anyone comes within earshot of her cries for help.

'Her right arm is hanging uselessly at her side, but she scrabbles at the door with her left hand, trying desperately to find a way of opening it. She bangs as hard as she can on the door and shouts frantically for help. In the cellar there's no way of telling how time is passing, but it must have been less than four or five hours later that she loses her balance and falls back down the stairs again. Maybe she fainted with the pain or maybe she slipped on the stone steps as she hammered desperately on the door: either way, down she goes, breaking her collar bone on the way down and cracking her head on the floor at the bottom.

'She's probably unconscious by now as the bleeding in her brain gradually ends her life. She can't hear when Adam West comes looking for her around about lunchtime, worried that he hasn't seen her around the farmyard all morning. She can't call out to let him know where she is. He goes out again, thinking she must have gone to visit her husband's grave, not knowing that if he'd gone into the cellar he might even then have been in time to save her, and not knowing that he was going to have to answer questions about whether he threw her down the steps and closed the door on her and left her to die.'

'I thought she hit her head and died instantly,' Rhoda said quietly. 'I'm sure that's what I was told.'

'Everyone tried to play down the mother's suffering for Gemma's sake,' Peter told her. 'They all thought the child had been through enough, what with already having lost her father and now her mother. So nobody told her about the broken nails on her mother's left hand and the scratches on the inside of the door where she had scraped frantically at the wood trying to find a way out. She didn't know about the bleeding fingertips or the bloody smears on the door and doorframe. She didn't see the X-rays of multiple fractures or read the report of massive bleeding in the brain and a ruptured spleen. She didn't-'

'OK. That's enough. I get the picture,' Rhoda interrupted, showing signs of annoyance for the first time.

'As far as Gemma was concerned,' Peter resumed, 'it was all very similar to when her father died: he deserted her and went away to heaven; now her mother had gone away too, down into the darkness of the cellar.'

'It's hardly the same though,' Rhoda began.

'Only this time,' Peter went on, ignoring her, 'Gemma was in control. Her mother was planning to desert her in favour of Adam. Life would never be the same if they got married. But Gemma had stopped all that. She couldn't prevent her mother leaving her, but at least she has decided how she went. And, if she couldn't keep her mother, at least Adam hasn't got her either. And, in a strange sort of way, her mother's death actually brings Gemma's father back to her, because this time she's considered old enough to attend the funeral and she discovers that her father was actually buried in a grave in the churchyard in the next village and her mother is buried with him – which is another triumph for Gemma because she isn't with the usurping Adam.'

'This is all supposition, you know,' Rhoda observed. 'Gemma could have been telling the truth when she said her mother must have slipped on the cellar steps while she was out at school.'

'And then the door swung closed by itself,' Peter continued for her. 'I admit that, by the time the neighbours arrived and started looking for Mrs Markham, the door was unlocked, so it could have been unlocked all the time and in her panic she just didn't manage to get it open. But, when I read the pathologist's report about the bruises on her hand and the way her nails were torn and then I look at the forensic report which said her blood was all over the door including the door knob, I can't help thinking that if the door really wasn't locked she'd have managed to get out.'

'So you're saying Gemma locked her mother in before she went to school and then unlocked it before fetching the neighbours after she got back?'

That's right. She claimed that, when he mother wasn't there when she got home, she went round to the neighbours to ask them if they had seen her, but we only have her word for it that she didn't know full well where her mother was all the time. What I'd like to know from you is: does my alternative version of events square with Gemma's state of mind? We know she wasn't keen on her mother re-marrying, but was she angry enough about it to lash out at her mother like that and then not do anything to help her after she fell?'

'Anything I say would only be speculation,' Rhoda

began cautiously.

'Alright, how about this then,' Peter said, seeing that she was not about to commit herself to an opinion. 'Will you accept for the moment that the door was locked and that's why Mrs Markham couldn't get out?'

'I don't know. If it's as clear as you're making out, why didn't the coroner say so in his report?'

'Because nobody wanted to think that a fourteen-year-old girl could have locked her mother in the cellar and then gone off to school, apparently without a care in the world. But, I'm not sure it needs to have been as callous as that sounds. What if Mrs Markham fell down the cellar steps while Gemma was there – maybe because Gemma pushed her, but maybe just accidentally – and Gemma thought that she was dead? Could she have locked the door to shut out the awful scene?'

'How do you mean?' Rhoda asked, appearing more interested now.

'I'm imagining her going down the steps after her mother and finding her lying unconscious and thinking she must be dead. It's the first time she's seen a dead body and it frightens her. So she runs back up and locks the door because she can't bear to look or even to think about it. And she goes off to school, trying to behave as if it hadn't happened, maybe even convincing herself that if she does that then she'll come back and find that it really hasn't happened.'

'You know, I think you might have something there,' Rhoda broke in. 'Let's suppose for the moment that it was just an accident. Then it might seem to Gemma as if her mother had deserted her in the same way as her father did. It brought back all the trauma from eight years earlier and all she wanted to do was to get away and block it out. Afterwards she may even genuinely not have remembered what happened-'

'Except that she did have the presence of mind to unlock the cellar door,' Peter pointed out.

'Yes, I suppose she must have realised that she might be blamed if people found her mother locked in,' Rhoda conceded, talking slowly as she tried to think things through. 'Ah! But that doesn't mean she was guilty of anything more than lying to the police. How about this? Suppose she wasn't even in the kitchen when her mother fell down the cellar. She comes in on her way out to school, completely unaware that anything has happened, and she sees the cellar door swinging open. They have a rule that it's always kept closed and locked – so that nobody can fall down the steps – so she closes it and locks it, quite unaware that her mother is down there. Then, when she comes home and can't find her mother she looks in the cellar and finds the body and panics that people will think she shut her in deliberately.'

'But surely she'd check her mother wasn't in the cellar before closing the door?'

'Maybe she did. She could have called down, got no reply and assumed her mum was somewhere else – out in the farmyard feeding the chickens or something.'

'Yes,' Peter said slowly, 'it could have been like that. So Gemma could have been telling the truth when she said that, as far as she was concerned her mother was alive and well when she went to school, even if she had in fact inadvertently locked her in the cellar before going out.'

'I'm just suggesting that your bloody door knob and broken fingernails don't necessarily prove that Gemma pushed her down the steps.'

'OK. Let's leave Pat Markham's death for the time being and think about what happened to Gemma after that. She had no living relatives so she was taken into care. She seems to have been less disturbed than you might have expected after losing both her parents in violent accidents. She settled into the home apparently quite well, although she didn't make any close friends. My guess is that she was wary of committing herself to anyone after her experience of losing the only two people she ever cared about. Does that make sense psychologically?'

'Sounds reasonable enough to me,' Rhoda agreed.

'The only person she seems to have got at all close to during that period of her life is a boy called Paul Godwin, who was a couple of years younger than her. He only stayed in the home for a few months and was subject to a lot of bullying from some of the other boys. Gemma rather took him under her wing.'

'Really? She never mentioned him. She seemed very detached at that time. As you say, not wanting to commit in case she got hurt.'

'Anyway, she left care and trained as a hairdresser and seemed to be doing pretty well for herself. But still no boyfriends or any close friends, until 1999 when she meets an Australian called Robert White. He's a research assistant at the university, over here on a three-year research project. They hit it off and it's not long before she moves in with him. For the first time since her mother died, Gemma has allowed her happiness to depend on someone else, but that's not a problem because Robert is completely devoted to her.

'But then she starts having doubts. The insecurity that has dogged her ever since her father died kicks in again and she starts worrying that Robert may one day go off and leave her. She finds it increasingly difficult to bear letting him out of her sight. When he goes off on field trips she's tormented with the thought that he may never come back. She becomes ever more demanding of his time.

'And Robert, in his turn, finds Gemma's attitude increasingly oppressive. The more she wants him with her, the more he wants to find excuses to keep away. He'd stopped working late when he started going out with Gemma, now he starts staying in his department in the evenings again and goes in early every morning so he won't have to listen to Gemma over breakfast asking him what time he'll be back that day. In the end, he decides he can't go on like this much longer. His contract is coming to an end and he turns down the offer of a renewal and says he's going back to Australia to be closer to his family. He books his flight and tells his parents when to expect him. His colleagues are surprised at his change of heart, but not unduly so, and they notice that he seems happier now that he has made the decision to go home.

'But one person who is going to be very surprised and very upset when he tells her is Gemma. So he puts off saying anything until it's only a few weeks before he's due to leave. At last he can't put it off any longer, so he books a table at a restaurant and takes her out for what he intends to be their last dinner together. He's worried that she won't listen properly to what he has to say, so he writes a letter explaining everything and takes it with him to the restaurant.

'What he doesn't realise is that Gemma has already got wind of his plan to go back to Australia. She's been surreptitiously checking his phone and his laptop to make sure he's not being unfaithful to her and she's discovered about the one-way ticket he's booked to Australia and about him turning down the new job in Oxford. So she's been planning how she can stop him going off and leaving her the way everyone else in her life has gone off and left her.

'As Robert expected, Gemma seems devastated by the news, but after a bit of heated argument they manage to finish the meal without attracting too much attention. He finishes up with a cup of strong coffee, which is just perfect for her to slip some Rohypnol into without him noticing any difference. Then they leave to walk the short distance home together. It's raining hard so there's nobody much about. As they're crossing the river, Gemma starts talking about how unfair he is, going off and leaving her and how pointless her life is going to be without him. She climbs up on the parapet at the side of the road and points down at the river below and threatens to jump in and end it all. Robert is starting to feel woozy from the drug, but he manages to climb up beside her and start reasoning with her to get down and come home. That gives her the opportunity she's waiting for and she gives him a little push – just like the little push that she gave her mother all those years before – and down he goes into the water!

'And now you're investigating this Robert White's death?' Rhoda asked.

'Unfortunately not,' Peter admitted 'The case was closed several months ago. The inquest verdict was suicide. At the time I thought that was the most likely explanation, but I'm not so sure now. In fact, I'm pretty convinced it was Gemma who was responsible for his death and she very cleverly dressed it up as suicide to put us off the scent. This is how I think it was:

'She gets down off the wall and walks home. It's still raining hard so there's nobody about to see her arriving back on her own. When she gets to the door of her flat, she makes a bit of a disturbance, shouting out Robert's name and talking in a loud voice as if he were there with her, so that her neighbour in the next flat is prepared to swear that she heard them both come back together. She waits until the following evening and then reports Robert missing to the police, who tell her not to worry because most missing persons come back of their own accord.

'Then, when his body turns up in the river the following morning, she acts all surprised and shocked. She starts getting a bit anxious when the police look as if they suspect Robert might have been murdered, so she has a look at the letter he wrote to her and finds that, by tearing off the top section where he talks about going back to Australia, it can be made to look like a very convincing suicide note. So she tears the paper and throws away the bit she doesn't want and rings up the police to say that she just found a note behind the toaster. She puts the rest of the bottle of Rohypnol tablets, which she bought on the black market, in the bathroom cabinet and claims that they belong to Robert and that he told her they were for hay fever. So we assume that he took the drug himself, either as a sleeping tablet or as a preliminary to topping himself by jumping in the Thames.'

'So what made you change your mind? Why don't you buy the suicide theory anymore? This all sounds desperately complicated. Aren't the simplest explanations usually the true ones?'

'Do you remember me mentioning a boy she met in the care home?'

'Paul something-or-other wasn't it?'

'That's right, Paul Godwin. Well, he went on to become Detective Sergeant Godwin and, by a complete coincidence, he worked with me on the investigation of Robert White's death.'

'I suppose he's the friend that you believe is in danger from Gemma now?'

'That's right. He recognised Gemma from when they were teenagers together and remembered her fondly as the one person who had been kind to him then. After the police investigation was closed, they started going out together. It wasn't long before she moved in with him. For a while, he seemed happier than I'd ever known him, but then, just like with Robert White, things started to go downhill. His work's been suffering: I seem to spend all my time now covering up for him.'

'Maybe he's just starting to get a better work-life balance,' Rhoda suggested. 'Have you considered whether you may have made unreasonable demands on him in the past?'

'I'm not just talking about the way he's always off like a hare at the end of each shift or the way he's become so reluctant to do any extra hours when they're needed; I'm talking about him never seeming to have his mind on the job anymore and-'

'He's in love: it'll pass.'

'It was fine when he was in love! When he was just in

love, he was bright and cheerful and eager to do anything to help anyone. This is different. He's always metaphorically looking over his shoulder in case Gemma might be checking up on him. And she keeps ringing him at work to make sure that's really where he is. And it isn't just his work that's being affected: he's starting to let other people down too. There's this little girl that he's fond of. She's only two and doesn't understand any of this. He keeps promising to do things with her and then pulling out at the last minute because Gemma wants him with her instead. It's ruining his life and I can see he's starting to realise that things can't go on like this much longer; and if he decides to end it with Gemma then will she find a way of giving him a little push down the stairs or off a bridge or out of a high window?'

'Aren't you being a bit melodramatic?'

'I don't think so, but that's what I was hoping you might be able to help me decide. Do you think my assessment of Gemma's personality could be right? Has she been so damaged by the trauma of her father's death that she can't bear anyone she loves to have anything else that matters to them apart from herself? Does it ring true to you that she could have been responsible for her mother's death – or at very least did nothing to prevent it – and the death of her previous boyfriend?'

'Now you're really putting me on the spot,' Rhoda said thoughtfully. 'I'm loath to suggest that she's a killer, but there is something about what you've said …'

Peter waited in anxious silence for her to continue.

'I do think,' Rhoda resumed slowly, 'that she was very, very traumatised by her father's death – much more than anyone accepted at the time. That's why I wasn't brought in until so long afterwards, when they started to think she ought to have got over it and she clearly hadn't. And I think you put your finger on it when you said that she saw it as a betrayal and found it hard to trust people after that. I really believed what she said about her mother's death, but then nobody told me about how her mother had been alive in the cellar for hours after she fell down, which does make one think, doesn't it? I can't put my hand on my heart and say that Gemma couldn't have pushed her mother down those cellar steps. In fact … in fact the more I think about it, the more I start to believe that it could have happened that way. Maybe not a deliberate act, but she was a very, very angry young woman and she certainly could have preferred to lose her mother altogether than to have to share her with a stepfather.'

She looked up at Peter with a pleading expression in her eyes.

'I really do hope you're wrong,' she said quietly, 'but I've a horrible suspicion you may be right.'

CHAPTER 36

Peter returned from his visit to Rhoda, feeling all the more convinced that Gemma Markham had killed both her mother and her lover and that Paul was now in serious danger from her if he were to give her any cause to suspect that he was less than a hundred percent devoted to her. Consequently, he was even more determined to gather the evidence to enable her to be brought to justice for White's murder, which seemed to him to be the only way of protecting his friend. This would have to wait, however, because the next day was Lucy's third birthday and everything else was secondary to making it a day for her to remember.

Peter had arranged to be on an early shift that day, so as to be free to collect his son, Eddie, who was coming down from Manchester for the party, from the station during the afternoon and to take him on to Bernie's house. He was please to discover that Paul had arranged to take a day's leave in order to prepare an entertainment for the guests. At least he seemed keen to make amends for having let the little girl down over past weeks, but it was a pity that he had been forced to use some of his precious leave in order to avoid Gemma's ever-present demands. She, presumably, was at work and probably did not know that he was not.

Shortly after half past three, Peter, Angie and Eddie arrived at Bernie's house and were greeted by an ecstatic

Lucy, who immediately took Peter by the hand and led him into the living room to show him all her new toys. For a few minutes, everyone was engrossed in her demonstration of a plastic engineering set, with which she and Bernie had been constructing a model crane. Then Eddie managed to attract her attention to the parcels that they had brought with them and she sat down on the floor, intent on unwrapping them.

While Lucy was thus occupied, Bernie turned anxiously to Peter.

'Have you heard anything from Paul today?' she asked. 'He said he'd be here at lunch time to set up his puppet theatre, but we haven't heard a thing from him and his mobile's turned off.'

'No,' Peter shook his head, 'he was on leave all day. He said he needed to work on the puppets this morning.'

'Do you think he's alright?' Bernie asked in a low voice to prevent Lucy from hearing. 'I know he hasn't exactly been the most reliable person in the world recently, but he was very definite that he was going to be here today.'

Peter thought for a moment.

'Give me a few minutes and I'll make some checks,' he said, heading for the door.

He slipped out into the hall and sat down on the stairs. First, he tried ringing Paul's flat and then his mobile number. Sure enough, neither elicited any response. Then he picked up a copy of the Yellow Pages, which lay on the old-fashioned hall-stand, and thumbed through until he found the entry for the hair salon where Gemma worked. He rang the number and asked to speak to her.

'I'm sorry,' the receptionist told him, 'she isn't in today. She phoned in sick this morning.'

Peter thanked her and rang off. His mind was racing. Was this the moment he'd been dreading, when Gemma decided that Paul couldn't be trusted to stick with her and that she had to take action to make it impossible for him ever to leave her? After a few moments' thought, he put his head round the living room door and beckoned Bernie to come out.

Paul had been having a most unsatisfactory day. He had somehow managed to let slip to Gemma over breakfast that he was taking the day off work to prepare for Lucy's birthday party and she immediately declared the intention of staying at home herself. He had remonstrated with her vainly and in the end, he had given up and started work on the new puppets that he was making. She hung around watching him, chattering away and every so often plying him with unwanted cups of coffee and cans of lager. He bore it as patiently as he could until the moment when she leaned across to kiss him, joggling his arm as she did so, and caused him to send the pieces of the new hairy mongrel puppet, which he had just painstakingly assembled but not yet fastened together, clattering to the floor.

'What did you do that for?' he shouted, unable to hold back his rising anger any longer.

He got down on his hands and knees and started searching for the pieces. The dog's body was easy to locate, but the small wooden tubes that made up its limbs and tail had rolled in all directions across the smooth kitchen floor. He counted them out on to the table. There was still a piece missing. Back down on the floor, he peered under the fridge and washing machine. Then he moved them away from the wall and inspected the space behind each.

'Look at all that mess!' Gemma exclaimed. 'I'll get the brush and clean it up.'

'No! Leave it alone!' Paul said sharply, speaking louder than he intended, in his agitation at the thought that she might sweep up the missing section of his dog's foreleg and throw it away with the dried up frozen peas and cobwebby bottle-tops.

Gemma flounced out of the room and Paul felt a guilty

sense of relief at the thought that she might sulk for long enough that he could complete his project in peace. As soon as she was gone, he spotted the missing piece lying hard up against the skirting board next to the door. He picked it up and started reassembling the puppet. For the next hour or two, he remained engrossed in his work and made good progress. He was just putting the new puppets into their boxes, ready to take them to Bernie's house, when Gemma came back in and announced that she needed the kitchen to prepare lunch.

Sighing silently, Paul cleared his tools and puppet-making materials from the table and carried them through into the living room. Then he started transporting the puppets down to his car. He toyed with the idea of setting off straight away without telling Gemma, but he could not quite bring himself to that level of deceit. Besides, it would only make things worse when he came home that evening.

As they ate, Gemma chatted cheerfully while Paul remained silent. He knew he could not go on like this, but neither could he bring himself to break with the only woman he had ever loved. If only he could make her understand that she could be the first, most important thing in his life without being the only thing that mattered at all!

As soon as the meal was over, Paul picked up his car keys and prepared to set off for Bernie's house, but Gemma stopped him.

'Don't go yet,' she pleaded. 'You can't need to be there so early. I thought you said it was a tea party.'

'It is, but I want to get the puppet theatre set up before Peter and his family get there. And I want to have time for a bit of a rehearsal with the new puppets. I got behind with making them so I haven't had time to practise properly.'

'Oh! You'll be alright,' Gemma argued. 'She's only three, remember: she won't be able to tell whether you've practised or not.'

'Still, I'd like to get it right. And, anyway, I told Bernie to expect me by two.'

'A few minutes late won't matter. Please! I thought we could have a walk round some of our old haunts today. I've got it all planned. We can go and see Willowbank and then-'

'We can't visit Willowbank – not without an appointment!' Paul protested. 'They won't be expecting us. It wouldn't be fair. Anyway,' he said, remembering what Peter had said, 'it doesn't do to go back.'

'I didn't mean go into Willowbank – just have a look at it from the outside – and then go for a little walk around where we used to go. It won't take long, and it's something I've been wanting to do for ages. Please!'

'Oh all right!' Paul gave in, deciding that the sooner they got on with whatever it was Gemma had planned the sooner he would be able to get away to Lucy's party. 'But I must be at Bernie's by three at the very latest.'

As they were leaving the building, Paul's mobile phone rang. He fished it out of his pocket and was about to answer it when Gemma grabbed it from him and switched it off. She put it in her own pocket and strode on ahead, down the path to the road. Paul caught up with her as she waited by the car for him to unlock it.

'What did you do that for?' he demanded. 'It may have been urgent.'

'Not so urgent it can't wait until after we've been for our little walk. Please, Paul! You're off duty today: can't we have just one hour to ourselves without you expecting to be called away any minute?'

Paul opened the driver's side door without replying. He could see that, with Gemma in this mood, argument was pointless. He decided to go with the flow and just hope that she would become more reasonable if he allowed her to have her way for a few hours.

'I'll drive, she said suddenly. 'I know a good place to park.'

'OK', he agreed, handing over the keys and walking

round to the other side. Somehow, it all seemed so much easier simply to do as Gemma wanted. He wondered why he had never thought of this course of action before. He leaned back in his seat and closed his eyes. That was where he had been going wrong, he decided, everything would be all right now he had worked out the way to make their relationship work.

They drove the short distance to the part of north Oxford where Gemma had spent her last few years of adolescence, before being launched, at the tender age of sixteen, into the adult world. Paul looked dreamily out of the window as they passed the Care Home where they had met all those years ago. It looked smaller and less imposing than he had remembered. Gemma drove on a little way to where the houses started to give way to countryside. Then she pulled in at the kerbside and switched off the engine.

'Come with me,' she said, 'I want to show you something.'

Bernie got up from the floor as unobtrusively as she could and slipped out of the room to join Peter. He closed the door firmly behind them and led her a little way away to make sure that they would not be overheard.

'I may be overreacting,' he said in a low voice, 'but I'm worried about Paul. Gemma didn't go into work this morning – she phoned in sick. Were you expecting her to come with Paul this afternoon?'

'No. I told him she was welcome to come as well, but he said she would be working until five. I suggested she could come on after, but he didn't think she'd want to. Maybe she *is* sick and Paul's staying at home to look after her,' Bernie suggested reasonably.

'But in that case, why hasn't he rung you? You know what I think happened with her previous boyfriend – I'm afraid this may be the point at which she's going to try the same with Paul.'

'Is that what that child psychologist you were seeing

yesterday thinks?' Bernie asked, remembering Peter's appointment with Rhoda.

'Well, she wouldn't commit herself – these people never do – but she did agree that my ideas about Gemma's state of mind were consistent with what she knew of her.'

'So what exactly do you think she's planning to do?' Bernie asked sceptically. 'Paul's not going to be a pushover for her. He's a fit young man; surely he'll be a match for anything she can do?'

'In both the other cases, either by luck or design, she got her victims into situations where she didn't need to be strong enough to overpower them. She just gave them a little push and down they went: tumbling down a flight of stone steps or plunging into a raging torrent!'

'A little push,' Bernie repeated slowly. 'Just a little push …Oh Peter! I've just had a thought! Did Paul ever tell you he once considered suicide himself?'

'No. When was this? I had no idea!'

'It was ages ago, when he was in care. He had it all planned out, but Gemma talked him out of it. He was going to jump off the Godstow Road railway bridge under a passing train. He'd been very systematic about it apparently. He'd timed how long it took for a train to get from one side of the bridge to the other – with a stopwatch no less – and the time that it took for an object to fall to the ground from the top of the bridge. He reckoned he could time it just right so that he hit the ground just before the train came out of the tunnel and the driver would have no chance of seeing him and stopping the train.'

'And you say he told all this to Gemma?'

'That's right. The way he sees it, she saved his life by persuading him not to go through with it.'

'That's it!' Peter declared suddenly. 'I'm off to Godstow Road. I'm probably just imagining things, but I won't be able to rest until I'm sure she hasn't lured him there to his death!'

'You're not going alone,' Bernie said firmly.

'Well you're sure as hell not coming with me,' Peter retorted. 'It could get dangerous.'

'Which is precisely why you mustn't go on your own,' Bernie insisted. 'But I wasn't suggesting I would come. You need someone tall enough and strong enough to restrain two young people who are planning on jumping off a railway bridge. I'd be useless: if they're perched up on the parapet, I'd be too short even to reach their knees never mind haul them down! Take Eddie.'

Peter looked unconvinced.

'Go on,' Bernie urged. 'He's fit and strong and *not a policeman*,' She added meaningfully.

'OK. I'll take Eddie. He can drive and leave me free to look out for Paul and Gemma.

Gemma led Paul to where the road rose up on to a bridge, first over the Oxford Canal and then over the railway. There was a footbridge at one side of the road bridge, with railings to prevent pedestrians from falling on to the track. Paul felt tired and wished she would slow down, but she pulled him along on to the bridge.

'Do you remember?' she asked, her voice sounding strangely far away. 'You brought me here and told me you were going to jump off under a train.'

'And you told me that things couldn't be as bad as that and it would be a waste if I did it,' Paul answered, trying to picture the scene in his mind, but finding it all very confused and fuzzy. 'That's what I meant when I said you saved my life,' he added, remembering their conversation on the day he and Peter had broken the news of Robert White's death.

'Show me again how you planned to do it,' Gemma said eagerly, putting both feet on the bottom rail between the upright struts of the railings and leaning over the barrier to look down at the track below.

'Get down, Gemma,' Paul urged. 'Don't lean over like

that; you could fall.'

'I'm OK,' she insisted, swinging one leg over the railings and standing astride them, looking back at him.

She beckoned to him to climb up beside her.

'Come on! You're not afraid are you?'

'That's Paul's car,' Peter said suddenly, pointing out of the window as Eddie drove them slowly along Godstow Road. 'And look up ahead! There are a couple of people fooling about on the footbridge.'

Eddie followed his father's pointing finger and saw two figures on the bridge, standing taller than he would have expected. One of them was waving its hands about, while the other had head bowed and shoulders slumped.

'Drive past,' Peter instructed. 'Just go at a normal pace, as if you were just on your way somewhere. Don't let them see we're looking at them. In fact, don't you look their way at all, leave it to me to check out if it's them.'

Eddie drove obediently on, over the bridge and down the other side. As he passed the two figures, he glanced across at them and noted that the more animated one was a dark-haired woman and the one who now seemed to be slumped over the rail was a tall man with broad shoulders and curly brown hair.

'That's Paul alright,' Peter said. 'Carry on as if nothing had happened and pull in further down where they won't notice us. I'm going to call for backup.'

A few minutes later, they were on their way back towards the bridge on foot, walking briskly, but trying not to draw attention to themselves by hurrying too much.

'If it comes to restraining them from jumping off,' Peter said to his son in a low voice, 'you take Paul and I'll look after Gemma.'

'OK Dad,' Eddie answered, feeling both proud and nervous at being involved in a real-life police drama.

'But don't touch either of them unless we have to. Any sudden movements could frighten her into doing something we'll all regret.'

Paul and Gemma were too absorbed in their own conversation to notice the two men approaching. Gemma had her back to them, perched rather precariously astride the railings. Paul had both feet on the bottom rail and was leaning over the barrier, with his head down as if he were staring at something on the track below. He looked up briefly at the sound of Peter's voice as he addressed Gemma and then let his head drop again, as if it were too much effort to hold it up.

'Good afternoon Miss Markham,' Peter said in a matter-of-fact voice. 'I think it would be a good idea if you got down off there. You could easily fall and hurt yourself badly.'

'I know what I'm doing,' Gemma retorted. 'Go away and leave us in peace.'

'I'm afraid I can't do that,' Peter answered calmly. 'I've got this whole section of railway line closed until we get the two of you out of danger. It's standard procedure when someone looks as if they may be going to jump. There won't be any trains going into or out of Oxford to the north or west until you two come off the bridge. Now, why don't you come with me back to the car and we can talk it all through in a civilised manner? And I can let all those poor passengers, who are stuck at red signals wondering whatever's going on, continue their journeys.'

'I don't believe you!' Gemma said, glaring at Peter who looked back mildly. 'You wouldn't be able to do that – not unless we said we were going to jump.'

'So that isn't what you're planning? I'm very glad to hear it. In that case you won't mind getting down and coming with me, will you?'

Peter put his arm out in an offer to help her down, but Gemma drew back and reached out to take Paul by the shoulder, pulling him towards her. Peter backed away, holding his hands up in front of him to show that he did not intend to take hold of her.

'Take it easy,' he said gently. 'Why don't you tell me what this is all about?'

'Just go away!' Gemma shouted. 'Leave us alone.'

'Peter?' Paul mumbled, twisting round to look at him for the first time. 'What're you doing here?'

'I've come to take you to Bernie's,' Peter said, trying to stay calm and speak normally. 'It's time for Lucy's party and she's expecting you.'

'Yes. That's right,' Paul agreed, with slightly slurred speech. 'I'm sorry Gemma, I'll have to go.'

'No!'

She leaned forward and grasped his shoulders with both hands, pulling him towards her and trying to drag him forcibly over the safety barrier. Eddie stepped forward and grabbed Paul about the waist. Gemma's grip loosened and suddenly she jerked backwards. Peter reached out to catch hold of her but he found himself grasping thin air as she overbalanced and fell on to the railway line. At the same time, Eddie and Paul collapsed backwards and found themselves lying in a heap on the path.

For a moment, Peter stood aghast, looking helplessly down at the crumpled body lying across the northbound track. Then he took out his phone and started dialling for help. While he was still in the process of summoning an ambulance, a police patrol car pulled up and two uniformed officers got out.

'We heard you'd got a jumper sir,' one of them said, recognising Peter. 'Is that him?' he added looking down at Paul, who was lying huddled in Eddie's arms.

'No. I'm afraid she's down there,' Peter replied, putting away the phone and pointing towards Gemma's motionless body. 'She only just fell. The ambulance is on its way.'

The uniformed men took over the incident scene, donning high visibility jackets and clambering down the embankment to make an initial assessment of Gemma's condition and to move her off the track in case of any failure by the signalling staff to prevent trains passing along the line. Peter and Eddie helped Paul into his car and Peter drove him back to his flat to sleep off the effects of the drug that Gemma had put into his food at lunchtime.

Eddie was dispatched back to Bernie's house in Peter's car, with strict instructions not to say anything to frighten Lucy. Fortunately, the little girl was too busy playing with her new toys to question him when he explained that Paul was 'not very well' and Peter needed to stay with him for a while to look after him.

It was only once Lucy was safely packed off to bed that Eddie could explain to his mother and Bernie what had gone on at the railway bridge. Angie's immediate reaction was to propose that she should go at once to Paul's flat to apply her nursing skills. Bernie too wanted to get in on the act and suggested that they bring Paul back to stay with her for a while. Eddie, however, eventually persuaded them that this was a matter for Peter and Paul to sort out between them man-to-man and that their well-meaning attentions would not be welcome.

Meanwhile, Peter was watching at Paul's bedside as his colleague gradually regained consciousness and started looking around with a bewildered expression on his face.

'The traditional thing to say in these circumstances,' Peter said with a smile, 'is "where am I?"'

'I can see where I am,' Paul answered, pushing himself up into a sitting position, 'I just can't work out how I got here.'

'What's the last thing you remember?'

'Putting the puppets in the back of the car. What time is it now? Have I missed Lucy's party?'

'I'm afraid so, but don't worry about that: you can take them over another time and give her the show. So, you don't remember going with Gemma to Godstow Road and standing on the railway bridge?'

'No.' Paul looked worried as he shook his head. 'What happened? Did I bang my head or something? And where's Gemma? Is she alright?'

'She's badly injured, but she should pull through.'

'So what happened?' Paul's voice sounded scared. 'And why don't I remember it, if I was there?'

'Lie back and try not to worry,' Peter said, perfectly aware how difficult it would be for Paul to follow these instructions. 'I'm afraid there's no nice way to tell you this. Your memory loss is a result of the drug that Gemma put in something she gave you to eat or drink – Rohypnol most likely.'

'But why?' Paul sat up straight and looked at Peter, wild-eyed.

'She was afraid of losing you,' Peter said, gently pushing Paul back down on to the pillows. 'She was jealous of anything and anyone that took you away from her for a moment: your job, your friends, your hobbies ...'

'But-'

'The same thing happened with Robert White,' Peter went on, his hand still resting on Paul's shoulder. 'She couldn't bear to let him out of her sight in case he went off and left her; but that only made him feel smothered and imprisoned and he started to look for a way out. When it started looking to her as if she was going to lose him, she decided to stop him and the only way she could think of was to push him into the river to drown. She'd made up her mind to do the same sort of thing with you.'

'I don't believe it! Gemma would never ...'

'I'm afraid she did,' Peter insisted gently. 'We'll have to wait for the results of tests on the blood sample we took from you, but I'm pretty confident that they'll show that you were given a similar dose of Rohypnol to the one that Robert White had before he went into the Thames. And I saw her with my own eyes trying to tip you off the footbridge on to the railway line this afternoon. She fell and hurt herself, but it's only bruises and a few broken bones: no head or spinal injuries as far as anyone can see.'

'It's my fault,' Paul said quietly. 'I gave her the idea of jumping under a train. I even-'

'I know about that,' Peter interrupted. 'Bernie told me. But none of this is your fault. Gemma's a very damaged young woman. She never really got over her father's death all those years ago. If it hadn't been that way, she'd have found another. At least Bernie was able to point me in the right direction because of what you'd said to her, so we found you in time.'

Paul thought about this for a while, leaning his head back on the pillows and staring into space.'

'Do you think I'll ever remember?' he asked at last. 'It feels dreadful having that gap in my memory, as if I'd lost a few hours of my life.'

'I don't know. Everyone's different. I dare say it may come back eventually – if you don't try too hard. The best thing to do is to try not to think about it and then maybe the memories will gradually start coming back.'

Peter did not say what he was thinking, which was that it would be far better if Paul never did remember the events of that afternoon. He himself would give a lot to be able to forget the sight of Gemma's body falling through the air – taking far longer to reach the ground below than you would have thought possible – and the sickening thud as it hit the railway track.

EPILOGUE

Physically, Gemma made a full recovery. Under police questioning, she admitted to having deliberately left her mother to die after pushing her down the cellar steps in a fit of anger. She also confirmed that she had drugged Robert White and then lured him on to the wall of Folly Bridge and pushed him into the river and that she had been attempting to do away with Paul in a similar fashion. She pleaded guilty to two counts of manslaughter and one of assault. The prosecution dropped charges of murder and attempted murder, on the grounds that her mental state meant that she was not fully responsible for her actions. She was committed to a secure mental unit for an indefinite time.

Paul at first cherished the hope that she would eventually be released and might become the lifelong partner that he had hoped for. He visited her regularly until he was asked to desist by her psychiatrist, who told him that his continued attentions made her agitated and anxious and were inhibiting any chance of her regaining her mental equilibrium. He threw himself into his work with a determination that Peter found almost frightening and spent his free time immersed in his models.

Peter came to rely more and more on Paul's assistance in his work, finding him always willing to go the extra mile in furthering any investigation, but he worried that this devotion to duty was a sign that he had given up hope of finding happiness outside of his job. He was relieved that his young colleague continued to pay frequent calls on Bernie, who retained a motherly interest in Paul, including making several unsuccessful attempts at finding a soul mate for him from within her own circles of university and church acquaintances.

On his return to university, Eddie became, for a time, quite a celebrity among his fellow students for the part he had played in a criminal case which was reported, albeit only briefly, in the national press.

On the other side of the world, Bernard and Samantha White had mixed feelings on being informed of the true story behind their son's death. It was a relief to know that he had not, after all, taken his own life, but it was highly unsettling to think that they had met and spoken to and even sympathised with his killer.

Lucy continued to grow up surrounded by doting adults and, against the odds, somehow managed to remain quite unspoilt by their attentions. Paul installed the puppet theatre permanently in a corner of the large living room, and she looked forward every week to Saturday afternoon when, if he was not on duty, he would come and put on a show for her own private entertainment.

Sergeant Adams watched the growing closeness between DI Johns and DS Godwin and tried to start a rumour that there was more to their relationship than met the eye. But, somehow, the story never seemed to catch on and Peter and Paul were able to continue to work together in harmony until the time came for Paul to seek promotion and move away from Oxford and the painful memories it held for him.

THANK YOU

Thank you for taking the time to read TWO LITTLE DICKIE BIRDS. If you enjoyed it, please consider telling your friends or posting a short review. Word of mouth is an author's best friend and much appreciated. Thank you,

Judy

MORE ABOUT BERNIE AND HER FRIENDS

Bernie and Peter feature in six more books.

- **Awayday**: a traditional detective story set among the dons of an Oxford college.
- **Changing Scenes of Life**: Jonah Porter's life story, told through the medium of his favourite hymns.
- **Despise not your Mother**: the story of Bernie's quest to learn about her dead husband's past.
- **Murder of a Martian**: a double murder for Peter and Jonah to solve.
- **Death on the Algarve:** a mystery for Bernie and her friends to tackle while on holiday in Portugal.
- **My Life of Crime:** the collected memoirs of DI Peter Johns.

Read more about Bernie Fazakerley and her friends and family at https://sites.google.com/site/llanwrdafamily/

Visit the Bernie Fazakerley Publications Facebook page here:
https://www.facebook.com/Bernie.Fazakerley.Publications

Follow Bernie on Twitter: https://twitter.com/BernieFaz.

ABOUT THE AUTHOR

Like her main character, Bernie Fazakerley, Judy Ford is an Oxford graduate and a mathematician. Unlike Bernie, Judy grew up in a middle-class family in the South London stockbroker belt. After moving to the North West and working in Liverpool, Judy fell in love with the Scouse people and created Bernie to reflect their unique qualities.

As a Methodist Local Preacher, Judy often tells her congregation, "I see my role as asking the questions and leaving you to think out your own answers." She carries this philosophy forward into her writing and she hopes that readers will find themselves challenged to think as well as being entertained.